She stare
as if stur

The glossy cream-colored pearls looked terrific on her. "I shouldn't do this," she said, though she made no move to undo the clasp. "It isn't mine."

"You're only trying it on," Jeremy replied. "Alison wouldn't care."

Marlo shook her head. "This is stupid," she said, her tone brimming with self-reproach. "I shouldn't want things like this."

"Why not?" It bothered him that she behaved as if she didn't think she deserved such luxuries. He glided his hand through the dense black waves of her hair. "You're so beautiful, Marlo."

She issued a short, dry laugh. "Any woman can be beautiful if you hang enough pearls around her neck." Turning from him, she unfastened the clasp and dropped the pearls onto the vanity table. Only someone observing her closely, as Jeremy was, would have noticed her hand was trembling....

ABOUT THE AUTHOR

We are thrilled to welcome well-known writer Judith Arnold to our ranks. The popular author of twenty-one Harlequin American Romance novels brings a fresh, lively touch to the Superromance line with this exciting and heartwarming tale. Judith lives in Massachusetts with her husband and two young sons. Her second Superromance novel, *The Woman Downstairs,* will be published next year.

Books by Judith Arnold

HARLEQUIN AMERICAN ROMANCE

205—COMMITMENTS*
209—DREAMS*
225—COMFORT AND JOY
240—TWILIGHT
255—GOING BACK
259—HARVEST THE SUN
281—ONE WHIFF OF SCANDAL
304—INDEPENDENCE DAY
330—SURVIVORS
342—LUCKY PENNY
362—CHANGE OF LIFE
378—ONE GOOD TURN
389—A > LOVERBOY

*KEEPING THE FAITH SUBSERIES

Raising the Stakes

JUDITH ARNOLD

Harlequin Books

TORONTO • NEW YORK • LONDON
AMSTERDAM • PARIS • SYDNEY • HAMBURG
STOCKHOLM • ATHENS • TOKYO • MILAN

Published July 1991

ISBN 0-373-70460-7

RAISING THE STAKES

Porter's upper lip had curled with distaste. "My darling ex-wife is honeymooning in Europe this summer with her new husband. The guy is younger than you, Jeremy, if you catch my drift. She's gone and hitched herself to a cute little boy. Alison hasn't taken the situation too well."

"She probably needs you right now," Jeremy had advised, although as a carefree bachelor he'd felt a little presumptuous explaining paternal responsibility to Porter. "Maybe this is your chance to get to know your daughter better."

Porter hadn't seemed thrilled by the prospect. As far as Jeremy could tell, getting to know his daughter had never been a high priority for him. "What are we supposed to do, sit around shooting the breeze?" he'd complained. "I've got a business to run. I know how to make money and pay her bills, not how to talk to her. What in God's name am I going to do with her for the whole summer?"

"Entertain her," Jeremy had proposed.

"Sure." Porter had snorted. "My idea of entertainment is negotiating a juicy land transaction. Here's a thought, though," he'd said, eyeing his young colleague with an unnerving smile. "*You* could entertain her."

"Me?"

"You're closer in age to her."

"Porter—she's a college kid!"

"And you're, what—twelve, thirteen years older than her. You're single and a hell of a lot more charming than me. You could show her a good time, Jeremy. She's a nice girl, and a hundred times better looking than that lady you brought with you to the Pace & Hartley Christmas party. All you'd have to do is take her to the club, the beach, whatever.... What's the harm in escorting a pretty young lady around for a few weeks? Just until she starts making some friends around here."

Jeremy hadn't seen the harm in it, either. He and Brenda, the woman he'd brought to the Pace & Hartley Christmas party, had gone their separate ways months ago, and he wasn't involved with anyone else at the moment. He had no objection to keeping a visitor to his part of Connecticut amused, particularly if in doing so he was helping out a business associate.

So he'd started socializing with Alison, bringing her to the beach, inviting her to play tennis, including her in his friends' dinner parties. The more time he spent with her, ironically, the more he realized that he was helping her at least as much as he was helping her father. She was painfully lonely, and bitter about her mother's remarriage. She had no one to confide in, no one to lean on. Despite her nonchalant facade she seemed pathetically lost. Jeremy felt sorry for her.

A car passed them going the opposite direction on the shoreline road. As the sound of its engine receded behind them, he heard her sigh. He gave her a quick look, appreciating her beauty in a detached way. She was wearing a stylish jumpsuit of ivory silk, with a seductively low-cut top, plunging cutouts below her arms and loose-fitting trousers. It had undoubtedly cost a fortune. When it came to his daughter, Porter Havelock was as free with his money as he was stingy with his time.

"Would you rather not come along to these dinner parties?" Jeremy asked.

"And sit around at home alone?" The possibility clearly appalled her.

"Haven't you got any friends from school who live nearby?"

"They mostly live in New Jersey," she said, extending her lower lip even farther. "They always kid me about being from another country just because my mother lives in Manhattan. They must think Connecticut's on a different planet."

"Look." Jeremy slowed the car slightly around a sharp curve. "I know my friends don't excite you, but I'm doing my best."

"I don't blame you, Jeremy. Really." Her eyes shone with sincerity. "You've been a whole lot nicer to me than my father, and I appreciate it."

"You can't blame him, either," Jeremy said. "Consider the situation from his side. You've been living with your mother for years and years. You and your father are practically strangers."

"And he isn't exactly going out of his way to change that," she snapped. "My mother was right about him—he doesn't give a damn about anybody but himself. All he wants to do is marry me off and get me out of his hair—what little he's got left." She issued a short, humorless laugh. "If you don't watch out, Jeremy, he's going to marry me off to you."

Jeremy couldn't refute her. More than once since he'd started seeing Alison, Porter had dropped some leaden hints about what a spectacular catch she was. He'd besieged Jeremy with pointed comments concerning Alison's inherited wealth and reminders about her striking beauty. More than once Porter had mentioned, rather ominously, that he thought of Jeremy as a son.

"I'm sure your father only wants you to be happy," he said, sounding less convincing than he'd intended.

"Yeah, right. He figures if I'm happy I'll leave him alone." She stared for a moment at the passing scenery—the stark modern beach houses and the dwarfed trees, the uneven stone seawall and the receding tide. "Bob was really boring tonight, wasn't he? All that talk about the Federal Reserve System . . . I thought I'd die."

"The Federal Reserve System is important," Jeremy argued, defending his friend.

"Not so important you've got to talk about it all during dinner. And what was that stuff Melanie served, anyway? Squid or something?"

"Smoked eel."

"Ugh." Alison grimaced.

"It was delicious."

"It looked disgusting."

"Not that anyone forced you to look at it. You weren't even at the table for most of dinner. You were on the telephone."

"I was not."

"You excused yourself from the table at least three times—"

"Because nobody answered the first two times."

"Who was so important that you had to call them in the middle of a dinner party?"

Alison shot him a scathing look and then resurrected her pout. She folded her arms across the blousy bodice of her jumpsuit and scoured the road ahead of them with her gaze. They had cruised away from the beach and were heading toward a barren stretch of marshland. The moon and the car's headlights offered the only illumination along the twisting road.

"I knew you were eager to leave," Jeremy went on in an ameliorating tone. "And yet there I was, finally ready to hit the road, and you had to run off and make another telephone call."

"Don't yell at me," Alison grumbled, sulking.

"I'm not yelling at you," he said evenly, refusing to be drawn into an argument with her. "All I'm saying is it was rude."

"Bob was rude to lecture everyone for hours about the Federal Reserve System." She shifted in her seat, presenting Jeremy with her shoulder. Her gaze remained on the road ahead.

"And I suppose Melanie was rude for serving eel." He was grinning, but with her back to him Alison couldn't see that.

"She was. Eel is about as rude as you can get."

"Some people consider it a gourmet treat."

"Some people are gross."

"I take it I'm one of them?" he commented.

Alison didn't say anything. She leaned forward, her hands gripping the dashboard and her teeth clamped around her lower lip as if she were bracing herself for a collision. Scowling, Jeremy swung his gaze back to the road in time to see a sky-blue van emerge from a dirt drive hidden by the marsh grass. It charged onto the road directly in front of the MG. Flooring the brake pedal, he downshifted and steered for his life. His car skidded onto the shoulder and bumped to a halt.

He let out a shaky breath. "Are you all right?" he asked, giving Alison a swift, anxious appraisal. She was pale and wide-eyed, her hands white-knuckled on the dashboard. He saw no blood or bruises on her, thank goodness, no signs of injury.

"I'm okay," she said, then let loose with a giddy laugh that Jeremy ascribed to nerves.

"I don't know where the hell that van came from," he muttered, stunned by his failure to have noticed it before it was almost too late. He glanced toward the road and saw that the van had pulled to a stop on the shoulder a few yards ahead. The driver's door opened and a young man emerged. He swaggered along the side of the road toward Jeremy's car.

"Hey, it's all right," Jeremy called to him. There was something sinister about the man, something about his unshaven jaw and his bulging biceps that made Jeremy reluctant to exchange addresses with him. He'd prefer it if they would both just drive off and forget the incident. "No damage done, and no one got hurt."

The stranger swept Jeremy's compact sports car with a contemptuous gaze, then strolled to the side door of his van. Pivoting on one sneakered foot, he unlatched the door and slid it open. Two other young men leaped out brandishing revolvers.

Guns. Jeremy shut his eyes and then opened them. The guns hadn't vanished. He hadn't hallucinated them. He tried to memorize the men's faces, their attire, any identifying characteristics—but his gaze insisted on traveling inexorably back to those evil-looking guns. They appeared hard and heavy and deadly. Their silver-gray barrels ended in menacing black holes. Bullets, Jeremy knew, came out of those holes.

This was bad, really bad.

Jeremy was a smart man. He had a degree from the University of Pennsylvania's School of Architecture and a job he treasured. He was six feet tall, weighed a trim one hundred sixty-eight pounds, played squash three times a week, ate oat bran and avoided salt.

But he was no match for three thugs, two of them armed with guns.

"Stay calm," he whispered to Alison, doing his best to keep his own panic at bay. His heart was ricocheting against his ribs and sending a crazy pulse through his body, making him dizzy. His vision seemed unable to register anything but those damned black bores at the ends of the two pistols. He wanted to scream, curse and throw up—not necessarily in that order.

He clung to his tenuous self-control. He had to maintain a level head; he had to protect Alison. He had to be brave enough for both of them.

"Stay calm, Alison," he repeated under his breath as the men neared the MG. "If we do as they say we won't get hurt."

"They haven't said anything," Alison pointed out, her voice brimming with excitement.

It occurred to Jeremy that, in her youthful naïveté, she considered this roadside hijacking perversely thrilling. He glimpsed the elegant gold watch on her wrist and the triple strand of freshwater pearls at her throat. He was wearing a gold watch, too, and there were his wallet and her purse, and the MG, fourteen years old but lovingly restored.... Would it be enough to buy their survival?

The three men surrounded the car and peered in. Jeremy promised himself that he would never again own a convertible. He felt painfully exposed in the roofless vehicle, completely vulnerable to the men and their weapons.

"Get out," the van driver said to Alison, wrenching open her door and grabbing her arm.

"Hey!" Jeremy reflexively reached for her other arm. "Don't you dare touch her!"

One of the gunmen swatted Jeremy's hand away, then hauled him out of the car as well.

This was it, then. His number was up. He was going to die. As he was led along the gravelly shoulder of the road, he contemplated the fact that death was imminent, that his final resting place was going to be amid some tangled reeds a quarter mile from the water's edge, that the last conversation of his tragically abbreviated life was going to have dealt with smoked eel. He hoped it wouldn't hurt, that was all. He prayed to God that dying wouldn't hurt—and that the men wouldn't harm Alison.

"Leave her alone," he demanded, reassured by the firm authority in his tone. As frightened as he was, he wouldn't quake and quail before these creeps. He wouldn't beg. "Do what you want to me, but for God's sake leave her alone."

"Shut up," one of the gunmen barked before shoving Jeremy against the rear of the car and pinning his arm behind his back. Jeremy kept his eyes on Alison; she was being led to the van by the driver and the other gunman.

"Where are you taking her?"

"Shut up," the gunman ordered him.

"So help me, if you do anything to her—"

"I said, shut up."

He watched helplessly as the driver and the other gunman ushered Alison to the open side door of the van. She spun around and sent Jeremy a look of wide-eyed astonishment. He issued a few more silent prayers: that they wouldn't touch her, that if they killed him she wouldn't have to watch, that they'd be clean and swift, that there was such a thing as heaven, that he'd wake up and find out this was all a bad dream. He wanted to shout some reassurance to her, but what could he say? That he was sorry this jerk was going to murder him? That he wished her better luck in the future? That he wished her a future, period?

She turned to the driver. "Please, don't hurt him," he heard her say just before she was lifted up into the van.

He felt a sharp, swift pain at the back of his skull. His vision filled with an explosion of spinning stars, and then darkness closed around him.

CHAPTER ONE

MARLO MCGINNIS MARCHED up the slate walk to what she presumed was the front door. With these weird modern houses you couldn't always tell which side was the front and which was the back. Jeremy Kent's house was high and narrow, landscaped with too much gravel and scrubby bushes and not enough grass. An abundance of windows overlooked the water; although Long Island Sound was a couple of miles in the distance, the house stood on a promontory that offered a dramatic view.

Even without having seen his house, she could have guessed that he would be rich. Porter Havelock would not have allowed his daughter to become engaged to anyone who wasn't. Havelock hadn't told Marlo much about his daughter's fiancé, only that he was thirty-three years old, from a "good" family, that he was the chief architect of the office complex Havelock was currently developing in northern Stamford, and that he'd been through a traumatic experience and needed to be treated gently.

Marlo wasn't sure why Havelock had felt it necessary to remind her to be gentle. Did he expect her to browbeat the guy? Practice her judo on him? All she wanted was to get a firsthand report on Alison's abduction. Just because Jeremy Kent was young, rich and successful didn't mean Marlo couldn't treat him with civility.

She adjusted her blazer, smoothed her blouse along the waistband of her skirt and rang the doorbell. The air smelled of cedar and pine; the sky was flocked with high, wispy clouds. The small wedge of lawn bordering the driveway where she'd left her car glistened with dew.

No one answered. She was certain Jeremy Kent was at home; Havelock had phoned ahead to alert him that a private investigator was on her way over to interview him, and he'd assured Havelock that he had no plans to go anywhere. Before she'd approached Jeremy Kent's door she'd peeked through one of the garage windows and seen a classy-looking MG convertible parked inside.

She checked her watch: nine o'clock. Maybe Jeremy had gone back to bed. After all, the previous night hadn't been exactly restful for him. He'd spent time at the police station, time at the hospital, more time talking to Havelock. The poor man was probably exhausted.

She couldn't stand around waiting for him to catch up on his beauty rest, though. Havelock was anxious to get his daughter back—preferably with a minimum of publicity and without having to part with any ransom money. If Alison didn't turn up in a few hours, the FBI would be brought into the case, and once they were involved, the press would follow, blaring sensational headlines: "Rich, Beautiful Coed From Connecticut's Gold Coast Snatched from Beau's Car On Beach Road...."

Marlo rang the bell again. The door swung open and she found herself staring at a bare, gloriously masculine chest. The sturdy rib cage was upholstered by a supple layer of lean muscle, which was in turn covered by evenly suntanned skin and a delectable mat of wiry golden hair. She let her eyes stray down as far as the drawstring waist of a pair of sweatpants, then ran her gaze back up past a flat stomach and those well-toned pectorals. She lingered for a moment on a sinewy ridge of shoulder before raising her eyes to view a strikingly handsome face.

Jeremy Kent might have had a traumatic night, but other than his eyes, which were bloodshot and ringed with shadow, he appeared to have survived his trauma remarkably well. His dark blond hair was mussed, his brow furrowed, his lips curved in a scowl and his square jaw darkened by an overnight growth of beard. And he was gorgeous.

Young, rich, successful and handsome. It was a bit much, but Marlo would try to forgive him. "Hello," she said brightly, ignoring his forbidding scowl. "I'm Marlo McGinnis. Porter Havelock sent me over to talk to you."

He stared at her for a minute, his frown intensifying. Marlo focused on the soft gray shade of his irises, the same muted color as pussy willows. Narrow lines radiated from the outer corners of his eyes and a deep crease marked the bridge of his nose. He lifted one hand to the back of his head and rubbed it, then grimaced. "Marlo McGinnis," he repeated in a hoarse, weary voice.

"May I come in?"

He sized her up again, obviously skeptical. "Porter said he was sending over a private investigator."

Marlo dutifully pulled her license out of her purse and presented it to him.

He squinted at it, then handed it back. "I thought I met someone named McGinnis who works for him—but the person I met was a man."

"My father," Marlo explained. "Stan McGinnis. We're partners. He does a lot of security work for Mr. Havelock, but it was decided that I would handle this. May I come in?"

He hesitated a moment longer, then waved her inside. He shut the door behind her and shuffled barefoot down a hall to an airy two-story high living room furnished with expensive-looking pieces: a sectional couch of brown leather, a rocking chair, a few scattered tables, a floor lamp and a sickly coleus in a clay pot. Two pillows lay at one end of the couch, and indentations in the cushions indicated that Jeremy had been stretched out on the couch when she'd rung his doorbell.

"Feel free to lie back down," she invited him, gesturing toward the pillows. "I understand you took quite a bang on the head last night."

He scrutinized her warily, then moved back toward the hallway. "Let me put on a shirt first," he said. "I wasn't expecting a woman."

She almost called after him that he needn't trouble himself on her account—she thought he looked great just the way he was. But she kept her mouth shut. The man was out-of-bounds: even if he wasn't already promised to Alison Havelock, he was way beyond Marlo's reach. Too affluent, too upper-class. Too dangerously good-looking.

She listened to him trudge up the stairs and then paced the living room, mentally recording every detail: the thin residue of ashes in the fireplace, undoubtedly left over from the previous winter; the collection of hardcover nonfiction and paperback novels filling the built-in shelves; the blank legal pad lying on the coffee table next to a pair of thin-rimmed tortoiseshell eyeglasses and a mug with an inch of cold black coffee at the bottom. The dhurrie rug, the panoramic windows, the dying plant.

Jeremy Kent was apparently not the sort to knock himself out trying to impress others. He might own a fancy house but he hadn't exerted himself to decorate the interior. Nor had he made much of an effort to water his coleus.

She was on her way down a hall to snoop in a few other rooms when she heard his footsteps on the stairs. She hurried back to the living room, arriving a few seconds ahead of him. He had put on a clean oxford shirt, khaki trousers and socks, but he hadn't bothered to shave or comb his hair. He pointed vaguely toward the rocker, then collapsed onto the couch and rubbed the back of his head again.

"Have you taken any aspirin?" she asked solicitously.

He grunted. "You ought to save your worrying for Alison. God only knows where she is or what they've done to her...." He closed his eyes and shuddered.

"God may be the only one who knows right now," Marlo noted briskly, "but I intend to find out soon. I'm sure you'd rather be resting right now, Mr. Kent, but if you can answer just a few questions—"

"I'll do whatever I can to help," he said fervently. "I've already answered a million questions for the police, though. Have you seen their report?"

Marlo nodded. "I won't ask you a million questions," she promised, keenly aware of his exhaustion. "Just a few." She pulled a pad and pen out of her purse and flipped to a clean page. Clicking open the pen, she glanced up to find Jeremy staring at her, apparently puzzled. "What's the matter?" she asked. "Did I get ink on my nose?"

A feeble grin crossed his lips. "You just don't look like a private eye, that's all."

"What do I look like?"

He studied her neatly arranged black hair, her lightweight suit and shell blouse and low-heeled pumps. "Right now, you look like a secretary about to take dictation."

She smiled tolerantly. "Most people expect P.I.'s to wear rumpled raincoats, smoke cigarettes and pack a weapon. The truth is, most of my work involves asking questions, gathering evidence and fitting it together. It's cerebral, Mr. Kent, and I can do it in a skirt."

"Your father..." He leaned back in the couch and appraised her thoughtfully. "He's a detective, too?"

"Yes." She didn't mind answering his questions before she asked hers. If he approved of her answers he'd be more relaxed with her, more likely to open up. "My father and I are partners," she explained. "A great deal of his work over the past few years has been for Porter Havelock—setting up security systems in the office complexes he builds, helping him with background searches on employees and so on. But yes, we're both investigators."

Jeremy continued to stare at her, rubbing the back of his head slowly and thoughtfully. "That's nice, working with your father," he finally said.

"I have no complaints. Can we get started now?"

Jeremy hesitated. "Marlo is an unusual name," he remarked. For someone eager to do whatever he could to help solve the mystery of Alison's disappearance, he seemed peculiarly willing to waste time on trivia.

"I was named after Phillip Marlowe," Marlo told him. "My father's a Raymond Chandler fan. My mother changed the spelling to M-A-R-L-O, like the actress."

Jeremy smiled. Marlo found herself drawn in by the sweet, soft gray of his eyes. She wondered whether he'd look as handsome in his glasses as he did without them. Would they obscure his eyes or magnify them? Would they emphasize the smoky color?

These were absurd thoughts, and she concertedly shoved them from her mind and tackled the business at hand. "As I indicated, I've read the statement you gave the police. Do you recall anything more about the license plate on the van than what you told them? Any letters or numbers, anything that may have come to you after you got home?"

He shook his head. "Just what I told the police—that it was a New Jersey plate."

"One of the old black-and-white plates, or a blue-and-yellow plate?"

"A blue-and-yellow one," he said.

That wasn't terribly surprising; most vehicles registered in New Jersey had changed over to the newer plates. Even so, the police should have recorded that detail. It would help to narrow down the year the van might have been registered. "You didn't catch the make of the van?" Marlo asked.

"I'm afraid not."

"American or foreign?"

He meditated for a minute. "I don't know. I think it was pretty new—one of those vans with the sloping fronts."

"Was there a logo on the back? Maybe a pentagon or an ellipse or something?"

Jeremy closed his eyes in an apparent attempt to conjure up the scene. When he opened his eyes again, he appeared oddly startled. "Now that you mention it . . . I think there was an oval shape near the bumper."

Ford Aerostar, Marlo scribbled onto her pad. "Anything else? Any bumper stickers? Dents or scratches? A yellow square sign stuck to the window reading Criminals On Board?"

Jeremy seemed unsure of how to take Marlo's dry humor. "There might have been a sticker on the bumper, a parking sticker of some sort," he said.

The police hadn't made a note of that, either. Marlo jotted the information onto her pad, then lifted her gaze back to him. He returned her stare, and she sensed that, despite their gentle color, his eyes were sharp and all-seeing even without the aid of glasses. A ripple of self-consciousness fluttered through her, but she ignored it. "Was Alison scared when the kidnapping occurred?" she asked.

"She was petrified," he answered automatically. "We both were."

Marlo continued to watch him, trying to tap into his subconscious. She and her father had spent quite a while with Porter Havelock that morning, and while her father had questioned Havelock directly, Marlo had concentrated on the nuances, on what was left unspoken. Havelock had told her father that Alison was always getting herself into scrapes, and Marlo had interpreted his statement to mean that Alison was anxious for attention. Havelock had declared that Alison had spent much of the past month moping around the house and complaining of boredom, and Marlo had absorbed that Alison needed excitement. The girl had spent a lot of time lately on the phone on long-distance calls with a couple of college friends, Havelock had related, male friends—but whenever he had inquired about her relationship with these male friends, Alison had insisted that she adored Jeremy and wanted only to be with him. Marlo had stored it all in her mental files, positive that once she'd processed all the information, the pieces would fall into place.

Jeremy's claim that Alison had been petrified during the abduction might be true—or the truth might be that he was viewing Alison's reaction through his own terror. "Did she scream?" Marlo asked.

"Well . . . no. But neither did I."

"You're a man. She's a woman, much younger than you."

Jeremy meditated. "No," he repeated. "She didn't scream."

Marlo could feel a hunch taking shape—an inkling of a hunch. She'd been doing detective work long enough to trust her hunches implicitly. "Did anything unusual happen during the evening?" she pressed Jeremy. "You and Alison had been the dinner guests of some friends here in Westport, right?"

"That's right."

"Was Alison at all nervous during the course of the evening? Did she act strangely?"

Jeremy gave Marlo a baffled look, as if he were trying to figure out what she was getting at. "No," he replied. "She acted pretty normally."

"She just lounged around making chitchat with your friends all evening?"

"Actually . . ." He paused, mulling over his words. "She didn't enjoy the dinner much," he said carefully, as if weighing how much he should reveal. Marlo considered reminding him that she was working for his future father-in-law, but he continued before she could chide him about his reticence. "She doesn't much care for gourmet food, and she isn't terribly fond of the couple who hosted the dinner."

"So what did she do? How did she get through this unpleasant evening?"

"It wasn't unpleasant," he retorted. "And she got through it just fine."

"Sitting at the table and watching everyone else eat gourmet food?"

He reflected. "To be totally honest . . . she entertained herself by making telephone calls."

Telephone calls. Just like the telephone calls she'd been making from her father's house recently? To the same friends from college? "Do you know who she called?"

"I wouldn't presume to ask," he said coolly.

"How many calls did she make?"

"I wasn't counting."

Marlo grinned. It was all coming together. "Alison goes to college in New Jersey, doesn't she?"

"Yes— Fairleigh Dickinson University."

New Jersey license plate, New Jersey college. "Did the kidnappers use force getting her into the van?"

Jeremy's gaze narrowed. "I'd say waving a gun around constitutes using force. Wouldn't you?"

"They could have picked her up and carried her to the van, couldn't they?"

"They didn't have to," he pointed out. "Flaunting their guns did the trick." He closed his eyes and sighed. "God help me—I told her to do whatever they said so she wouldn't get hurt. Maybe it's my fault she—"

"It's not your fault." Marlo swiftly cut him off. He had no reason to be racked with guilt. No matter how this thing had gone down, no matter whether or not Marlo's hunch panned out, Jeremy had been nothing but an innocent bystander. "Did she resist climbing into the van?" she asked, eager to visualize the actual kidnapping as clearly as possible.

He didn't answer immediately. Opening his eyes, he gazed for several seconds toward the broad panes of glass lining the wall. When he turned back to Marlo his expression was quizzical, nearly accusing. "What exactly are you getting at, Ms. McGinnis?"

"The truth," Marlo answered succinctly. She recalled Havelock's request that she treat Jeremy gently and wondered whether her insistence on extracting every trivial detail from his memory of last night constituted browbeating. But she couldn't stop. The more information she had, the more specific Jeremy was, the faster she'd be able to solve this mess. "Did she resist the kidnappers in any way?" she asked in what she hoped was a compassionate tone of voice.

"No," he admitted, then rallied. "But she begged them not to hurt me."

"Oh?" Marlo lifted her pen. "What did she say?"

"'Please, don't hurt him.'"

"How did she say it?"

"What do you mean?"

"I mean," Marlo said with all the patience she could muster, "did she shout it? Cry? Grab hold of her captor's shirt and shake him?"

Jeremy scowled. Once again, he seemed to be regarding Marlo with suspicion. "What was she supposed to do?" he snapped. "The men had guns, and—"

"And did she scream it or did she just say it?"

"She just said it," he replied curtly. "But I don't see—"

"*How* did she say it? Can you say it exactly the way she did?"

He was clearly exasperated. "She just said it, Ms. McGinnis. She said, 'Please, don't hurt him.' What is this, an audition?"

Marlo ignored his sarcasm. That Alison Havelock hadn't screamed, hadn't wept, hadn't pleaded for her own life, hadn't struggled . . . that her last words were a calmly stated request on Jeremy's behalf . . . It was coming together into a clear picture. Marlo's hunch had to be right.

"Don't worry about Alison," she declared as she rose from the rocker and folded her pad shut. "I have the feeling she's just fine."

In spite of his obvious fatigue, Jeremy sprang to his feet. "How can you be so...so blasé about this?" he charged. "Alison's been kidnapped, for God's sake!"

"I'm not being blasé," Marlo said placidly, returning her pad and pen to her purse and adjusting its strap on her shoulder. "Just logical. You've been very helpful, Mr. Kent," she continued, starting down the hallway. "I appreciate—"

In one long stride he caught up to her and grasped her arm. His fingers were strong but not crushing, his grip holding her without much pressure. Her gaze flew from his hand to his face just inches above hers. His eyes met hers and she sensed more in them than simply impatience and suspicion. She saw his confusion—almost felt it. Confusion and contrition and something else, something she couldn't decipher.

His gaze held hers for a pregnant moment. Then, abashed, he let go of her. "Forgive me," he said, "but I don't think you're taking this situation seriously."

"Oh, I am," she assured him, trying to ignore his clean, male scent, the tingling sensation his hand had imparted to her upper arm, the warmth of his body so close to hers. For an insane instant she envisioned the way he'd looked when he'd opened the door to her, clad in nothing but a pair of sweatpants. She pictured his magnificent chest and his sleepy, unfocused eyes, his tousled hair and his broad, rugged shoulders.

Jeremy Kent was one sexy guy, she acknowledged. Alison Havelock was one lucky girl to have won his heart.

So why had she pulled this outrageous stunt? Why in heaven's name had she staged her own kidnapping?

"I've got to get back to my office," said Marlo, pleased that her tone betrayed nothing of her thoughts. "I'll be keeping Porter Havelock apprised of all developments, so—"

"I'm coming with you," Jeremy said abruptly.

"What?"

"I'll come with you."

Again she found herself drawn by the hypnotic power of his gray eyes. What was he after? What did he want? The only rational explanation she could come up with for his eagerness to accompany her was that he was deeply devoted to Alison.

She wondered how he'd take it when he learned that his beloved girlfriend had faked the previous night's roadside melodrama, that for reasons known only to herself she'd deliberately chosen to abscond with a trio of phony kidnappers. It would probably break his heart.

Marlo wasn't about to share her theory with Jeremy— not only because she wanted to spare his feelings, but because, if she was correct, the entire incident could cause enormous embarrassment to Porter Havelock. He was the man paying her fee; she owed it to him to pursue the case of his daughter's disappearance as discreetly as possible. She wanted to avoid any tabloid headlines, but particularly such headlines as "Rich, Beautiful Coed From Connecticut Gold Coast Deceives Father And Fiancé."

And, of course, there was always the possibility that Marlo was wrong. In which case, she'd be facing tons of catch-up work. She definitely didn't want Alison's lover around to slow her down.

"I'd rather go alone," she told Jeremy, taking a deliberate step back. Standing so close to him was hazardous; she was far too conscious of his riveting good looks. "It's going to be monotonous work—real basic, tedious stuff. Making phone calls, running through lists, that kind of thing."

"What lists?"

"Mr. Kent . . ." She manufactured a smile and stalked down the hall, suddenly anxious to leave. "I'll have Alison's father get in touch with you if there's any news. Thanks for your time." She reached for the doorknob.

"I want to help," he insisted. "I could run through the lists with you."

"Or you could take some aspirin and lie down. I really think that's what you ought to do." Marlo swung open the door and stepped outside, compelled to get away from Jeremy before she blew everything by grabbing those alluring shoulders of his, giving him a teeth-rattling shake and saying, "Your pea-brained sweetheart is bluffing. She let you get popped in the skull just for kicks. You're wasting your heart on her."

What she said, in an admirably restrained voice, was, "Don't worry about Alison—I'll get her back. You take care of yourself." Then she strode briskly down the front walk to her car and around to the driver's side.

She slid in behind the wheel, started the engine and let out a long breath. "You can start worrying about her *after* I get her back, chump," she muttered, aware that Jeremy Kent was about to learn some pretty unsettling things about his beloved young girlfriend.

HE WATCHED through the screen door as Marlo McGinnis folded her tall, slim body inside the Honda parked in his driveway, revved the engine and drove down to the street and out of sight. Then he reached behind his head to rub the throbbing egg-shaped lump at the base of his skull.

The past twelve hours had dissolved into a murky montage of images in his mind: regaining consciousness to discover himself lying among the weeds at the side of the road, his car untouched beside him and his head hammering with pain. Rising shakily to his feet and finding his keys still in the ignition, his wristwatch still on his wrist and his wallet in his pocket. Driving through town until he reached the police station, staggering inside, collaring the first uniformed officer he saw and babbling incoherently about what had happened.

A ride to the hospital in a police cruiser. More police interviews as he waited to be examined. A brain scan that revealed no serious damage. A ride with the police to Porter's Southport estate. Porter yelling at him that he ought to have taken better care of Alison, that he'd been entrusted with her, that he shouldn't have let this dreadful thing happen to her. Police intervention on Jeremy's behalf. Porter storming off to get a drink, then returning and apologizing for his outburst, acknowledging that Jeremy had undoubtedly been through a lot and couldn't be blamed for what had happened to Alison. A ride back to the station house in Westport to pick up the MG. Home. Four Excedrin. Fitful sleep.

Phantasmagoric images, one bleeding into the next, until now. Until a tall, raven-haired woman with long legs and a quick mouth invaded his house, cutting through his mental blur with her knowing smile, her perceptive brown eyes and her husky voice.

He ought to be worried about Alison. He ought to be frantic.

But all he could think of was that he shouldn't have let Marlo McGinnis get away.

CHAPTER TWO

GUNS! SHE HADN'T KNOWN they were going to use guns.

Alison shifted under the blanket. Hot and sweaty, she was dying to throw off the covers and come up for air. They must have driven out of Connecticut by now. And even if they hadn't, she was wearing one of Ned's shirts over her jumpsuit and she'd braided her hair and tied a scarf around her head, so it wasn't like anyone was going to recognize her through the car windows. Besides, Dave's mother had already seen her because they'd been making so much noise when they arrived at his house to swap his van for Peter's Volvo. Two o'clock in the morning, and Mrs. Sawyer had insisted on fixing them pancakes. Alison hadn't had any appetite, but the guys had sat around the kitchen table stuffing their faces for an hour. Really. It wasn't as though this whole kidnapping thing was much of a secret anymore.

But Ned had insisted that she stay hidden when they drove back through Connecticut on their way north. "Keep the blanket on," he'd said. "Keep your eyes closed. Pretend you're sleeping." He'd insisted on sitting in the back seat with her, just to make sure she did it right.

She wanted to ask him where he'd found the guns. She figured he had to be the one who'd gotten them; Dave and Peter were good guys but kind of dorky. They wouldn't know the first thing about how to go about obtaining a gun, let alone how to use it. She'd almost laughed out loud when she'd seen the way they handled their weapons—like two nerds pretending to be Clint Eastwood or something. It would have been funny—if they hadn't gone and hurt Jeremy.

Hurting people had never been part of the plan. Especially hurting Jeremy. He was the only good thing about this whole awful summer, as far as Alison was concerned. He was old, sure—not bad looking, but old just the same. And he sometimes treated her condescendingly. But at least he talked to her and did things with her. At least he listened when she talked to him.

Which was more than she could say for her father.

She'd exaggerated when she told her father about her relationship with Jeremy. She'd let the old man believe that she and Jeremy were real close, that they were in love. It enabled her to get out of the house whenever Jeremy phoned her—no questions asked, no rules laid down. Her father didn't even give her a curfew as long as he knew she'd be with Jeremy. All he said was, "Jeremy's a fine man—you couldn't do better," and that kind of thing. "He comes from a good family, he earns a nice living, and he'd make a wonderful son-in-law." Not a wonderful husband, oh no. Alison's father always saw things from his own perspective.

So, okay, she'd let him think they were getting serious. It kept him off her case. She could just imagine what he'd think if she ever introduced him to Ned. Ned might have come from a family her father would approve of, but since he'd graduated from Fairleigh Dickinson last year the only job he'd had was as lifeguard at a country club—and after all of a month he'd gotten fired for talking back to his boss. Ned was dumb that way. But he was exciting, and he knew things. Like where to get guns.

"Are we out of Connecticut yet?" she asked. Her words were muffled by the blanket.

"Shh," he hissed.

"I'm hot."

"Shut up. It's rush hour. We're in a traffic jam in Hartford."

She tried to lift her head high enough to peek out the window, but Ned pushed her back down. She was beginning to think that maybe he was getting into his role a little too wholeheartedly. It was one thing to let him kidnap her so she could give her father a well-deserved scare and spend a little time up at Peter's summer house. But it was quite another thing to get shoved around, and to see a nice guy like Jeremy get whacked on the head with a gun butt.

"Jeremy didn't really get hurt, did he?" she asked through the folds of gray wool.

"Nah."

"Because the way he fell—"

"He's okay. Dave hardly touched him. Right, Dave?"

"I didn't hear any bones breaking," Dave called back over his shoulder.

"Because if you hurt him, you could get charged with assault or something," Alison pointed out.

She felt Ned's hand through the blanket tightening on her hip. "Hey, listen, toots, it's up to you to make sure nobody gets charged with anything, right? That was the deal we made. If any of us get caught, you've got to make sure we don't get in trouble over this. We're doing it all for you, so you've got to come through for us. That was the deal."

The deal didn't include guns, she retorted silently. It was just supposed to be a gag, a few days away from her father's stifling world, a chance to party with her friends and shake her father up and make her mother feel guilty for having flown off to Europe with Lucian, her creepy new underage husband. Nobody was supposed to get hurt.

She really, really hoped Ned understood that.

MCGINNIS & MCGINNIS, INC., was located on the third floor of a nondescript office building in the heart of Bridgeport. The front room resembled a dentist's waiting room minus the syrupy music: a couple of tweedy sofas, a coffee table covered with out-of-date magazines, a potted plant, a receptionist's desk. A door led into the back room where Marlo and her father worked. Two steel desks stood facing each other, Stan's cluttered and Marlo's tidy. A side table held the computer, and every available inch of wall space was lined with file cabinets and shelves. The south-facing windows let in plenty of sunshine.

Ida, the receptionist/bookkeeper, never came in on weekends, and Marlo's father was still at Porter Havelock's house, so Marlo had the office to herself. She'd taken a brief detour home to change out of her skirt and blazer and into some comfortably broken-in jeans and a sweatshirt, then headed for the office. A phone call to an acquaintance who worked in New Jersey's central motor vehicle department produced a list of several hundred metallic-blue Ford Aerostars that had been registered in the past five years; of that list, thirty-two had been registered in Bergen County, where Fairleigh Dickinson University was located. If Marlo's theory was wrong she'd have a lot of backtracking to do, but she trusted her instincts on this one.

She telephoned the college switchboard. A clerk answered and at Marlo's request connected her to the security department—usually the department in charge of issuing campus parking stickers. "I'm hoping you can help me," Marlo told the man who took her call. "Last night I dented a van in a parking lot with my car, and I just drove away without leaving a note or anything. Now I feel so guilty, I've got to do something. The van had a Fairleigh Dickinson sticker on the bumper. I'm hoping you might be able to tell me who it belonged to so I can contact them and pay them for the damage."

"And who says honesty is out of fashion?" the man exclaimed, clearly impressed by Marlo's alleged bout of conscience. "Have you got the license plate number?"

"Actually, I've got several," said Marlo, not bothering to elaborate. She'd learned that, when lying, she was best off explaining as little as possible. "I'm sure one of them is the right one, if only you can tell me which one belongs to a Fairleigh Dickinson student or a faculty member." *Please,* she added silently, shooting a prayerful look heavenward, *let one of these licenses pan out.* Into the phone, she slowly started to recite her list of license plate numbers.

She struck gold on her eleventh try. "Yes, we've got a record on that one," the man told her. "It belongs to David Sawyer of Montclair. A senior here at the school."

"David Sawyer," Marlo reiterated, writing it down. "Have you got his address?"

The security man hedged. "Um . . . I don't know that I ought to give that information out."

"His phone number, then?"

"I guess that would be all right," the security man said, then provided the number.

Marlo sent another prayer heavenward, this one in gratitude not only for having found a Fairleigh Dickinson student who owned a light blue Aerostar but also for having been connected to a gullible security officer. As soon as she thanked the man and hung up, she went to the shelf where she and her father stored their extensive collection of United States telephone directories. She pulled out the Bergen County directory, opened it to the *S*'s, and searched the Sawyer listings until she found one with a phone number that matched.

"Bingo," she whispered, jotting down the address and returning the directory to the shelf. She grabbed her purse from the bottom drawer of her desk and started toward the door. Curling her hand around the knob, she felt it turn from the other side. She pulled the door open and came face to face with Jeremy Kent.

Marlo didn't much like being sneaked up on. Worse yet was being sneaked up on by someone as devastatingly handsome as Jeremy. Since she'd left his house two and a half hours ago he'd shaved and combed his hair. The whites of his eyes were clear, and when he smiled she noticed a faint dimple at the corner of his mouth.

Her first impulse was to yell at him for having startled her. She suppressed the urge and ordered herself to remain polite and pleasant. He might have come to her office because he remembered something important about the previous night's abduction. He might have tried to telephone her and gotten a busy signal, and he'd driven here to tell her in person.

"Mr. Kent—what can I do for you?" she asked, regarding him with a circumspect smile.

He didn't answer right away. Instead, he took his time assessing the change in her appearance since he'd last seen her. While he'd become more well-groomed, she'd become less so. Her makeup had faded and her hair was messy from the many minutes she'd spent with a telephone receiver pinned to her ear. Her white leather sneakers were scuffed and her sweatshirt had telltale reddish spots on one sleeve from when she'd helped her father restain his redwood deck furniture a couple of Sundays ago. This was her off-hours-on-the-telephone garb, not her meeting-with-rich-clients attire.

No point in apologizing for her appearance, however. If Jeremy was going to barge in on her unannounced, he'd have to take her as she was.

His silence continued. "Did you remember something you wanted to tell me about the van? Or the kidnappers?" she asked.

"I want to help," he said quietly, his edgy smile vanishing. "I felt so useless sitting around my house."

"You're more use to me there than anywhere else," Marlo informed him, taking a step back in an effort to escape the subtle, enticing fragrance of his after-shave. "That way I know where you are if I've got any questions."

"You'd know where I was if I was with you," he pointed out.

"Mr. Kent, I told you—this is the boring meat-and-potatoes stuff. There's really nothing for you to do here but twiddle your thumbs."

"Call me Jeremy," he said.

She sighed. It wasn't unusual for her to use a client's first name, but she preferred to maintain a certain formality with Jeremy, if only because when she thought of him in informal terms she thought of him bare-chested—which was without a doubt a perilous thing to do.

"Look," he said, crossing the threshold. "I'll do whatever you want: man the phones, make coffee, whatever. I just want to be a part of it, that's all."

"You're already a part of it," Marlo reminded him. "You've got a nice big bruise on your skull to prove it."

"I mean, part of the solution." His eyes were bright as they scanned the office. "I just can't sit around idly. I've got to *do* something. Alison's out there, somewhere—"

"You don't have to worry about her," Marlo reassured him. "I'm going to find her. Maybe today."

His gaze traveled from the row of file cabinets back to Marlo. It didn't take him long to notice that her purse was slung by its strap over her shoulder and she was clutching her key ring. "You're on your way out."

"That's right. And since we're not open for business, I plan to lock up the office."

"Meaning I should go home?"

"Exactly." She brushed past him on her way to the door.

He halted her, curving his hand over her shoulder. "I want to come with you," he said.

His voice was low and oddly persuasive. She neither needed nor wanted a tagalong for her jaunt to Montclair, and yet . . . he looked so hopeful, so imploring.

She didn't expect any violence when she confronted David Sawyer—if she managed to track him down. The way she figured it, one of three things was likely to happen when she rang the Sawyer doorbell: she would find Sawyer and he'd confess and hand Alison over; she'd find Sawyer and he'd turn out not to have had anything to do with Alison's abduction; or she wouldn't find Sawyer.

Given those three possibilities, Jeremy truly wouldn't be that much trouble to have along. He was in love with Alison and justifiably frantic about her well-being. He wanted to see his sweetheart. Marlo couldn't blame him.

"I'm going to New Jersey," she alerted him. "It's going to take a couple of hours."

His hand relaxed on her shoulder but he didn't remove it. His fingers remained molded around her, warm and firm, his fingertips brushing the edge of her collarbone. "Is that where you think Alison is?"

"There's someone there I want to talk to who might know where she is," Marlo said cryptically.

"I'll come with you." In his mind, apparently, the matter had already been decided.

Not in hers, though. There was something to be said for bringing him along: if Alison saw him she might come to her senses more quickly. She might feel remorseful—or even relieved. The arguments against bringing him along didn't seem all that decisive: it wasn't professional, he might get in the way, it was generally unwise to deviate from standard practice.

And then the most conclusive argument against having Jeremy Kent spend the next several hours with her: he was too handsome, too desirable, too damned attractive.

"All right, you can come," she muttered, capitulating in spite of herself. Some small voice of sanity inside her warned that this was a bad idea. The same reliable instincts that told her David Sawyer would lead her to Alison Havelock also told her she ought to steer clear of Jeremy Kent.

But sometimes, just sometimes, instincts were meant to be ignored.

"YOU KNOW, I DON'T ordinarily do this," Marlo said.

"Do what?"

"Allow a client to accompany me on a job."

Jeremy wondered what sort of jobs she usually took on—and what sort of clients. Her office hadn't been anything like what he'd imagined. It had lacked the smoke-filled seediness he might have associated with her namesake Phillip Marlowe, as well as the glamorous decor he might have expected from an attractive female detective. Rather, it had looked like a place of business, unadorned and functional.

They were cruising south on I-95 in her Honda sedan. The car, he noticed, had an air-conditioning button on the dashboard but Marlo didn't turn it on. Instead she had the windows open, and hot July air blasted through the car, tangling the black waves of her shoulder-length hair and sweeping it back from her face. Her skin was clear and peach-toned, her eyes nearly as dark as her hair, her nose long and narrow, nicely balanced by a long, narrow chin. Her lips were thin, and even when she was frowning they turned up at the outer corners, giving her a perpetually ironic look that fascinated him.

His gaze traveled from her face to her body, her wonderfully long legs covered by snugly fitting denim and her torso hidden beneath the baggy folds of her oversized white sweatshirt. The shirt's loose neckline drooped slightly to one side, revealing her swan-like neck and a bit of her right shoulder. She'd shoved up the sleeves, exposing her slender forearms and wrists. Her only jewelry was a plain wristwatch on a black leather strap.

He wondered what the dark red stains spotting the sweatshirt were from. They looked like dried blood—and contemplating what might have created them was distinctly unappetizing. Had he talked himself into accompanying this woman on a shoot-out? She'd made that little speech at his house about how most people expected private eyes to pack a weapon—but she'd never specifically told him she *didn't* pack one.

Why on earth had he demanded that she bring him along? Had he survived the kidnapping only to be shot during the rescue? He wished he could be as stoical about the situation as she was. She sat calmly beside him, her eyes on the road, her left elbow resting on the sill of the open window and her right hand manipulating the gear stick with finesse, managing to execute shifts without dislodging the receiver of the cellular phone installed between the seats. If the car was, in fact, carrying them to an ambush she appeared to be remarkably unconcerned.

"Is this going to be dangerous?" he asked, manfully keeping his voice free of anxiety.

She tossed him a swift glance, then turned her gaze back to the highway and shrugged. "I hope not."

"You don't seem scared."

"Fear doesn't do me much good, so I tune it out," she explained vaguely. "If you're scared, though—"

"I'm not," he said quickly.

She cracked a smile. "Forget about danger. If these jerks were dangerous they would have done more than hit you on the head last night. My guess is they're amateurs."

"What makes you say that?"

"If they were pros, Havelock would have received a ransom demand by now, probably with a lock of Alison's hair taped to it as proof that they had her. Pros wouldn't waste time; they'd get right down to business."

What Marlo said made sense, and Jeremy took comfort in it—but only for a second. "What if they kidnapped Alison for something other than money?" he asked anxiously.

"You mean her body?" Marlo asked. Jeremy nodded. "Forget it," she said, shooting him another brief look. "Sex criminals operate differently—and, frankly, if I thought that was what this case was about, I *would* be scared. I'd let the police handle it. I steer clear of violence whenever possible.''

He was reassured—until his eyes strayed to those mysterious red stains on her shirt. "That isn't blood, is it?" he asked nervously.

She glanced down to where he was pointing, then laughed. "No, Jeremy. It's redwood stain."

He sighed with relief.

"I'm not saying there's no risk whatsoever here," she added, jolting him out of his complacency. "I wouldn't have let you come along, except that you're Alison's fiancé."

He gaped at Marlo. "Her what?"

She focused on the road. "Well, all right, Havelock said you and Alison haven't made an official announcement yet, so maybe I'm not supposed to know. But don't be angry with him. He filled me in on your relationship with Alison only because he knew that the more he told me about her, the easier it would make my job. I'm sorry if I've stumbled onto something private."

"Private," Jeremy echoed, stunned. How in God's name had Porter come up with the idiotic notion that he and Alison intended to get married? "Exactly what did Porter say about Alison and me?"

"He said you were in love and you made her very happy. He thinks of you as a son, and he's really quite pleased with the way things are developing between the two of you. It's all very touching, Jeremy—and I'll tell you, it's only because you're her future husband that you're here in my car right now."

Her future husband? Bad enough that Porter had blown the friendship way out of proportion—Jeremy had never even kissed Alison, for crying out loud! But why did he have to go and say such ridiculous things to Marlo

McGinnis, of all people? If Jeremy felt anything toward Alison, it was essentially the sort of fondness a protective older brother might feel toward a flighty younger sister. He supposed he'd made her happier, lately, than her own parents did. But he wasn't in love with her—and he certainly wasn't her fiancé.

He had to set Marlo straight. "I think...maybe you misunderstood Porter."

Marlo let up on the gas pedal and eyed him accusingly. "Which means what? You're tagging along for the fun of it? Because you couldn't think of anything better to do today?"

"No, I—"

"I don't need this, Jeremy. I brought you along because I was figuring maybe it would help Alison if you were there when I found her. Now you're telling me you and she aren't—what? You aren't engaged, you aren't close—"

"We *are* close," he insisted.

Marlo eyed him speculatively. "You won't be of any use if you *aren't* close to her," she pointed out.

"We're close," he said in desperation, aware that Marlo was ready to kick him out of the car. "I swear, we're close."

Marlo shot him one final look, then pressed the accelerator, picking up speed. "All right," she yielded.

Far from relieved, Jeremy felt troubled. He wanted to participate in solving this crime not only because he felt guilty for having been unable to prevent it from occurring, nor because he found sitting on the sidelines extremely frustrating, but because he wanted to be with Marlo. He wanted to look at her, to admire her beauty; he wanted to watch her as she worked, to see her lively mind in action. He wanted to learn what made her so fearless—and he wanted to test the limits of his own fearlessness.

He wanted to ask her out—as soon as Alison was safe and sound, of course. As soon as this entire nightmare was behind him.

It galled him to think that the only way he could remain in Marlo's company was to pretend he was Alison's boyfriend. He consoled himself with the knowledge that if Marlo was right, if Alison's rescue was a mere matter of hours away, he wouldn't have to maintain the pretense for long.

Marlo changed lanes as the highway forked north and south at the New York state line. "I understand you're an architect," she said.

"That's right."

"Did you design that house of yours?"

"No." The subtle twist in her voice left him little doubt that she didn't like his house. He wasn't sure why—it was a good design. But he wasn't going to let her put him on the defensive. "I generally work on office buildings, shopping complexes, that sort of thing," he told her.

"That's where the money is, huh."

Once again he sensed a strain of sarcasm in her tone. He supposed skepticism was a healthy trait for a private eye, but even so, he didn't like the way it made him feel the need to justify himself. "I went into designing office buildings because I grew up surrounded by them in Manhattan," he told her. "So many of the buildings there had a sameness about them—they were so bland and uninspiring. I thought it would be rewarding to design more aesthetically pleasing office buildings so that the people working in them would be surrounded by an attractive environment. Money wasn't a factor."

She eyed him dubiously but said nothing.

"How about you?" he asked, forestalling further grilling. "Why did you go into detective work?"

"My father," she replied.

"He made you?"

She chuckled. "He begged me not to. Money *was* a factor. He wanted me to do something where I could earn a fortune. Law, business, computer engineering ... Anything but detective work."

"And you defied him," Jeremy summarized with a smile.

"He went absolutely nuts when I decided to attend the police academy instead of college. I even joined the Bridgeport P.D. It drove him up the wall. 'Anything!' he begged. 'I'll even let you be my partner. Just quit the damned force!' "

"Why? Doesn't he like policemen?"

"He has nothing against them," she explained. "But they have to handle drug dealers, muggers, rapists, wife beaters. Murderers. They get killed. My father didn't like that. To tell you the truth, neither did I."

"I'd hardly consider kidnapping nonviolent."

Marlo considered his statement as she followed the signs to the George Washington Bridge. "Most of what my father and I handle is pretty pedestrian stuff," she told him. "My father specializes in security—background checks, shoplifting prevention, stuff like that. I deal more with social situations—missing persons, adulterers, an occasional corporate embezzler for variety's sake. The most dangerous case I ever had was a runaway dog. I found the beast, and when I went to put a leash on him he bit my finger. I needed three stitches."

She extended her right arm in Jeremy's direction. He focused for a moment on her satin-smooth skin, the delicate protrusion of her wrist bone, the slender bones radiating out toward her knuckles.

Then he noticed the scar on her right index finger—a pale pink line marring the middle joint. It could have been worse, he thought. The dog could have severed a tendon or an artery—or bitten off an entire joint. It could have lunged for her face....

And yet, being bitten by a frenzied dog seemed rather trivial when compared to what they'd have to contend with once they came upon Alison's captors. Closing his eyes, he envisioned the steroid-fed muscles of the van driver and the formidable guns of his two accomplices. He recalled the gruff voice of the gunman who'd held him, the steel in his grip as he'd pinned Jeremy's arm against his back and the heartless ease with which he'd knocked Jeremy unconscious.

Jeremy would take an ill-tempered dog over three human goons any day.

But he wasn't going to give in to fear. He had his pride. If this willowy woman with her luminous brown eyes and her lush mane of hair wasn't intimidated by the prospect of facing off with a trio of thick-necked kidnappers, Jeremy sure as hell wouldn't be intimidated, either.

He'd be just as brave as she was.

CHAPTER THREE

"OH, MY GOD—THAT'S IT!"

Jeremy froze in his seat, his hands clenched into fists and his gaze riveted to the light blue Ford van parked innocuously inside the open two-car garage of a grand brick colonial. They'd made a quick stop at the Montclair fire station— "A town's fire station always has the best local street maps," Marlo had informed him—and from there had meandered through a pleasant upper-middle-class subdivision to this house, which sat squarely on an acre of neatly mown grass. The house appeared well maintained, with curtains at the windows, flowering shrubs flanking the flagstone porch and a decorative brass knocker on the front door. It didn't look like the home of a felon.

Marlo gave the house a cursory glance, then continued past it to the corner. Jeremy twisted in his seat to stare out the rear window. "That was it, Marlo. That was the van. Why didn't you stop?"

She turned the corner and pulled to the curb. "I'll go back," she said calmly, shifting into neutral, applying the parking brake and lifting her purse from the floor behind her seat. She opened it and poked around inside.

"Don't tell me you've got a pearl-handled pistol in there," he muttered, unable to see inside the purse.

She tossed him a grin. "All right— I won't tell you," she obliged.

His heart began to race, partly from anxiety and partly from sheer excitement. Before last night, his only intimate exposure to a gun had occurred when he'd received a toy "Man From U.N.C.L.E." pistol for Christmas two and a half decades ago. Now, for the second time in twenty-four hours, he might be within touching distance of a gun.

He'd lived such a tame life: a privileged childhood in a posh apartment on Manhattan's Upper East Side, surrounded by adoring parents, an indulgent housekeeper and a younger brother who fairly idolized him. An estimable career at the Collegiate School followed by four productive years at Williams College and graduate studies at Penn. A partnership-track position at Pace & Hartley, an award for his design of an office building in Norwalk, an active social life, a wicked serve on the squash court.

All in all, it was about as boring as the Federal Reserve System.

He had the wisdom to be frightened by the prospect of Marlo and the kidnappers engaging in a shoot-out on a tree-lined block in a sleepy northern New Jersey community. But he couldn't ignore the intoxicating macho vengeance pumping through his veins. He wanted to take on those gorillas. He wanted to beat them up, trounce them, maybe kick in their teeth for good measure. Not kill them—of course not. He was a civilized man. But he'd sure like to rough them up a little.

Correction: he'd like to rough them up a lot.

His vindictive fantasies faltered when he saw Marlo pull from her purse not a handgun but her pen and pad. "You're going to rescue Alison with *that*?" he asked, incredulous and undeniably disappointed.

"No. I'm going to go talk to the owner of the van and take some notes." She shifted her car back into gear, executed a U-turn and cruised back around the corner to the house with the blue van in the garage.

"What should I do while you're taking notes?" Jeremy asked as she parked in front of the house and shut off the engine.

"Sit tight," she said succinctly.

He scowled. He hadn't badgered Marlo into bringing him on this rescue mission just to sit tight while she took all the risks. "But—"

"Jeremy," she cut him off, her tone offensively reasonable. "If Alison happens to be in there and the kidnappers see you, they might get spooked and make a run for it. I've got a much better chance of getting inside the door if I'm alone."

"Sure," he grumbled. "You go on in by yourself. Let them have two hostages instead of one."

Marlo laughed. "They aren't going to hold me for ransom. Unlike Porter Havelock, my father's broke. I'm definitely not worth risking a prison sentence over." With that, she swung out of the car and shut the door.

Stewing, Jeremy watched her saunter confidently up the driveway to the open garage, where she spent several minutes inspecting the van. Then she headed to the front door. She lifted the brass knocker, dropped it, and waited. The door was opened by a plump middle-aged woman dressed in tennis whites. She and Marlo talked for a minute, and then Marlo vanished into the house with the woman.

Staring at the closed door, Jeremy entertained a series of thoughts: that Marlo was in danger. That Alison *wasn't* in danger. That the woman in the tennis whites looked a great deal more like a suburban matron than a latter-day Ma Barker. That Marlo looked sexier in a voluminous sweatshirt and faded jeans than Alison had looked in her haute couture silk jumpsuit. That Marlo looked sexier not because of her attire but because of her gloriously long legs, her graceful posture, her wind-tossed hair, her bright, animated eyes, her courage and humor and wit and the way even when she was angry or solemn her lips hinted at a smile.

He watched the house and counted the minutes, wondering how many would have to elapse before he could tell her the truth about his relationship with Alison. A swift surge of remorse washed away that thought. For God's sake, Alison's life might be in danger. He shouldn't be thinking about how to win Marlo's affection.

The door opened and Marlo emerged, followed by the woman. On the porch they chatted a bit longer, their voices distorted by the hot afternoon breeze. Finally Marlo nodded, handed the woman a business card of some sort and then jogged across the lawn to the car.

So much for a quick rescue of Alison. If she had been in the house, apparently Marlo hadn't been able to secure her release. Jeremy suffered a confusion of emotions, among them dismay and a small amount of spiteful glee that Marlo hadn't been able to pull off this mission single-handedly. Maybe she would need his assistance, after all. Maybe he'd prove to be indispensable. Maybe, after last night's debacle, he would have an opportunity to redeem himself with some grand heroics.

He tried to guess from Marlo's expression what had transpired inside the house, but she remained poker-faced as she got into the car. She tossed her purse into the back seat, started the engine and pulled away from the curb.

"Well?" he asked, impatience getting the better of him.

"Maine."

"Main? Is there a Main Street in this town?"

"Not Main Street," Marlo corrected him. "Maine, the state. That's where Alison is."

"How do you know that?"

Marlo eyed him briefly. "I've worked long and hard to master the necessary skills of this business," she pointed out. "I graduated in the top tenth of my class at the police academy, I've trained myself both physically and mentally and I've developed my powers of logic to a high degree. I'm a pro, Jeremy. Do you honestly expect me to reveal my trade secrets?"

Her bragging irritated him. "I honestly expect you to reveal how you came up with Maine, of all places," he retorted.

She shook her head and grinned smugly. "This sort of expertise has to be earned. I know how to gather even the most inconspicuous evidence, how to reason through what I've got, how to know what information to use and what to discard—"

"Spare me the lecture," he interrupted. "Just tell me how the hell you figure Alison's in Maine."

Marlo considered her answer for several seconds. Then she shrugged and said, "The woman at the house told me."

IN FACT, MRS. SAWYER had told Marlo a lot more than that. As she drove back toward the parkway, Marlo cast a surreptitious glance at her cellular phone. She wanted to call her father, to fill him in on what she'd learned and to pass along to Porter Havelock the news that his daughter was apparently among friends. But she didn't want to say anything in front of Jeremy. She didn't want to be the one to break the news to him that his fiancée was a first-class twit.

Spotting a gas station up ahead on the road, she decided to opt for discretion. She pulled into the station's parking area and stopped the car. "I'll be right back," she said, shoving open her door.

He looked toward the rest room door and nodded. "Okay."

She felt obligated to enter the lavatory. Since she didn't have to use the facilities, she spent a few minutes inspecting her reflection in the cracked mirror above the sink. Her hair was mussed and her complexion appeared a wan olive shade in the glaring fluorescent light. She should have worn something prettier than her old sweatshirt, she thought glumly. Some earrings and a little makeup might have helped.

They wouldn't have helped enough. No matter how hard she tried, she would never have the polished, moneyed look that women like Alison Havelock were blessed with from birth on, thanks to their refined genes and their parents' overflowing bank accounts. Marlo could have her hair restyled, bankrupt herself at Bloomingdale's and paint her face with Elizabeth Arden's top-of-the-line cosmetics, but she'd still look like the Irish-Scottish-Italian-Polish hybrid she was—too tall, too gawky, too working-class.

It was stupid, letting Jeremy's presence put her in such a funky mood. She couldn't afford to feel insecure and inferior. That he was the best looking man she'd ever laid eyes on should have been reason enough for her to have refused to let him accompany her on this outing. That he was so deeply enamored of Alison was even more reason.

That Alison appeared to be a spoiled brat who amused herself by leading her father's private investigator on a wild-goose chase all over the Northeast made matters infinitely worse.

Alison Havelock didn't deserve the love of a man like Jeremy. But then, Marlo supposed, when you had baby-blue eyes and a cute little button nose, fiery auburn hair and a trust fund worth half a million dollars, men tended to be more than willing to overlook certain character flaws.

Sighing, Marlo inched open the rest room door and spied on Jeremy. He was seated in the car exactly as she'd left him. She edged the door open a bit wider, slipped out and strode around to the glass-walled office and inside. "Have you got a pay phone?" she asked the attendant. He nodded toward a wall phone near the door.

Marlo shoved a coin into the phone, recited her credit-card number to the operator and supplied the operator with her father's home phone number. If nobody answered, she'd try to reach him at Havelock's.

He was home. "Stan McGinnis here," he said.

"Hi, Dad. I'm in New Jersey. I found the van the kidnappers were driving."

"Hey, Marlo—good work!" Despite his attempts to steer his daughter into a safer, more lucrative profession, Stan McGinnis had never made a secret of the pride he took in his daughter's talent as a detective. An only child, she'd always been the proverbial apple of his eye, and after her mother's death fifteen years ago Marlo had also become her father's confidant and sounding board. Stan McGinnis had friends and didn't lack for company. But he and Marlo had a special relationship, a closeness forged in shared ambitions, shared interests and shared sorrows.

"Any sign of Alison?" he asked her now.

"She's in Maine. I talked to the mother of the van owner. He's a friend of Alison's from Fairleigh Dickinson."

"Uh-huh. Porter's been contacted, by the way."

"He has?"

"A quick phone call, about an hour ago. 'We have your daughter, don't call the police, we'll be in touch.' Real useless stuff. Angie Russo down at the telephone company traced it to a pay phone in New Hampshire."

"I guess they made a pit stop along the way. According to Mrs. Sawyer, her son and a few of his old school buddies—including a pretty red-haired girl—rolled in after midnight last night, waking her up with all the noise they made. When she asked her son what was going on, he said he and his pals were heading up to Maine for a while. Seems one of them—his name is Peter Olson, she thinks—anyway, he has the use of his family's vacation place up in a town called Beresford. Mrs. Sawyer said she hasn't got an address or a telephone number for this Olson place, but as far as she knows it's just a nice old country farmhouse and the gang from college hangs out there all the time."

"What gang?" her father grumbled. "Haven't these kids got jobs?"

"They're rich," Marlo reminded him.

"They could all use a good shaping up," he muttered. "Staging a kidnap, knocking people around with guns... They could all of 'em use a firm hand on the backside—especially Porter's daughter, for putting him through this nonsense." Marlo knew from personal experience that her father was a true believer in discipline. She'd spent many weekends of her adolescence confined to her bedroom, grounded over some infraction or other. "Well," he continued, "I'll let Porter know you were right about the whole thing being a sham. He'll be relieved to know she's safe."

"Has the FBI joined the effort yet?"

"They sent someone over to Porter's house after he got the call from New Hampshire. The fellow's a real know-nothing, though. You could stand this guy on the middle of the Golden Gate Bridge and he wouldn't be able to find San Francisco. Not that I'm complaining, mind you. If he locates Alison before you, it's going to be in all the papers."

"Don't worry about it. My strategy at this point is to cruise up to Beresford before Alison and her band of merry men move on to someone else's vacation place. I'll probably stop back home to pack a bag—" and drop Jeremy off, she added silently "—and then head on up north tonight. That way I can get an early start in Beresford tomorrow."

"Where is Beresford, anyway?"

"Beats me. I'll have to pick up a map at the office."

"Well, give me a buzz whenever you can," her father requested. "Keep me posted. I'll try your car phone if I need to reach you."

"All right."

"And keep your lip buttoned. I don't think Porter would take too kindly to anyone finding out about his daughter's shenanigans."

"Yes, Dad."

"And be careful, sweetheart. These kids—who knows? They did have guns."

"Which they didn't fire," she reminded him, rolling her eyes at his paternal admonishments. "Which they probably don't even know how to fire."

"Even so, they're crazy kids. Don't underestimate them."

Marlo groaned. His tone of voice bore an uncanny resemblance to the tone of voice he used to use whenever she was about to go out on a date. "Remember, Marlo, all boys are after one thing only, and once they've got it they'll leave you high and dry," he'd warn her. "Don't let your guard down or they'll catch you unawares."

"Yes, Dad," she said, the same singsong way she used to respond as an adolescent. "I'll be careful."

"Keep in touch."

"I will." Marlo said goodbye and hung up. With a wave to the attendant, she strode out of the office and across the lot to her car.

"Why didn't you use your car phone?" Jeremy asked as she settled herself in the driver's seat.

She had hoped she wouldn't have to face that question. "Well..." she hedged, scrambling for an answer and coming up with nothing better than the truth: "I didn't want you to hear what I had to tell my father."

Jeremy frowned. "What didn't you want me to hear? Is Alison hurt?"

"No." She started the engine and drove out of the gas station, thinking once more that anyone who pulled a stunt like this fake kidnapping didn't deserve to have a man like Jeremy Kent tormenting himself over her well-being.

"Has Porter received a ransom demand?"

"No."

"Then what? Something the woman said, right? Did she tell you something important that I'm not supposed to know about?"

Marlo sighed. If she didn't toss him a scrap he'd continue to pester her all the way back to Connecticut. "You want to know what she told me? She told me her son is a good boy, and so are his friends."

"Good boys? Oh, of course," Jeremy said sardonically. "Those good boys knocked me unconscious and kidnapped Alison. Prime candidates for sainthood, aren't they."

"Jeremy—the point is, they aren't going to hurt Alison. All right? Mostly the woman talked about how her son lost ten pounds last month on a grapefruit diet. I honestly wish she'd told me more, but other than the stuff about how they were heading up to a vacation house in Maine she was pretty useless." Except for the fact that she'd confirmed Marlo's hunch about the incident being a hoax. Marlo wasn't about to share that vital information with Jeremy, though.

He appeared dubious. "If she was so useless, you could have reported to your father on the car phone."

She shot him an annoyed look. "I'm entitled to talk to my own father in privacy, aren't I?"

Jeremy stared at her. Even with her attention focused on the road she was acutely aware of his gaze on her, his dazzling gray eyes absorbing her angular profile, attempting to divine what she might know about Alison, what she might have told her father, what she wanted to prevent Jeremy from hearing. "If you needed privacy," he said, his voice taut, "you could have asked me to leave the car."

"Look, Jeremy," she said sharply, "I'm not used to having company while I work, all right? I'm not used to having some stranger tagging along, asking me lots of questions. I'm not real clear on the etiquette here. Next time I promise I'll boot you out of the car."

She wasn't sure what sort of reaction she'd expected, but it certainly wasn't the one she got: a slowly spreading smile. "Next time," he murmured. "I'm glad we're agreed on that."

"Agreed on what?" she asked apprehensively. For some reason the carefully honed detective skills that served her so well when she was trying to puzzle out what Alison Havelock was up to seemed to deteriorate when it came to figuring out Jeremy Kent.

"I'm coming to Maine with you," he explained.

"Oh no, you're not!" She shouldn't have brought him on this brief jaunt to New Jersey. She certainly wasn't going to compound her mistake by letting him accompany her on what might amount to a several-days-long outing to the rock-strewn wilds of Maine.

He continued to gaze at her, making her self-conscious. "Why not?" he asked with deceptive innocence.

Because he was too distracting, that was why not. Because those pussy-willow eyes of his were too bewitching, and his chin was too strong, and the chest hidden beneath his crisp cotton shirt was too tantalizing. Because he was attached to a woman who was too young for him, too pampered, too petty—and because he was committed to that woman in a way no man had ever committed himself to Marlo.

Because she resented the hell out of Jeremy, that was why.

"It simply isn't done," she said, trying to match his even tone.

"But you brought me along for this part of it."

"Much to my regret," she muttered.

"Why do you regret it? What did I do? I sat here beside you and stayed out of your way. And if you had needed a backup—"

"A backup!" She hooted a laugh. "What sort of backup would you provide?"

He bristled, his male ego wounded to the quick. "Your highly developed powers of logic seem to have failed you, Marlo," he retorted. "It just so happens that I'm smart and strong, and that if you'd gotten into trouble in that house you would have been damned glad that I was there."

She smothered her laughter. Sure, if she'd been in trouble she would have been glad, but that was a specious *if*. Part of her skill as a detective entailed being able to predict, ahead of time, whether there was going to be trouble and then acting accordingly. If she'd thought there was anything the least bit risky in entering the Sawyer house, she wouldn't have gone in without a backup. But her backup would have been her father, not some gorgeous country-clubber from Connecticut's Gold Coast.

Still, she had no call to insult him. "I didn't mean to laugh at you, Jeremy," she apologized. "It's just that I can't have you interfering with my work. I can't be worrying about you. I've got to concentrate on finding Alison."

"Fine," he concurred. "Don't worry about me. We'll both concentrate on finding Alison."

"But you don't know the first thing—"

"Then teach me. I'm a fast learner."

She sent him a bewildered look. "What you are, Jeremy, is an architect. What do you want to learn detective work for?"

He studied her thoughtfully. "I've just met this detective who's made quite an impression on me," he said, his voice low and steady, all traces of indignation gone. "I want to spend some more time with her, to see how she goes about doing things, how she thinks. How she manages to be so brave.''

Marlo swallowed and kept her eyes focused on the road so she wouldn't have to look at him. She might be brave when it came to marching up to strange houses, barging in on the residents and peppering them with questions about the vehicles parked in their garages. But Jeremy's unexpected declaration drained her of her bravery. It made her want to run for cover.

Only a fool would interpret his words as a come-on. He couldn't really have meant to insinuate that he was interested in Marlo. He was interested in her profession, that was all. People always thought detective work was exotic.

She followed the parkway signs to the George Washington Bridge, permitting herself a fleeting glance at him. He had turned to face forward again. His legs were crowded into the narrow space beneath the dashboard, and his sun-streaked hair danced in the humid breeze gusting in through his open window. His eyelids were lowered against the glare of the mid-afternoon sun, and she noticed that his lashes were a paler blond than his hair.

''If you went to Maine with me,'' she noted, determined to talk him out of accompanying her, ''you'd miss work. This trip is probably going to take a couple of days. You'd lose income and get in trouble with your firm.''

''As if that matters. The bulk of my work these days is for Porter Havelock. I doubt he's going to be pushing ahead with the office park in Stamford while his daughter is being held by a bunch of thugs.''

Marlo disagreed. From what her father had told her and from what she herself had observed, Porter Havelock was passionately in love with his work. She couldn't imagine what would keep him from his current project—but surely the bogus kidnapping of his daughter by a few of her college classmates wouldn't.

"It's a long trip," she argued, groping for any way to convince Jeremy that he could back down without sacrificing his self-esteem. "This car isn't really that comfortable for long drives. Look at you—your legs are all cramped."

"My legs are fine," he countered. "It is kind of stuffy in here, though. Why don't you use your air conditioner?"

"It's broken," she told him, pleased that he was willing to acknowledge her car's shortcomings. Whatever worked, she thought. Anything to get him to retreat with dignity. She didn't want to have to force him out of her car. She wanted it to be his decision.

"Broken, huh." He pushed the dashboard button, and a blast of scorching air blew out of the vents. "The fan works," he observed, shutting it off.

"No kidding. I could use it in January, instead of the heater."

"When was the last time you had it recharged?"

"Recharged?"

He sent her a reproachful look. "You're supposed to recharge your air conditioner on a regular basis. I'll bet that's what's wrong with it."

"Swell. Maybe I should forget about finding Alison and make an appointment with the repair shop."

"What I was thinking," he clarified, "is that we could take my car up to Maine instead."

"First of all," she said sternly, "I haven't said you could come to Maine."

"It's not up to you to say I can't."

"It is up to me," she declared, no longer bothering to spare his feelings. "Listen to me, Jeremy: *You can't.*"

"Since when did they close the border? I can drive up to Maine as easily as you can, Marlo. It would make more sense if we both traveled in the same car."

And it would be more pleasant, she admitted to herself. Jeremy was an interesting companion. This jaunt to New Jersey would have been pretty dull without him along.

But he couldn't come to Maine with her. She wouldn't allow it. As scintillating as he was, as disturbingly handsome, as bright and stubborn and all-around intriguing, she simply couldn't bring him along. In fact, the more she found to like about him, the more imperative it was for her to put some distance between them. He was Alison's boyfriend, for crying out loud.

"If you'd seriously consider driving that car of yours all the way up to Maine, you must be playing with half a deck," she muttered. "I wouldn't trust it on a trip to the supermarket. It's an antique."

He sat up straighter. "How do you know about my car?"

She smiled triumphantly. "I'm a detective, Jeremy. I know all kinds of things." There was no need to disillusion him by reminding him that any passerby could peek through the windows in his garage and see what was parked inside.

He gave an amiable shrug. "Granted, the MG hasn't got air conditioning. But it's got a convertible roof and..." He drifted off, his smile disappearing.

"And what?"

"Nothing," he said pensively.

She tried to make sense of his sudden change in mood. She'd been hoping to rid him of his bravado, but now that she'd succeeded she didn't like it. She preferred Jeremy when he was boastful and confident, even if his cockiness exasperated her.

"It's a great car," she reassured him. "It's just kind of old for taking long drives, don't you think?"

"Sure," he grunted.

"The truth is, I adore convertibles," she went on, eager to cheer him up. "My Uncle Gordy used to have an old Mustang convertible when I was a kid, turquoise with a white interior and a white roof. He used to drive me out to the beach at Hammonassett State Park every Saturday during the summer, and all the ladies would swarm around the car in the parking lot. He'd send me off to play in the sand so he could flirt with them. I think they were more interested in the car than they were in him. It was a classic."

"A Mustang," Jeremy echoed blandly.

Compared to a restored MG, Jeremy probably considered a Mustang a car for the lowly proletariat. Then again, in his social circle, people probably didn't go to the state beach at Hammonassett, either. They all undoubtedly belonged to private beach clubs.

"Does your uncle still have the car?" he asked when her silence extended beyond a minute.

She gave a short laugh and shook her head. "That was twenty years ago. He's a middle-aged man now, and he drives one of those station wagons with the fake wood on the sides. He's got a wife and three kids and a potbelly."

"Too bad."

"Yeah. I keep telling him he ought to go on a diet."

"No—I meant too bad about the car. The original Mustangs were wonderful."

She peered at Jeremy with newfound respect. Maybe he wasn't such a rich snob, after all. "So what don't you like about convertibles?" she asked him.

"I like them just fine." The tension in his voice belied his words.

"Come on, Jeremy—tell me. It's the middle of the summer. You don't drive around in your MG with the top up, do you?" She knew he didn't. The top had been down when she'd inspected his car through the garage window.

He stared out at the slate-colored water of the Hudson River as they crossed the bridge into the Bronx. His expression was impassive except for his eyes. Whenever Marlo caught a glimpse of them, they appeared turbulent with emotion.

"Is it because you associate your car with the kidnapping?" she probed.

"Yes."

She realized how difficult it must have been for him to reveal his fear. Men hated to admit they were afraid of anything. "That's a normal reaction," she said.

"I love that car," he confessed. "I earned the money to buy it the summer after I graduated from high school, and I've rebuilt the engine twice. That car has taken me to California, to Florida, to Nova Scotia.... I've had some great times in that car. And now..." He drifted off, sighing. Marlo noticed that the bridge of his nose was once again scored with a deep crease.

"Hey, Jeremy—it's okay. They didn't damage the car or anything. You drove it into Bridgeport when you came to my office, didn't you?"

"I wasn't thinking then," he mumbled. "I guess it just didn't occur to me..."

Delayed reaction. She knew all about it. "In time you'll get over the shock," she assured him.

"They had guns, Marlo." His voice shrank to a mere rasp. "The top was down, and suddenly, they had those guns aimed at us. We were so...so exposed." He shuddered.

She ought to tell him right now that the entire affair had been a hoax. She ought to let him know his life had never truly been at risk—if only because she didn't want him to go home and attack his beloved MG with a sledgehammer.

But would he really feel any better knowing that the guns probably hadn't been loaded? Would the news that his fiancée had had her school chum conk him on the head hard enough to knock him unconscious truly erase all his negative feelings about his car? Not a chance. If anything, the truth would probably cause his negative feelings to expand until they encompassed Alison—and Marlo, too. As the bearer of bad news, she'd win his everlasting wrath. She'd be better off leaving him in ignorance.

"You'll get over it," she said sympathetically.

"What makes you so sure?"

"I've been there," she said. "I've had a gun pointed at me, too. When I was with the Bridgeport Police."

"How long did it take you to get over it?"

She gave him a sidelong glance and exhaled. She was tired of lying to him, tired of keeping everything hidden. "Years," she admitted. "In all honesty, Jeremy, I still have nightmares every once in a while. It's a horrible thing to go through."

"How did you cope with it? What happened to you?"

She lapsed into a memory of that morning—a bright, crisp Wednesday morning in October. "My partner and

I were patrolling downtown," she related. "We saw some kids in an alley, and since they should have been in school we assumed they were up to no good. So we got out of the cruiser and went to investigate. One of the kids pulled a gun on me."

Jeremy winced. "What did you do?"

"What did I do?" She issued a short, self-deprecating laugh. "I swiped the gun out of his hand, cuffed him, read him his rights and ran him in. I booked him on charges of possession of an unlicensed weapon. Then—" she tossed Jeremy another look "—I handed in my resignation."

"Really? Just like that?"

"You bet. One whiff of my own mortality, and I'd had it. So much for my supposed bravery."

"And you still have nightmares?"

"Not very often," she said. "Every now and then, when a whole lot else is going wrong. If I'm having a bad dream, as often as not all the nasties in it have that kid's face."

"I had bad dreams," Jeremy murmured, staring at his knees. "Last night, when I finally fell asleep, I dreamed about the kidnappers, again and again. It was ghastly, Marlo."

She wanted to tell him not to worry. She wanted to recite a few bromides, simplistic words of consolation, something to mitigate the horror. But she knew there were no easy cures for what he was experiencing. She'd been through it herself. She knew.

"All right," she said softly. She couldn't abandon Jeremy when he'd shared his innermost feelings with her, his deepest dread. She wanted to pull off the road and give him a hug, tell him that only a fool would remain undaunted with a gun trained on his nose, and that only

an immensely brave man would confess his fear. She
wanted to assure Jeremy that he'd survive the nightmares as he'd survived the crime, that in time he'd grow
to love his MG again, that after a while he'd develop a
different perspective on the situation. She wanted to
gather him to herself and comfort him, and whisper that
she'd do whatever she could to help him get over it.

Her brain warned her she was making a big mistake.
But her heart told her she couldn't leave him behind.
"You can come to Maine with me," she said.

CHAPTER FOUR

"HE'S IN THERE, in the study," said Dolores. "You go right on in."

Stan McGinnis nodded at Porter's housekeeper. He had been to Porter's house enough times to have gotten used to the young woman's West Indian patois, although he still found it easier to translate her facial expressions than her lilting, accented speech. Right now, her expression was telling him that Porter needed to be whipped into shape, and her shy but hopeful smile was telling him that he was the man to do the whipping.

Stan pondered how amazing it was that rich people were always so dependent on those of the lower classes to pull their lives together for them. Porter would never be able to function without Dolores. She put up with his temper, his occasionally despotic demands, his ribald humor and his questionable taste. She kept his floors clean, his shirts ironed and his pantry stocked. She answered his door, his telephone and too many other day-to-day needs to count. Heaven help Porter if the Immigration and Naturalization Service ever found out about her.

Not that they would. By Stan's estimate, there were more undocumented workers pruning shrubs, dusting heirlooms and changing babies' diapers behind the walls of Fairfield County's estates than sewing buttons in Manhattan's garment district, but the authorities would never perform a sweep of the Gold Coast mansions. The people who employed all these illegal aliens were too wealthy to have to play by the rules.

Following Dolores's outstretched hand, Stan sauntered down the marble-tiled hallway to Porter's study. It was Porter's favorite room. Unlike the other thirteen rooms in the house, Porter had decorated this one himself, and it showed. The cherry-wood floor was covered with a rug featuring an excessively busy Persian design, and the walls were adorned with framed plat maps of Porter's most lucrative construction projects. An oversize globe, with oceans so bright a blue they strained Stan's eyes, stood on a gleaming chrome base in one corner of the room; an entire shelf of the built-in bookcase occupying one wall held an assortment of liquor bottles. Although he could have afforded a desk of solid mahogany or teak, the desk Porter had placed in the center of the room was composed of black steel with a laminated fake-maple top, just like the desk he used in his on-site trailer. The sofa and armchairs were upholstered in a cranberry-colored leather that clashed with the rug. The curtains featured flocks of mallard ducks winging across a faded gray background.

Porter was seated at his desk, his head bowed and his hands molded around a glass of Scotch. Taking in his slumped shoulders and downturned face, Stan felt a momentary pang of sympathy for the man. He recovered quickly and strode across the room. "Hey, Porter," he said, rapping the desk with his knuckles as if he were knocking on Porter's door.

Porter lifted his head. His blunt, tough features were screwed into a grimace. "Stan," he grunted.

"You're supposed to be happy. Alison's safe, she's among friends and we know where she's headed. Let's see a big smile, now."

Porter didn't oblige. He lifted his glass to his lips, took a sip of Scotch and cursed. "The ice diluted all the flavor out of this. Dolores!" he shouted toward the doorway.

"Uh-uh." Stan removed the glass from Porter's hand, then crossed to the door and closed it. "You've had more than enough to drink, Porter."

"How do you know how much I've had to drink?"

Stan knew because during the two hours he'd spent in this room that morning Porter had downed two Scotches and admitted to having had a drink when Jeremy Kent and the police had come to the house in the wee hours. Mostly Stan knew because he'd seen the truth in Dolores's eyes.

He set the glass down on the liquor shelf, then moved to the couch and sat. The furniture was designed for someone with Porter's compact build, not for someone who was six feet three inches tall, most of it leg. Stan positioned his body at an angle so the stubby cushions would accommodate his lanky bulk. He drummed his fingers against the padded arm and regarded the woebegone man on the other side of the desk. "Alison's safe," he repeated. "I called you as soon as Marlo called me. We've got a line on her. We've called off the cops and the feds. You ought to be doing a victory dance, Porter, not drowning your sorrows."

Porter grunted again. He ran his hands through the sparse silvery strands of hair covering his scalp and sighed. "A victory dance," he echoed disdainfully. "The way I see this thing, my daughter has just chosen the wildest, most dangerous, most irresponsible way to inform me that she hates my guts, and I'm supposed to do a victory dance.''

"Would you prefer it if this kidnapping was for real?" Stan asked. He decided he wasn't comfortable seated as he was and tried a new position, hunching forward and resting his forearms on his knees. "Would you rather her life was in danger and thugs were hitting you up for millions of dollars?''

Porter gave him a withering look. "I would rather she'd had the decency to come to me and say, 'Dad, we've got problems, you and I.' ''

"You didn't need her to tell you that," Stan said gently. "You're the adult here, remember? You should have gone to her.''

"Right. I should've. I stink as a father, Stan—this isn't news. So why couldn't she just accept that she's stuck with a lousy father and get on with her life? Why did she have to humiliate me this way?''

"She's twenty years old," Stan reminded him. "You expect her to think rationally?''

There was a tap on the door and Dolores opened it, bearing a tray on which she'd arranged a coffee pot, two mugs, a matching creamer and sugar bowl and a plate heaped high with roast beef on rye sandwiches. "He hasn't eaten lunch," she told Stan. "He hasn't eaten breakfast, either. You make sure he eats. It's not good, the way he is." She set the tray down on a corner of Porter's desk and left the room, closing the door quietly behind her.

Porter glowered at the tray. "I'm not hungry.''

Stan would be willing to wager that Dolores had concocted this snack for the sole purpose of pumping some coffee into Porter's polluted bloodstream. "Eat anyway," he said, rising and crossing to the desk.

"I don't want to eat. I want a fresh drink."

"Fine." Stan poured him a mug of coffee. "Here's a fresh drink." He filled the other mug for himself, selected a sandwich and returned to the couch. "Sometimes," he added, just loud enough for Porter to overhear, "I think your daughter's more rational than you."

Porter swore under his breath, then issued a reluctant sigh and sipped the coffee.

Stan took a hearty bite of his sandwich and sent his silent thanks toward the door through which Dolores had vanished. Whether or not Porter was hungry, Stan himself was famished. It took a lot of food to keep his large body filled. "Have you heard anything more from the architect?"

"Jeremy?" Porter took another sip of coffee. "No."

"I guess we can take that to mean he's all right."

Porter concurred with a nod. "If he'd been seriously injured, the hospital wouldn't have released him. He got a bump on the head, that's all."

"Marlo called me from the office after she'd interviewed him. She said he seemed lucid."

"Jeremy Kent is an amazingly lucid young man," Porter declared. "If Alison were as rational as you seem to think she is, she would have wrangled a marriage proposal from him by now. They're perfect for each other."

"Words of wisdom from the man who hasn't got idea number one about what's going on inside his daughter's pretty little head," Stan commented dryly.

Porter attempted yet another scowl, which rapidly dissolved into a look of sheer plaintiveness. "Come on, Stan," he pleaded. "Help me out."

"I am helping you out. I've got Marlo on your daughter's tail. She should be getting back from Jersey within an hour, and then she'll refill the gas tank and strike out for Maine. Depending on where in the state Beresford is, she should be getting up there by—" he glanced at his watch and did a quick calculation "—oh, maybe nine, ten o'clock tonight. You might have Alison back in the bosom of the family sometime tomorrow."

"And then I'll *really* need help," Porter groaned. He plucked a sandwich from the heap, lifted the top slice of bread and gave the meat inside a suspicious look. Then he took a bite, chewed and swallowed, his canny blue eyes never leaving Stan. "You're a good father, Stan. You and Marlo are so close, you get along so well...." He took another bite and shook his head. "How do you make it work? Marlo must have been twenty years old once. How did you get to be so close to her? How did you do it?"

Stan gazed past Porter at the ugly mallard-duck curtains drawn across the window. How did he do it? By loving Marlo, that was how. By talking to her and listening to her. By making her the center of his life. Even before Catherine died, Marlo had been his doll, his princess, his touch-football quarterback, his best date for an ice cream at Friendly's. When he'd first started his own agency and money had been tight, Catherine had gone back to work and Marlo had spent her after-school hours at Stan's drearily quiet office, doing her homework or making long chains out of his paper clips while he tried to drum up business. Sometimes he used to let her dial the phone for him, or comb the newspapers in search of opportunities. If a new store was about to open in the Bridgeport area, the proprietor usually ran a classified advertisement calling for sales clerks. Marlo would circle the ads in red ink and then Stan would telephone the stores and ask if they wanted to hire a security consultant.

Even then Marlo had been his partner.

Catherine used to say that mother love was an automatic thing, inborn and natural. Father love wasn't. It had to be built brick by brick, with much greater care than Porter Havelock devoted to constructing his magnificent office parks and condominium developments.

That was how Stan and Marlo did it: slowly, incrementally but with boundless dedication.

"Marlo and I fought plenty when she was a kid," Stan observed. "There's nothing wrong with disagreements. You've just got to get past them, Porter. You've got to let Alison know she matters to you. If she really does, that is," he added, reading bristling skepticism in Porter's frown.

"Of course she matters to me," Porter snapped. "She's my daughter."

For whatever that's worth, Stan almost retorted. Right now Alison was less a daughter than a source of embarrassment to Porter. She had gone and thrown a doozy of a tantrum, and Porter was too incensed—and presently too inebriated—to look beyond the tantrum and treat the cause. Sure, what she'd done was humiliating. When Stan's next-door neighbor had discovered Marlo and some creep parked in Stan's driveway, necking in the back seat one Saturday night during Marlo's sixteenth year, Stan had been humiliated, too. So he'd grounded Marlo for a month, fumbled his way through an awkward discussion on birth control and the importance of a good reputation, and put the matter behind him. Humiliation wasn't fatal.

But failure to build a bridge to one's offspring could do irreversible damage. Porter was going to have to find a way to reach Alison soon or he would lose her forever.

Stan studied the pathetic man slouching in his swivel chair behind the desk. So much money, so much power, and the guy couldn't figure out how to connect with his daughter. It was pitiful, really pitiful. Stan would take his piles of unpaid bills, his cramped row house with its worn furnishings, his cranky old car and his modest income and his microscopic savings account over what Porter had any day—because the one thing he had that Porter didn't have was Marlo.

"WHAT'S THAT NOISE?" Jeremy asked.

Marlo shot him a quick glance. "What noise?"

He listened for a moment, frowning in concentration. "There. That groaning sound."

Marlo suppressed the derisive laugh that sprang to her lips. Jeremy must watch too much television. All those absurd detective shows teeming with shoot-outs and car chases and danger lurking around every corner! He'd seemed genuinely disappointed when she hadn't stormed the Sawyer house with guns blazing, and he'd actually thought a few splatters of redwood stain on the sweatshirt she'd been wearing earlier were blood. Now, as they cruised toward the New Hampshire border, he was hearing groans.

After they'd gotten back to her office from New Jersey, Jeremy had been openly reluctant to part ways with her and drive his own car home. But she'd promised several times that she would pick him up at his house in thirty minutes, and at last he'd left.

She wouldn't leave him behind, even though his departure had given her the opportunity. In spite of her reservations about bringing him along, Marlo realized how useful Jeremy's presence would be once she got to Maine. Alison was legally an adult, and Marlo couldn't force her to return to her father if she didn't want to go. But her devoted fiancé might be able to lure her back to Connecticut.

It was a good, sound rationalization. Marlo tried to convince herself that she had no other reason to bring Jeremy with her to Maine, that it had nothing to do with his mesmerizing gray eyes or the rugged contours of his chest or the touching vulnerability he'd exposed when he'd told her about his nightmares.

She also tried to convince herself, after she'd collected her road maps from the office and stopped off at home to pack an overnight bag, that the only reason she was exchanging her sweatshirt and jeans for a soft ramie sweater and tailored slacks was so she would appear legitimately professional if she should happen to locate Alison and her cohorts that night. She refused to entertain the possibility that she was dressing for Jeremy, that the dusting of makeup she applied to her face and the replacement of her pedestrian gold-post earrings with the textured gold hoops her father had given her for her thirtieth birthday had nothing to do with the man who would be accompanying her on the drive. He was taken, after all. And even if he weren't she would hardly be the one to take him.

She tossed her bag into the trunk and drove to Jeremy's house, where she found him standing in the driveway waiting for her, a leather two-suiter gripped in one hand. He hadn't changed his outfit for her, she noted, reminding herself that he had no interest in impressing her. Of course, he had been dressed more nicely to begin with, but even so, she didn't want to lose track of why he was traveling with her: not to impress her but to impress his beloved Alison.

They didn't talk much during the first couple of hours of the drive. Jeremy took charge of the radio, locating an album-rock station out of Hartford and commenting that if Marlo's job entailed long-distance driving she really ought to treat herself to a tape deck, to which she responded rather tartly that if she ever had a few hundred dollars to spare, she would do that. He asked her whether she'd spoken with her father before she'd left her office and she said no, she would call her father when she had something to tell him. She asked him if he'd informed anyone that he was going to Maine and he said no.

Really engrossing dialogue. She concentrated on her driving, trying not to exceed the speed limits by more than five miles an hour, trying not to resent Jeremy's carefree wealth and dazzling profile, trying to ignore the faint spicy scent of his after-shave. Every now and then she would glance away from the road and find him staring at her. Whenever she caught him in the act, he would swiftly look away and make some innocuous remark about the humidity or the song on the radio.

On the Mass Pike they made a pit stop. Agreeing to meet at the car in five minutes, Marlo and Jeremy parted outside the rest rooms. She watched him disappear into the men's room and then sped away to the bank of pay phones near a gift shop filled with huge, tacky sunglasses, plastic Pilgrim dolls, postcards with pictures of Cape Cod on them and T-shirts reading The Spirit of Massachusetts. She dialed her father's number and, when no one answered there, tracked him down at the Havelock residence.

"I'm just outside Sturbridge," she reported. "Beresford's pretty far north, near Bangor. I'm going to be getting into town pretty late."

"You'll get there when you get there," her father said. "I want you to drive safely."

Marlo made a face at his paternalistic admonition. "How's Havelock doing?" she asked.

"Drinking too much and whining about how humiliating this whole thing is. I've notified the police and they've been great about keeping the situation under wraps. I think Porter'll be able to cope much better if you keep things quiet up in Maine."

Marlo knew what her father meant by "keeping things quiet." Why else would she be relying on public pay phones instead of her car phone, if not to keep the truth about Alison's stunt a secret from Jeremy? Not that she would ever let on to her father that she'd brought Jeremy with her. If she did, he'd think she was nuts.

He would probably be right.

She met Jeremy out at the car as planned. He was holding a paper bag, and for an appalling moment she wondered whether he had actually blown some of his excess cash on a chintzy Spirit of Massachusetts souvenir. To her great relief, once he got into the car he pulled from the bag two cans of cola and a box of pretzels. "If we have a snack now," he explained, "maybe we won't have to stop for dinner until Maine."

"Good thinking," she said, taking a sip of soda and handing him the can to hold while she drove. "Thanks, Jeremy."

Her thank-you served to break the tension between them. When the radio broadcast the Eagles singing "Paradise" they both reminisced about where they'd been the first time they'd heard that song—Marlo at her Uncle Gordy's apartment and Jeremy, a budding adolescent, at his first boy-girl party. "All the girls wanted to play spin-the-bottle," he recalled, "but somebody put on this album and all the boys wanted to sit and listen to the music.''

"That's what they said," Marlo teased him. "The truth was, they just wanted to avoid kissing the girls.''

Jeremy laughed. "Most of those girls were wearing braces," he recollected. "Kissing them would have been about as thrilling as kissing the George Washington Bridge.''

They talked about inconsequential things, relaxed a little with each other, struggled through the Sunday afternoon home-from-Cape-Cod traffic on I-495. Shortly after the stream of cars thinned out near the New Hampshire state line Marlo accelerated back to the speed limit and Jeremy heard the groan.

"There it is again," he said. "Hit the gas, Marlo.''

"What do you mean, hit the gas?" The traffic had lightened but not disappeared completely. She wasn't going to risk a speeding ticket—let alone an accident—to indulge Jeremy's paranoia.

"Come on, just crank it up for a second.''

Sighing, Marlo pushed harder on the gas pedal. As the engine strained to pick up speed she heard it too: a low, rumbling sound.

"How old is your muffler?" Jeremy asked.

"How should I know?" she shot back. "It doesn't matter how old it is—it's under a warranty.''

"A warranty," he muttered.

Once he'd pointed the sound out to her she couldn't stop hearing it. The groan seemed to expand into a full-fledged rattle with bass overtones. "All right, look," she said, determined not to get pulled out of shape over a minor mechanical problem. "I can drive to Maine with a loose muffler. It's no big deal.''

As if to prove her wrong, the car resounded with a loud *clunk*, followed by a raucous scraping noise and menacing vibrations in the steering wheel. Jeremy twisted in his seat to peer out the back window. "Get off the road," he said unnecessarily; Marlo was already veering onto the shoulder. She yanked on the parking brake, shut off the engine and spat out a short, unladylike word.

Jeremy shoved open his door and climbed out. Marlo took a second to rein in her temper, then inched her door open. Cars whizzed past her in the highway's right lane, many of them crammed with vacation gear, others with bicycles strapped on top of the trunk or sailboards lashed to the roof. All of them threatened her with their nearness and speed. She edged cautiously toward the rear bumper.

Jeremy was kneeling on the loose gravel, his back bowed and his head nearly pressed to the ground as he peeked up at the underside of the car. He cradled the tail pipe with his hand, jiggled it, lowered his hand and watched the tail pipe descend to the shoulder. "Your muffler's falling off," he shouted above the din of the traffic.

Smothering the urge to curse again, Marlo hunkered down beside him. It was her car, not Jeremy's; getting her slacks as dirty as his was the least she could do.

"See?" He flattened himself against the ground and slithered deeper under the car to examine the problem. "There should be a bracket here. It's gone."

"Terrific," she said, forcing herself to stay calm. "What should I do?"

He wriggled back out into the air and sat up, dusting off his clothing. "You're going to need a new muffler."

"That's ridiculous," she protested. "The thing is on a warranty, Jeremy. It's supposed to be good for as long as I own the car."

"First of all," he said, as if explaining to a child, "those warranties have a lot of tiny print. The muffler may be guaranteed but not the exhaust pipes or the brackets. Those are the parts that break, Marlo, and you wind up having to pay to replace them." He stared at the dangling tail pipe grimly, then rose to his feet. "Which is neither here nor there. Have you got any tools?"

Marlo cringed. Her father was always nagging her to keep a decent tool kit in her trunk, but she'd never bothered, figuring that tools weren't going to do her any good since she didn't know how to use them. She was competent enough when it came to simple household maintenance, but automobiles stymied her. The last time she'd had to change a tire, she'd spent a half hour just trying to figure out how to assemble the portable jack.

"What kinds of tools do you need?" she asked nervously.

"Pliers, and a hanger."

"What kind of hanger?"

"A wire clothes hanger."

"Why would I have a wire clothes hanger in my car?"

"You've got suitcases in there," he pointed out.

She unlocked the trunk and let it swing open. He stared thoughtfully at the two suitcases—hers looking even grungier than usual next to his—as he rolled up the sleeves of his shirt. Marlo let her gaze linger briefly on his sinewy forearms with their dusting of golden hair, and then hastily looked away. "Whatever tools I've got are in the tire bay," she said, sliding the luggage out of the way and lifting up the board above the spare tire.

Nudging her aside, Jeremy removed the standard-issue tool pouch from the bay, opened it and examined its contents. Scowling, he shut it, tossed it back into the bay and lowered the board. Then he unbuckled his bag and pulled out a dress shirt on a hanger with a dry-cleaner bag still draped over it. In one deft movement he had the shirt and bag off the hanger. "Here," he said, tossing the shirt to her. "Fold this."

She didn't care for his dictatorial attitude, but she couldn't very well voice her disapproval when he was going to sacrifice his hanger to repair her muffler. Spreading the cleaner bag over the dusty bottom of her trunk, she laid out the shirt and folded it, watching Jeremy from the corner of her eye. He untwisted the hanger until its two ends were free, straightened out the kinks and bends as best he could, and then crawled under the car with it.

Placing his shirt neatly inside his bag, she resisted the instinctive temptation to investigate its contents. Instead, she squatted down beside him. "Can I help?"

"No," his voice drifted out to her.

She straightened up, feeling useless and not liking it. If Jeremy hadn't been here, she would have been up the creek right now—but if he hadn't come, he wouldn't have had the chance to make her feel so inept and ill-prepared for this emergency.

Well, she thought with a wry grin, there were her priorities in a nutshell. She'd prefer to be stranded on the side of the highway, unable to return the fugitive Miss Havelock and collect her retainer, as long as her pride remained intact. She lived her life on the premise that having one's pride was more important than having money—undoubtedly because she had plenty of the former and not much of the latter.

Lacking anything better to do, she watched Jeremy work. More accurately, she watched him from the waist down; his upper half was hidden underneath the car. He had a lean abdomen and well-proportioned legs, and they shifted with limber grace against the pavement as he stretched and groped along the car's underside. The twisting motion of his hips was unintentionally sexy, and Marlo deliberately steered her gaze down below his knees. His feet, shod in leather deck shoes, weren't too big. Given that she herself wore a size nine and hated the fact, she tended to notice how large other people's feet were. His were just right.

She truly hoped there was something wrong with him: his legs too hairy or not hairy enough; his high forehead given to periodic outbreaks of acne; his knees ugly. She hoped he snored. She hoped he was on the verge of going bald, or given to unexpected attacks of gas. It simply wasn't fair that everything about him should be perfect, from his upper-crust heritage to his lucrative career, from his dazzling eyes to his feet. It wasn't fair.

Well, he'd get his comeuppance soon enough, when he found out he was engaged to marry a ninny.

With a lithe wiggling motion he slid out from under the car and sat up. His shirt was soiled in spots and his hands were grimy. A greasy gray streak marred one flawlessly sculpted cheek. The wire hanger was nowhere in sight.

"Is it fixed?" she asked, sounding more timorous than she intended.

"Temporarily." He dusted off his hands, rubbed his thumbs over the more stubborn smears of grease on his palms, and then started to hoist himself up. Marlo reflexively extended her hands to him and he clasped them, using her for leverage as he stood. His grip was warm and strong, his hands more calloused than she would have expected. His fingers were long, easily closing around her slender wrists. As soon as he was on his feet, he let go of her and frowned at the faint smudges of dirt he'd left on her hands.

"How temporary?" she asked.

He shrugged. "I strung the muffler back on with the hanger. It ought to hold for a while—I don't know how long. If time weren't of the essence I'd suggest leaving the highway at the nearest town, finding a repair shop and having the job done properly."

"I'm not going to do that," Marlo argued, not because time was of the essence but because money was. "I've got a warranty. I shouldn't have to pay."

"Marlo," he chided her, although his tone was patient and his eyes sparkled with amusement. "I told you, those warranties never cover what you need. Maybe..." His voice drifted as he contemplated the situation. "We can probably get up to Maine. Then we can rent a car, and you can have the repair done up there while we go after Alison."

"What are the odds the muffler won't fall off again before we get to Maine?"

He scrutinized the rear bumper. "Fifty-fifty."

She checked her wristwatch and scowled. Even if her warranty were good, none of the franchised muffler dealers would be open at four o'clock on a Sunday afternoon. She might as well find a service station, bite the bullet and have the job done correctly. Killing an hour wouldn't affect the outcome of this case, but repeated hassles with a jerry-rigged tail pipe would irritate Marlo no end.

"Let's go get it fixed," she said resignedly, gesturing toward the passenger side and then heading for her own door, so lost in her thoughts that she barely noticed the cars whizzing perilously past her on the highway. She joined Jeremy inside the car, started the engine and turned to him. He had strapped on his seat belt and was scraping his right thumb over his left palm, trying to rub off the dirt there.

She studied the sharp lines of his profile, the firm angle of his jaw, the depth of his concentration. There was something disconcertingly modest about him. Another man might berate Marlo for the sorry condition of her car or gloat about having saved the day.

He *had* saved the day. No matter how uneasy that made Marlo, she was too honest to deny it. "Jeremy?" she said quietly.

He glanced up.

"I—uh . . . Thank you," she said.

He gauged the sound of the idling motor for a moment, then shrugged. "Better hold that thought until we make it to a repair shop. I don't think I did such a great job."

"You did a better job than I could have done."

He chuckled. "I'll show you how to do it someday, if you'd like."

"I'd like that a lot," she said at once. She wanted to believe her speed in accepting his offer arose from a desire to improve her mechanical know-how, but deep inside, she suspected it arose from a desire to see Jeremy again after this pseudo kidnapping was straightened out. That was a stupid desire, and she ordered herself to put it out of her mind. "You're pretty messy," she observed, deciding it was safer to focus on his hands than on his riveting eyes.

"I'll wash up when we stop."

"What about your shirt? You ought to let me pay the cleaning bill—"

He silenced her with a laugh.

"Look, it's my car. It's my fault that you got yourself filthy trying to fix it."

"Forget it," he said, leaning back in his seat as she merged with the traffic. "I like tinkering with cars."

"On the shoulder of a busy highway?"

"Well, you can't always plan where to have a breakdown. You didn't know your tail pipe was going to get loose."

"I should have known. If I'd had a newer car—"

"Your car is fine," he assured her, though his critical glance at her nonfunctioning air conditioner and her low-fidelity radio contradicted his words. "Old cars need a little more attention, that's all. Parts start to go. You've got to give them TLC."

Spotting a sign marking the exit ramp into Haverhill, she signaled to leave the highway. She couldn't imagine lavishing TLC on a creaky old car, but then, she didn't have abundant stores of tenderness to begin with. She had seen too much of the nasty side of life. During her days on the force, she'd seen the human destruction wrought by poverty and neglect and ignorance, and as a private investigator she'd borne witness to too much deceit, too many cheaters, too much emotional waste.

Maybe automobiles were more deserving of tender loving care than people, Marlo pondered as she drove down Route 125 into Haverhill, searching for a service station open for business on a Sunday afternoon. Cars, at least, wouldn't take you for granted. They might let you down, but they couldn't exploit you or condescend to you or rob you blind. They could break your bank account, but not your heart.

CHAPTER FIVE

THE FLOWERS DELIGHTED Alison.

She would never admit it, of course. To say out loud that she adored the late-blooming azaleas and rhododendrons, the untamed hedges of lilacs, the low-lying wild roses and scattered daisies and Indian paintbrushes would be uncool to the nth degree. Her father's house had no flowers at all, neither inside nor outside. He prided himself on being a practical man; to him, decorative landscaping was a marketing tool, useful for selling or renting units in his developments but not worth having around that Tudor-style mausoleum he called home.

Her mother, on the other hand, compensated for Manhattan's shortage of greenery by spending more than two hundred dollars a month on fresh flowers for her Park Avenue apartment. Alison had gotten used to being surrounded by pretty flowers, and after a few weeks at her father's house she'd come to miss them.

That the front yard of the Olsons' rambling white clapboard house, on a rise overlooking Penobscot Bay, was strewn with gorgeous blossoms made Alison feel a little better about what she'd done. She had been suffering misgivings ever since Dave had whacked Jeremy on the head last night. But the picturesque New England scenery, the traces of pink and lavender across the dusk sky, the fact that Ned had removed the blanket and let her sit up in the back seat of the car from Worcester on, and had put his arm around her like he really loved her... Maybe this whole thing hadn't been such a dumb idea, after all.

She followed the others up the winding slate walk to the broad veranda that stretched across the front of the house. Whitewashed Adirondack chairs faced the railing, and Alison thought about how nice it would be, once they'd gotten settled, to open a few beers and sit outside on the porch and watch the stars come out. But even though he'd lightened up a bit once they'd crossed the border out of Connecticut, Ned was still calling the shots. Alison wasn't about to make any suggestions at this point.

The kidnapping had been his idea. All she'd done was complain to him about what an awful summer she was having and how her father was ignoring her and everything, and the next thing she knew, Ned had cooked up this stunt. The way he described it, it had sounded exciting, and he'd assured her he would take care of all the details—like getting guns, she realized in retrospect. That was the sort of person Ned was: take-charge, in control, leader of the pack. He always had to have the last word, even when it came to deciding whether to spend the evening outside on a veranda or inside watching the tube. He had to be the boss.

In the weeks since she'd last seen him back in June, before she'd moved in with her father, Ned had had his coal-black hair refashioned into a modified flattop that displayed the tiny diamond stud in his earlobe. The style suited him, and so did the outfit he had on: a sleeveless T-shirt and an unbuttoned cotton shirt over it with the sleeves rolled high on his arms. The hems of his baggy khaki trousers were also rolled up to reveal his bare ankles above his punky sneakers. Ned hated wearing socks, even in the winter.

Despite the many hours they'd spent cooped up in the car, he looked a lot fresher than Dave and Peter, and especially Alison. Her silk jumpsuit was a mess of wrinkles, her makeup was smudged and her hair was unraveling from the braid. She couldn't wait to change into some clean clothes. As they'd planned, Ned had bought some new clothing for her and packed it inside his suitcase. She considered the notion of their clothes folded together inside a shared suitcase sexy, somehow. It was kind of like being married.

Peter unlocked the front door and they went inside. The spacious front parlor was cluttered with antimacassar-draped furniture and knickknack-cluttered shelves. Framed watercolors of hunting scenes hung on the walls and handwoven rugs covered the pegged-pine floorboards. It was obvious that the house had been recently occupied; the air lacked that musty smell of a closed house and the tabletops were clear of dust. In answer to her unvoiced question, Peter said, "We were just up here for the Fourth of July."

"And you're sure your folks won't be back any time soon?" Ned asked.

"Not for a week, at least. They're spending this week with my sister's in-laws on Martha's Vineyard." Peter set down his suitcase, crossed to a window and opened it to let in a brisk, clean breeze. "We're going to need some food."

Ned helped himself to Alison's purse and poked around inside. Finding it virtually empty—well, what did he expect? It wasn't like he'd kidnapped her on the way to the mall—he scowled and tossed it onto a sofa. Then he pulled out his own wallet and handed Peter a couple of twenties. "Why don't you and Dave pick up some stuff while I get Alison settled in? I don't think she ought to be seen in public right now."

"Yeah, all right. Sawyer?" Peter called to Dave, who was roaming around the room like an art critic, solemnly appraising each knickknack and watercolor. Unlike Peter and Ned, Dave was perhaps a dozen pounds overweight, ten of those pounds contributing to his mild beer gut and the rest softening the lines of his face, making his chin indistinct and his cheeks round. How such a teddy-bearish person could have knocked Jeremy unconscious was beyond Alison.

Now Peter... She could believe him capable of such a move. He and Ned had been tight all four years of college. Like Ned, Peter came from wealth; like Ned, he was always trying to prove something. Unlike Ned, however, he didn't have any charisma. He was just a rich kid with an attitude, as far as Alison could tell.

At Peter's summons, Dave nodded and headed for the door. "The bedrooms are all upstairs," Peter informed them as he stuffed Ned's money into the hip pocket of his jeans. "Mine's the one above the kitchen, so choose one of the others. I think all the beds are made up with clean linens—my mom always leaves the place ready for the next visit. Anything in particular you want us to buy at the store?"

"A couple of packs of cigarettes," Ned requested. "And a quart of Jack Daniel's."

"It's Sunday, man. They won't sell liquor on Sunday." When Ned reacted with a curse, Peter added, "Hey, maybe we could lift a little something from my dad's liquor cabinet without him finding out."

"Yeah, maybe," Ned muttered. "But I'm not a thief, you know."

Alison didn't think Ned had much basis for pleading innocent after he'd gotten hold of two guns and staged her kidnapping. But she kept her mouth shut as he waved off the others, closed and locked the door behind them, and then lifted his suitcase and ushered Alison down the hall to the stairs.

On the second floor, he insisted on checking out all six bedrooms before he selected one. The rooms were all lovely, each featuring a double or queen-size bed, a braided rug, a closet and a chest of drawers. Peter had been correct; all the beds were made with clean linens, and fresh towels hung from the brass towel rings in each bathroom. After careful deliberation, Ned finally chose the largest, a corner room with windows overlooking the rolling fields of a neighbor's farm and the stone-walled backyard of the Olson house. The bed had a quaintly carved maple headboard and an embroidered spread covering the wool blanket. A maple vanity with a three-way mirror and a cushioned stool stood in one corner. It reminded Alison of the vanity she'd had in her bedroom as a little girl, before her parents had split up.

Whatever happened to that vanity? Her mother hadn't moved it to New York City, and it was no longer at her father's house. Alison had forgotten about it until just this minute—and now she wanted to weep for having lost it.

She remained dry-eyed. Ned was being cool; she would be cool, too. If she started blubbering—especially over something as silly as a misplaced vanity—he would ride her mercilessly, and she couldn't afford to have him angry at her right now. Her mother and Lucian were on the Riviera somewhere, and her father... She wouldn't be surprised if he'd happily wiped his hands of her and headed off to his latest construction site for a nice, uninterrupted Sunday of work. Ned was her only ally in the world, and she couldn't risk doing anything to antagonize him.

She unclasped her pearls. They had been a gift from Lucian, one of his slimy attempts to win her over, and if they hadn't been so beautiful she would have thrown them back at his face. She never wore them around him, at least—she wouldn't give him the satisfaction of knowing she liked them.

After placing them in a heap on the vanity, she yanked the rubber band from her hair and unraveled the strands with her fingers. "Did you bring a brush for me?" she asked Ned.

He sprawled out across the bed, pulled a nearly empty pack of cigarettes from his shirt pocket and lifted a crystal ashtray from the nightstand. He nodded toward the suitcase and said, "Help yourself," then lit the cigarette and dropped the match into the ashtray. Alison didn't much care for the smell of cigarette smoke, but, again, she couldn't risk making Ned mad by asking him to stop.

She opened the windows, then returned to the suitcase. On her way she glimpsed Ned and paused. Even though this unhealthy habit had been partly responsible for his having lost his lifeguard job, she had to admit he looked foxy when he smoked. He dragged deep and exhaled through a sneer that made him look tough, masculine, invincible. Watching him smoke caused a feathery sensation in her belly, something dark and mysterious that her mother hadn't explained to her when she'd been explaining everything else. It was something Alison had never felt with any other man except Ned.

His eyes raked over her with lazy appreciation. They were as blue as hers—she often liked to imagine the beautiful blue-eyed babies they could have together. The sultry power of his gaze made the fluttering sensation in her belly increase and her cheeks grow warm. It didn't matter if he smoked, if he had access to firearms, if he was bossy and moody and unemployed. If he could make her feel so hot and quivery inside it must mean she loved him.

She lifted the suitcase up onto the foot of the bed and undid the leather buckles. Raising the top, she confronted a jumble of items—jeans, a few cotton T-shirts, knee-length shorts, a pair of size six Reeboks and, to her great relief, a brand-new hairbrush and toothbrush. She pulled the jeans and a clean T-shirt from the suitcase, then rifled through the contents a bit more. "Did you buy any underwear for me?" she asked Ned.

He exhaled a jet of smoke. "Nope."

"No?" A flare of panic shot through her. All she had were the panties she was wearing—not even a bra, since she couldn't wear one under the jumpsuit. She had specifically asked Ned to buy her three pairs of underpants and a bra when they were planning this thing. "Why not?"

"Why not?" He shrugged and snubbed his cigarette out in the ashtray. "What am I supposed to do, go into Macy's and buy a bunch of women's undies? Gimme a break!"

"Well, what am *I* supposed to do?" she retorted.

"I don't know. Skip wearing them, I guess."

The idea nauseated her. Going without underwear hadn't been part of the plan. The way Ned had described this trip, it was supposed to be fun, nothing heavy, nothing gross. Now all of a sudden there were guns and people getting hurt, hiding under blankets until she was achy and sweaty, and worst of all this: no clean underwear. She thought she'd die.

Being kidnapped wasn't all it was cracked up to be. She loved Ned, she really did, but sometimes he didn't seem to understand anything about her—and he didn't seem to care. Nobody cared about her. Nobody understood her.

At least Ned paid attention to her. For that, she could almost forgive him everything else.

Grabbing the T-shirt and jeans, she stormed into the bathroom. She would wash out the panties she had on now and hope they dried fast. Then, first thing tomorrow, she'd go into town and buy herself some new stuff. Nothing was going to stop her—not Ned, not the fear of getting caught, nothing.

JEREMY EMERGED FROM the service station lavatory, where he'd done a respectable job of scrubbing his hands clean. Apparently the mechanics used the same bathroom; someone had left a jar of heavy-duty grease-cutting soap beside the sink and Jeremy had helped himself to it. His shirt and slacks were in need of laundering, but that didn't bother him. He'd packed plenty of extra clothing.

Walking around the side of the building, he glanced first into the open bay where Marlo's car hovered six feet off the ground on a pneumatic lift, and then through the glass front wall of the office. Marlo was seated in one of the two vinyl chairs, hunched over a small black notepad and scowling. Jeremy watched her for a moment, admiring her angular profile, the wavy black tumble of her hair, her slender neck. Her arms, resting on the plastic arms of the chair, blocked her torso from his line of vision, but he had a great view of her legs.

While enticing, they didn't intrigue him in quite the way her face did at the moment. He was fascinated by the dent her frown etched into the narrow bridge of her nose, and by the uncharacteristically fragile contours of her cheeks. Most riveting of all were her lips, still hinting at a smile even though she was obviously displeased.

Nearing the door, Jeremy realized that the notepad she was poring over was in fact a checkbook. Her frown undoubtedly had more to do with the cost of the muffler repair than with the delay it had caused. When the mechanic had told her the job would run her something on the order of two hundred dollars, she'd winced as if someone had hurled a hardball into her stomach. Two hundred dollars didn't seem like much to Jeremy—Marlo would probably faint dead away if he ever told her how much he spent on parts alone for his MG—but to her, it was a staggering amount.

He continued to spy on her as she flipped back a page of the check register, read the notations and cringed. It would be so simple for him to pay for the repair, so natural for him to offer. Yet he stifled the urge, aware that if he ever did make such an offer, she'd hate him forever. Although he didn't know Marlo well, he understood that she wasn't the sort of woman who would take kindly to his generosity. She would probably consider it charity and accuse him of patronizing her.

He had never known a woman like her before. As a rule he felt self-confident with women, unafraid to speak his mind or act on his instincts. With Marlo, though, he had to be constantly on guard. Her attitude toward him implied that her decision to let him come to Maine with her had resulted from a momentary lapse in sanity, one she'd been regretting ever since. It had practically broken her heart just to thank him for performing first aid on her muffler. She didn't want to accept his assistance; she certainly wouldn't accept his money.

Sighing, he pulled open the heavy glass door and stepped inside the office. Marlo glanced up and attempted a wan smile. Then she folded her checkbook shut and dropped it into her purse. "They take Mastercard and Visa," he noted helpfully, pointing out the credit card decals affixed to the door.

"It doesn't matter whether I charge it or write a check," she grumbled. "Either way I'm out a lot of money."

He sat on the vinyl chair next to hers. "What sort of payment arrangement do you have with Porter Havelock?"

"Daily, plus expenses," she answered, discreetly refusing to divulge the amount per day she charged Porter. Jeremy assumed that amount varied from customer to customer.

"This repair could count as an expense. Why don't you just pass along the cost to him?"

Marlo shook her head. "That would be unethical. It's my car, my repair. I can charge him for gas and mileage, but not for maintenance costs."

Although he'd made the suggestion with her interests in mind, Jeremy admired her for rejecting the idea. A shady operator would find a way to incorporate the two-hundred-dollar charge into her client's bill, but not Marlo. She had too much integrity.

His gaze wandered around the room, from the candy and soda vending machines to the shelves stocked with plastic bottles of motor oil, to the windshield wiper racks, the coffee machine, the back issues of *Motor Trend* and *Road and Track* stacked on a table in the corner, the broad counter with its old-fashioned cash register, the round electric clock on the wall. Ten minutes past six o'clock. He grimaced. "Do you think we'll make it to Beresford tonight?"

"Not a chance."

She didn't seem nearly concerned enough. "Marlo, what if they get away?"

"Don't worry about it."

"Don't worry about it?" He gaped at her. "How can I not worry about it?"

"They aren't going to get away," she explained. "We know where they're going. Once they get there, that's where they'll stay. They'll head for a safe place and then sit tight."

"A *safe* place," he emphasized, finding her theory utterly unconvincing. "The fact that we know about this summer house proves it isn't safe."

"They don't know we know," Marlo reminded him.

"It was easy enough for us to find out about it," he argued, perplexed by her nonchalance. "All you did was ask that kid's mother and she told you. That's not safe."

"Jeremy." Marlo patted his hand consolingly. "They're amateurs, I told you. Beyond that, they're idiots. It wouldn't have occurred to them that we could trace them down to New Jersey, let alone that we'd reverse direction and trace them up to Maine."

"How can you be so sure they're idiots?" he charged. "What if it's a trick on their part to make us *think* they're idiots? Maybe they're actually geniuses."

Marlo gazed at him for a long minute. She seemed to be wrestling with her thoughts. Then she turned away. "Trust me," she said, staring through an inner door at the mechanic as he lifted a new muffler into place under her car. "They're idiots."

"You seem awfully positive of that."

"I am."

Swallowing his objections, he sat back in his chair. She was the experienced private investigator; he really had no choice but to accept her analysis of the situation.

Her eyes still on the mechanic, she asked Jeremy, "Have you ever heard of Peter Olson or David Sawyer?"

He frowned. "Should I have?"

"How about Ned Whitelaw?"

"Who are these people supposed to be?" he asked, annoyed that she kept throwing questions at him without responding to his.

"They're supposed to be the jerks who ran you off the road and absconded with your sweetheart."

His anger quickly dissipating, Jeremy puzzled over the names. "Are they well-known criminals? No," he answered himself. "You just said they're amateurs." He digested their names, silently contemplating each one: Sawyer, Olson, Whitelaw. Tom Sawyer; Folsom Prison; outlaw. These were not insights worth sharing with Marlo. "How did you find out their names?"

"Same way I found out where they were headed," she answered. "Sawyer's mother told me."

"If you know who they are, why don't you pass that information on to the authorities?"

"Havelock doesn't want the authorities in on this," she explained. "He wants to keep it hushed up."

"He's damned selfish," Jeremy muttered. "He's more worried about keeping his name out of the newspapers than saving his daughter's life." He recalled every gripe Alison had ever made about her father, every grievance she'd aired, and decided that far from exaggerating, she had been understating her father's egocentricity and his indifference toward her. "I think we ought to call up the police right now, and—"

Marlo gave him a sharp look. "Sure, why not? Let's call the police, the FBI and *U.S.A. Today*. Let's make a big splash. That'll really make everyone happy." Her tone lost its caustic edge, becoming low and earnest. "Do you have any idea what kidnappers do when you start making the wrong noises? I'll give you a hint, Jeremy—they don't go out and buy Godiva chocolates for the victim."

No, of course not. They did something gruesome to their captive. Marlo was right again, the seasoned professional reining him in and saving the world from his hotheadedness. It was just so hard sitting quietly, doing little and knowing that Alison was being held hostage by three animals. That they had names and at least one of them had a mother didn't make them seem any more human to him.

"Have *you* heard of them?" he asked. "Are they well known in law-enforcement circles?"

"No." She gazed at him for another long interval, her dark eyes alive with thought and her lips moving as she considered her words. Before she could speak, the mechanic bounded into the office through the open door, wiping his hands on a stained rag. "She's all ready," he announced brightly as he loped to the cash register to ring up Marlo's bill.

With tax, it came to two hundred thirty-eight dollars and fifty-six cents. Marlo squinted at the invoice, then shuddered. "This is a pretty high labor charge," she objected.

"It's Sunday night," the mechanic rationalized. "I'm here all by myself. It takes longer when only one person's working on a car. And anyway, I was supposed to be home for dinner an hour ago."

Groaning, Marlo wrote out a check and passed it to him. The mechanic demanded to see her driver's license and a credit card. He recorded a series of numbers on the back of the check, then stamped the invoice "paid" and gave it to her. "There you go, honey," he said, beaming a smile. "That muffler's guaranteed, now—as long as you own the car."

"Swell," she muttered under her breath. "Next time it breaks, I'll try to make sure I'm in Haverhill." Still muttering—words Jeremy thought it best not to pay attention to—she stalked out of the office.

In fifteen minutes they were back on the highway. The evening air had cooled considerably as the sun edged toward the western horizon, and the engine emitted a healthy purr through the open windows. Jeremy glanced at his watch. "If we really pushed hard, we might be able to get to Beresford before midnight," he calculated.

"Right. And we'll be bright-eyed and bushy-tailed when we get there, won't we. We'll prance through town, waking up the locals until we find someone who can tell us where the Olson house is, and we'll have enough energy to break in and sweep Alison away and take down three armed thugs without messing our hair."

"Sarcasm doesn't become you," he observed dryly. If criticizing her meant losing points with her, so be it. He wasn't going to be able to tolerate her sullen mood for the rest of this trip. If she tossed him out of her car for having dared to point out a character flaw, he'd hitchhike to a car rental establishment, get himself some wheels and go find Alison himself—with a police escort, if necessary.

The look Marlo gave him implied that tossing him out of her car was an idea she felt worthy of serious contemplation. She kept driving, however. "It's been a long day, all right? I'm tired and I've just blown half the money in my checking account on a new muffler with a useless warranty. Do you honestly expect me to be charming?''

"I expect you to stop taking your financial woes out on me.''

"Sorry if I'm lousy company, Jeremy. Sorry if I'm not quite up to your standards. You talked your way into that seat, don't forget. I didn't exactly invite you to join me.''

He wasn't sure how to interpret her little dig about his "standards," so he let it pass for the time being. "You might at least acknowledge that having me along hasn't been the worst thing in the world. For crying out loud, Marlo, if it hadn't been for me you'd still be stranded on the side of the road in Lawrence.''

"Something tells me you're going to be reminding me of that every chance you get.''

"All I'm saying is, remove the chip from your shoulder. I'm not your enemy.''

She shot him another look, her eyes glittering with fury. Maybe she thought he *was* her enemy, though he couldn't begin to fathom why. "Here's what you are, Jeremy," she said, fixing her gaze on the road ahead and tightening her grip on the steering wheel. "You're a big boy who got the wind knocked out of him and wants to get his revenge. If your only concern was Alison's safety, you would have stayed in Westport where you belong and let me find her and bring her home. But no—you want to go break someone's nose, don't you?''

"You said I could accompany you—''

"I made a mistake.''

"So live with it," he snapped, turning away and staring grumpily out the window.

He hadn't wanted to pick a fight with Marlo. He'd thought they were making headway, loosening up a little, stitching together the beginnings of a friendship. But her insufferable temper, her obstinacy, her open hostility...

Damn, but she turned him on. She irritated him, she exasperated him, she cut him down...and she excited him in an incomprehensible way. Even without looking at her he could picture her stubborn chin, her profoundly dark eyes, the delicate bones of her wrists and her tall, willowy body. Given the inauspicious start of this journey, he had pretty well lost hope that he'd ever get close to that body—let alone close to her flinty, fiery soul. But he could dream. He could imagine.

It looked as if he was fated to spend the next however-many-hours dreaming and imagining and building himself into a supreme state of frustration. He and Marlo would snipe at each other all the way to Maine. With luck they would rescue Alison, and then, their mission accomplished, they would snipe at each other all the way back to Connecticut, after which they'd never see each other again. A masochist's definition of bliss, he thought grimly.

But at least he'd get his revenge. At least he'd have the opportunity to break someone's nose. There was always that to look forward to.

OWING TO THE VACATION traffic, they didn't reach Portsmouth, near the Maine border, until an hour had elapsed, an hour of tense, brooding silence. Jeremy acknowledged that Marlo must be exhausted—it *had* been a long day, and she'd been on the go since early that morning, spending too much of the day behind the wheel. He would have offered to do some of the driving, but if he had she'd probably have bitten his head off.

She signaled to exit the highway. "We're stopping here for the night," she abruptly announced.

Jeremy didn't have the will to argue about her unilateral decision. If he and Marlo weren't going to be able to reach Alison before tomorrow, why knock themselves out trying to cover a few more miles? A motel sign was visible from the exit ramp, and Marlo drove unerringly down the frontage road until she reached the motel. She coasted into the half-filled parking lot and turned off the engine.

Jeremy peered out at the dingy two-story brick building. Its upper row of numbered doors opened onto an outdoor corridor with a breathtaking view of the highway, and its lower row opened directly onto the parking lot. The towering sign above the office flashed on and off with the name of the motel and "$37.95/nt Sun thru Thur" emblazoned on it. A smaller neon sign broadcast that the motel had vacancies, a fact Jeremy had little trouble believing. He doubted anyone on either side of his family had ever spent the night in a place this grim. Even his twelve-times-great grandparents must have had nicer accommodations on the *Mayflower*.

Trying not to let his revulsion show, he got out of the car with Marlo and followed her into the tiny office. The room reeked of cigar smoke in spite of the fact that the only person inside it was a gray-haired middle-aged woman minding the registration desk—or pretending to mind it. Her attention lay with the game show being broadcast on a portable television set that stood on a table behind the counter.

"We'd like two rooms for the night," Marlo said.

The woman seemed greatly annoyed by the interruption. She regarded Jeremy and Marlo with a hard, glowering stare that convinced Jeremy she was fully capable of chain-smoking cigars. "*Two* rooms?" she repeated, casting a disapproving look at him.

"Yes, two rooms," he confirmed tersely. He passed the clerk his Gold Card as Marlo pulled out her checkbook.

The clerk eyed them with increasing suspicion. "You want separate bills?"

"Yes."

She raised her eyebrows and took Jeremy's Gold Card. From her intense scrutiny of it, he inferred that she'd never seen one before. She flipped it over, squinted at his signature and then took an imprint of it.

"Where's the nearest restaurant?" Marlo asked as she wrote out a check.

"Oh, there's loads of 'em." The clerk waved vaguely toward the frontage road paralleling the highway. "McDonalds, Burger King, Friendly's, Pizza Hut." Her gaze drifted back to the television.

Jeremy cleared his throat to get her attention. "Can I have my card back, please?" he asked.

"Oh. Yeah." She passed him a pen to sign the charge slip, then slid two keys across the desk. They bore consecutive numbers, 111 and 112.

"How convenient," he grunted. It was bad enough that Marlo apparently loathed him, believed Alison to be his sweetheart and took him for an overzealous vengeance-seeking brawler. Worse was that, her negative opinion of him notwithstanding, he considered her the most enthralling woman he'd ever met. And now, to top it off, he was going to have to spend the night in a room adjacent to hers, knowing that she was just the thickness of a wall away from him, all alone in bed, resenting him while he fantasized about her like a smitten adolescent.

"Should we split a pizza?" he asked with a hopefulness he didn't feel.

Marlo glanced up at him and shook her head. "To tell you the truth, Jeremy, I'm bushed. I was thinking I'd just pick up a burger and fries and eat them in the room, and then sack out."

He could take a hint. "Fine," he said tautly, holding the office door open for her and trailing her out to the car.

They again lapsed into silence as Marlo cruised down the road to the strip of convenience stores and fast-food joints. She turned at the first burger place she came to and steered around the building to the drive-thru window. Jeremy ordered a couple of cheeseburgers and a soda for himself, knowing deep down that he was going to have a difficult time eating them. He was too weary, too edgy, too agitated to have much of an appetite.

"It smells good," Marlo observed as she passed the steaming bags of food over to Jeremy and accepted the ten-dollar bill he handed her. She passed it along to the chipper, uniformed teenager at the window, then gave Jeremy the singles and coins she received in change. "I'll pay you back when we get to the hotel," she promised.

"Why don't you let me pay for this?"

She cast him a quick look, then drove back to the frontage road. "It's a business expense. Havelock pays. Do me a favor, Jeremy, and pull the receipt out of the bag before it gets grease on it."

Jeremy rummaged around in the bags, then halted. This was ridiculous. The amount was trivial. And anyway, if this was as close as he was ever going to get to having dinner with Marlo, he sure as hell wasn't going to let Porter Havelock foot the bill. "If the receipt's in there I can't find it," he reported. "Let's just forget it, okay? I *want* to pay."

She sent him another quick, unreadable look, then turned onto the gravelly driveway to the motel's parking lot.

She parked near the building and shut off the engine. Jeremy insisted on carrying her suitcase for her, so she took both bags of food. They walked along the edge of the lot to their side-by-side rooms and he traded her suitcase for his dinner. He waited as she unlocked her door. Pocketing her key, she bent to lift her suitcase. When she straightened up her eye caught his, and she smiled—a nervous but genuine smile.

"Have a good night," he said, meaning it.

"Sleep tight," she returned, then stepped across the threshold and closed the door.

A long, doleful breath escaped him as he stared at her door. He wasn't sure what he expected—that she'd suddenly swing it open and cry, "What a fool I am! Let's have dinner together! Come on in!" After a minute he abandoned hope and let himself into his own room.

The drab interior depressed him, even though it was pretty much what he expected. The walls were an abject shade of yellow, the bedspread was an undefined olive green, the minimal furniture was constructed of Formica and the floor was covered with what felt like Astroturf. The windowless bathroom smelled of mildew. The walls were paper-thin; television noises from Room 113 seeped through the wall.

He picked listlessly at his food, flipped on the television in an attempt to drown out the noises from his unknown neighbor's TV—and to let Marlo know he was having a grand old time keeping himself entertained—and then retired to the bathroom for a shower. By ten o'clock he was in bed with the light out. The neighbor in

113 turned off his television set, leaving Jeremy awash in blessed silence.

He wondered if Marlo was in bed, too. His bed abutted the wall separating their rooms, and he wondered if hers did, too. He wondered if she wore a nightgown. She struck him as more the pajama type. Or maybe, like him, she slept in the buff.

The image made him groan.

He decided to distract himself by thinking about Alison. He wasn't as worried about her well-being now as he'd been that morning. Perhaps Marlo's unflappable approach to the rescue had influenced him to stop thinking of it as a life-or-death matter. It bothered him, though, that Marlo seemed so unconcerned about Alison's fate. He had to assume Marlo knew what she was doing, and yet... It didn't seem right to him. She knew more than she was letting on. She knew who the culprits were, she knew their names, their addresses. It didn't make sense.

Marlo McGinnis was clearly destined to drive him crazy in every possible way. Her mysterious approach to solving this kidnapping drove him crazy, as did her unjustifiable antipathy toward him, and that strange, ironic twist to her lips that made him ache with the longing to kiss her. She wasn't like the women he knew—and he wanted her in a way he didn't want the women he knew. He wanted to get through to her, to prove that he was more than just a big boy with a head wound and a vendetta. He wanted her to like him, to desire him, to accept him.

The possibility that she never would infuriated him even more than getting roughed up last night had. All his vindictive urges concentrated themselves onto the present, onto the woman in the next room. Restless and angry, he curled his hand into a fist and slammed it into the wall above the bed.

Silence surrounded him for an endless moment. Then he heard an answering knock on the wall, from Marlo's side.

CHAPTER SIX

SHE KNEW SHE WAS treating Jeremy abominably. It wasn't his fault that she drove an old, decrepit car and that he happened to be handy when it came to stopgap automotive repairs. It wasn't his fault that he had such mesmerizing eyes, such a dynamic chin, such a terrific physique. She'd even go so far as to allow that it wasn't completely his fault that he was rich.

Having chosen Alison Havelock to be his partner in life *was* his fault, however, and Marlo had every right to despise him for that.

She wasn't being cross and cranky with him because she despised him. It was simply a defense mechanism. If she didn't maintain some sort of barrier between them she might do something really stupid, like ask him to strip off his shirt so she could get another look at his marvelous chest.

If she despised anyone, it was herself. She'd been a dope to let him accompany her on this job. One instant of weakness, and now she was doomed to be tormented by his nearness all the way to Maine and back. Those moments of weakness were what always got you, she had learned years ago, during her training at the police academy. You had to be vigilant at all times; you couldn't let yourself be swayed by a display of vulnerability on your opponent's part. If you did, you might end up suckered—or worse.

She lay beneath the covers in the dreary motel room, clad in her favorite sleepwear—an oversize T-shirt—and tried to ignore the heavy aroma of grease and salt that lingered in the air from her dinner, which she'd tossed virtually untouched into the trash. She ought to have been ravenous, but she hadn't been able to bring herself to eat. She ought to have been tired, too, but an hour after showering, phoning her father and climbing into bed she was still wide awake and on edge. Her neck and shoulders were stiff from all the driving she'd done, her lower back was sore and her right thigh muscle was cramped from the constant pressure she'd exerted on the gas pedal.

What she wanted was sleep—but what she had was a keen awareness of the unattainable man in the room next door, a man who might have taken an interest in her if only she were ten years younger, five inches shorter, a million dollars richer....

What was she thinking? She had never met a rich person she could truly respect; she certainly had no desire to join the ranks of the wealthy herself. Rich people took too much for granted. They were spoiled. They thought nothing of wasting their money on nonsense. They had no grasp of reality. They got their way by manipulating others, preying on them, shutting their eyes to the human cost of their selfish demands. If a charity ball had to be planned, who cared that your private secretary was reeling from her chemotherapy treatments? You were rich; you could stamp your feet and scream until Catherine McGinnis crawled out of bed and dragged herself to Greenwich to help you organize your mailings and line up the caterers.

It didn't matter that Marlo's mother had been dying at the time. Marlo's father was self-employed and could scarcely afford the most minimal medical insurance. They had needed the money, and that harridan in Greenwich had had the money. So Marlo's mother had gone back to work.

Marlo tried to convince herself that the fact that her mother had spent the last two, painful years of her life struggling to keep her family out of debt, instead of marshalling all her energies to fight her disease, wasn't Jeremy's fault, either. But she couldn't help herself. She blamed them all, all those snooty Gold-Coast types who could afford every kind of insurance, the best doctors in the world, the finest state-of-the-art treatments. If Alison Havelock ever got cancer, she sure as hell wouldn't have to leave her sickbed at seven-thirty every morning to take dictation from a society matron in a waterfront mansion until finally one day she would be too weak to sit up, too weak to go on living.

Such negative thoughts weren't doing Marlo any good. She forced her mind to go blank, forced her eyelids to remain shut and regulated her breathing into a steady rhythm. For a while her fingers continued to clench and fidget against the blanket, but eventually her hands relaxed, and her arms, and even the knotted muscles in her shoulders. Sleep almost seemed within reach—until a sharp knock against the wall above her headboard startled her awake.

Her immediate reaction was fury. She'd been so close to drifting off when that too-handsome jerk shocked her nervous system back to full-alert status. It would take her hours to reach that level of drowsiness again.

Then, to her surprise, her rage transformed into wry amusement. Unless Jeremy was the sort to thrash about violently in his sleep, he was apparently suffering from insomnia, too. She wondered what thoughts were haunting him: misplaced concern for Alison's safety? Not-so-misplaced concern about the safety of Marlo's car?

Or anger at Marlo? Had her prickly demeanor gotten to him? Had she been too nasty? He had walloped the wall with enough force to imply that he was furious; the maudlin painting of a weepy clown above her bed had been jolted askew from the impact.

It pleased her to think Jeremy was as keyed up as she was. Impetuously, she knocked back.

Ten seconds elapsed. Fifteen. Then two polite taps on the wall.

She grinned and answered with two taps.

Her telephone rang. She turned on the bedside lamp and lifted the receiver.

"I can't sleep," Jeremy announced without preamble. She heard his voice in stereo, through the phone and through the tissue-thin wall.

"Neither can I," she admitted. "I shouldn't have drunk all that soda. It's got a lot of caffeine in it."

"Caffeine never affects me. I think it's just that I'm not used to going to bed this early."

"You're a night owl, huh?" Marlo's mind filled with an image of him dressed to the nines, partying with Alison at this or that glamorous night spot into the wee hours.

"No," he said, effectively erasing that image. "But ten o'clock is a bit early for me."

It was a bit early for her, too. But she'd been so fatigued, she had really believed she'd be coasting into dreamland within minutes of switching off the light.

"There's nothing on television," he went on. "Not even a baseball game."

"Are you a baseball fan?"

"I enjoy taking in a game every now and then."

"What team do you root for?"

"The Mets."

"Figures," she grunted, although she was chuckling.

"What's that supposed to mean?"

"The Mets are such a yuppie team. They draft their pitchers out of Yale, for heaven's sake."

"I take it you're a Yankee fan."

"Actually, the Red Sox. I know Bridgeport is closer to New York than Boston, but hey, I've got a few quarts of Irish blood in me."

Jeremy laughed. Then he grew quiet. "This is silly, Marlo, talking on the phone like this. Why don't we go someplace and get a drink?"

Because it's a lot easier for me to be friendly with you when we've got a wall separating us, she almost replied. "I'm not going anywhere," she said. "I can't bear the idea of getting back into the car right now."

"We could meet outside and talk," he suggested. "We could take a walk or something. It might help us unwind."

Hiding behind a wall was cowardly, Marlo admitted. And she *did* need to get some sleep. A short stroll in the balmy night air might work out the kinks in her nervous system. "I'll meet you outside in five minutes," she said, then hung up quickly, refusing herself the opportunity to change her mind.

Really, this wasn't a bad idea. A nice walk and a little companionable conversation tonight would not only relax her but also make it easier for her to deal with Jeremy tomorrow. If she didn't regain control of her anarchistic feelings about him soon, she was going to be a basket case, jittery from an emotional overload coupled with too little sleep. She crossed to her suitcase, which lay open on the laminated top of the dresser, and pulled out a pair of slim-fitting black jeans and a clean sweatshirt. After putting them on, she dug out her sneakers from the bottom of the suitcase and stepped into them. She ran her brush through her hair a few times, then scooped up her key and left the room.

Jeremy was already outside, leaning against one of the wrought-iron supports that held up the second-floor balcony. At her arrival, he straightened up and smiled. "It's so scenic around here," he joked, waving toward the crumbling asphalt of the parking lot, the strip of parched grass sloping down to the frontage road, the steady flow of cars just beyond the chain-link fence that separated it from the interstate.

Not just "scenic"—it was noisy. Even with functioning mufflers, the automobiles zipping along the highway at sixty miles per hour emitted a constant, irritating drone. "Maybe it's nicer behind the motel," she said, digging her hands into her pockets as a breeze swept across the parking lot. The air had cooled considerably, and the mugginess prevalent in southern Connecticut was nowhere in evidence this far north. She wasn't exactly chilly, but she was glad to be wearing long pants.

Jeremy had on jeans, too, and a clean shirt with the sleeves rolled up to his elbows. He sauntered beside her with a loose-limbed gait, his hands also in his pockets. Through the open window of one motel room they heard the cackle of canned laughter from a television; through another they heard the whining motor of a hair dryer and through another a woman giggling. Without speaking, without permitting themselves eye contact, they walked to the far edge of the building and turned the corner.

The side wall of the motel comprised a windowless stretch of brick on a rise overlooking the multicolored neon lights of the fast-food strip where they'd purchased their supper earlier that evening. Unmowed grass scattered with clover and dandelions covered the hill. "This isn't so bad," Jeremy remarked, gazing down at the almost festive-looking array of trademark-shaped lights below. Above them the overcast sky held a purplish hue; clouds obliterated the stars and reflected the headlights and shop lights illuminating this small corner of New Hampshire.

"Let's sit a while," said Marlo. The brief walk had reminded her of how stiff she was.

"Okay." Jeremy gestured for her to select a location. She settled against the motel wall, using it as a backrest. He lowered himself to sit next to her.

"I'm sore," she admitted. "Too much driving."

"I could spell you tomorrow," he offered.

For the first time since they'd met up outside their rooms, Marlo turned to look at him. His eyes, while still riveting, looked gentler in the night shadows, and his lips curved in a benign smile. He bent one leg and propped his forearm across the raised knee. His gaze lingered on the activity on the roadway below.

"How come you never wear your eyeglasses?" she asked.

He turned to her. "How did you know I wear eyeglasses?"

"I saw them on the coffee table in your living room this morning."

"Was that this morning? It feels like a year ago." He shook his head in amazement, then returned to her question. "I suffer from eyestrain sometimes," he explained. "I wear them if I've got a lot of fine-print reading to do, or if I'm concentrating hard on a blueprint, or if I have a headache."

"Do you get lots of headaches?"

"Not since I started using the eyeglasses," he answered, still smiling. "Of course, wearing eyeglasses doesn't do much to prevent a headache if I've gotten clubbed over the head."

"How's that injury, anyway?" Marlo asked.

"It's a bruise. Nothing much."

She scrutinized him, trying to ascertain whether it really didn't bother him anymore or if he was just being tough and stoical. She hoped it was the former. It disturbed her to think that he might be in pain, and hiding it from her.

He continued to stare at the road below them, seemingly hypnotized by the brightening of brake lights, the blinking of directional signals, the syncopated pattern of green to yellow to red to green at an intersection in the distance. Marlo's eyes journeyed from his outstretched leg to his bent one, to his balanced forearm with its spare overlay of golden hair, to the casual grace of his fingers in repose.

She tried to picture those fingers twining through Alison Havelock's luxurious auburn hair and came up blank. She could imagine the two of them partying in their designer fashions at some chic night spot but not smiling at each other, not truly enjoying each other. She could conceive of them forging a business agreement but not creating a loving marriage. As a detective she had to trust her instincts, and when it came to Jeremy Kent and Alison Havelock her instincts told her they made a dreadful match.

But she was in no position to counsel Jeremy on his social life. He was an adult; he had to live with his mistakes. In a way, she felt sorry for him.

Her unexpected twinge of sympathy did away with the resentment she'd been harboring toward him all evening. He was a man trapped in a dismal situation, entangled with a woman totally wrong for him, stuck with a future Marlo couldn't envy. Despite everything he had going for him, his life was far from perfect.

"I'm sorry," she murmured.

"Hmm?" He shifted to look at her. The motion drew her attention to his broad shoulders, to the V-shaped gap at the open collar of his shirt, to his hips. She recalled the motions of his body when he'd been working on her broken muffler, the way his lean male hips had flexed and twisted against the gravelly pavement, the way his movements had gotten her to fantasize about him.

Feeling her cheeks grow warm at the memory, she swallowed and turned away. "I'm sorry I've been so crabby," she said.

"Forget it." He waved off her apology. "You're just tired."

"I should have thanked you for fixing my car."

"You *did* thank me."

"Not enough." She took a deep breath, and another, willing herself not to give anything away, not to let Jeremy know she was indebted to him, attracted to him, uncomfortably vexed by him. She pressed her lips together to keep herself from revealing too much.

He cupped his hands under her chin and, gently but insistently, turned her head until their eyes met. She sensed at once that there was more than friendly reassurance in the gesture, more than simple forgiveness. The warmth of his fingers spread to her throat, up into her scalp and down into her chest. He held her face close to his, absorbing her with his gaze, probing her, searching beyond the panic in her wide eyes.

She prayed for him to say something, something banal and meaningless, something about her muffler and the service station and the worthlessness of guarantees. But she knew, in the instant before he caught her mouth with his, that speaking wasn't what he had in mind.

His lips were strong and persuasive. They grazed hers with quiet determination, exploring the full softness of her lower lip, the dainty notch in her upper lip, the surprisingly sensitive skin at each corner. It was less one single seamless kiss than a series of small, exploratory kisses, each one slightly less questioning than the last, slightly more assertive.

Patiently, carefully, he eroded her resistance, her sanity, her grip on reality, until her lips began to move with his. As soon as they did, as soon as her eyelids grew heavy and her breath deepened, he slid his hand around to the back of her head, plowing his fingers through the dense black waves of hair at the nape of her neck. The friction of his fingers on her skin sent a frisson of heat down her spine and she sighed.

That his hand was on her gave him an edge, and she attempted to equalize things by lifting her hand to his cheek. She felt the smoothness of his recent shave, the sharp angle of his jaw, the subtle movements of it as his mouth brushed hers at various angles, with varying pressure. Far from equalizing things, touching him had an utterly demoralizing effect on her. He felt so potent, so wonderfully male. Now that she'd touched him she didn't want to stop.

She ran her fingertips lightly along his jaw to his ear and behind it, into his thick dark-blond mane of hair. Lacing her fingers through the silky softness of it wasn't enough, though. His shoulders beckoned, firm and broad. As she slid one hand down into the hollow where his neck and shoulder met he groaned and opened his mouth against hers.

Kissing him like this was wrong, it was crazy, but it felt too good to stop. She lost herself to the minty taste of him, the searing thrusts of his tongue, the tensing of his hand at the base of her skull and the sweeping caresses of his other hand up and down her back and across her shoulder blades, drawing her closer, immersing her in sensations that thrilled her and left her yearning for more. She was helpless against her response, helpless against the lush heat that swelled inside her, causing her breasts to tingle and her hips to ache. Helpless against the understanding of what it would feel like to have more of Jeremy than just his lips and tongue, more than his arms wrapped around her and his hands stroking her, more than just a kiss.

Reveling in this spinning, luscious, pulsing helplessness was electrifying—but it was also dangerous, more dangerous even than chasing an armed teenage punk down an alley in a seedy neighborhood of Bridgeport. Marlo could not afford to be helpless.

Especially not with Jeremy.

Groaning with regret and dismay and seething frustration, she slid her hands forward to his upper chest and gave him a slight shove. He leaned back, gasping for breath. His eyes took a minute to come into focus. When they did, he gave her a heart-melting smile.

She refused to smile back. ''We can't do this,'' she said, her voice almost unrecognizably husky.

''Yes we can,'' he murmured, brushing her forehead with his lips.

Shuddering at the astonishing yearning he could awaken in her with such a chaste, tender kiss, she pushed him again, a bit more determinedly. ''No.''

His hands stilled on her back but he didn't remove them. Instead he stroked his fingers in a consoling pattern through her hair. "Look, Marlo," he said in a hoarse, rusty tone. He cleared his throat and tried again. "I like you. I think you're incredible. I think—"

"I think you're full of it, Jeremy," she retorted, annoyed that he would resort to stale sweet talk.

Stung by her rebuke, he frowned at her.

"I hate to be the one to remind you, pal," she said in a quieter tone, "but you're already spoken for."

He appeared momentarily puzzled, as if Alison had completely slipped his mind. As well she might have. Men tended to experience extraordinary mental lapses when their hormones were running the show. "Oh," he mumbled as understanding dawned. Then he shook his head. "It isn't what you think, Marlo—"

"Spare me," she snapped, shoving herself to her feet and folding her hands across her chest as if to hold in her emotions. "You don't know what I think. If you did, you sure as hell wouldn't like it. Good night." She pivoted on her heel and strode away, waiting until she was around the corner of the building, out of his line of sight, before she broke into a run.

GOOD NIGHT.

Never before had those two pleasant words been laden with so much bitterness. *Good night.* She might as easily have said, "Drop dead."

He sat leaning against the brick wall for a long time after she'd gone, staring down at the procession of cars and the display of lights without seeing anything. The ground was hard, the wall even harder, but the discomfort he was experiencing arose from Marlo, his desire for her, her rejection of him.

She hadn't rejected him right away, if that was any consolation. She had returned his kiss, at first with endearing shyness and gradually with enthusiasm. She'd tasted heavenly and felt even better. When her breath had mingled with his he'd felt infused with her spirit; when her tongue had moved against his, teasing and luring and skimming against him, he'd come close to losing control. And when his hand had journeyed down her back and he'd felt nothing beneath her shirt but her smooth skin, he'd had to fight the urge to guide her down onto the grass and press his mouth to her soft, unprotected breasts.

And she thought he belonged to Alison Havelock.

Alison. Remembering the reason for this trip sobered him, and he sat up straighter and felt the tension ebb from his chest and his groin. Saving Alison was more important than seducing Marlo. He was astounded to realize how close he'd come to telling Marlo the truth—that he and Alison were not, had never been and would never be lovers. Coming clean with Marlo would probably mean being summarily banished from this rescue mission.

Still, he would have to come clean with Marlo, not just to redeem himself in her eyes, but for the peace of mind honesty would bring. He couldn't maintain this ridiculous pretense any longer. It was wrong.

He would tell Marlo the truth first thing in the morning. If she dumped him, he'd deal with it. He had resources. He had his Gold Card; he could get his own transportation if he had to. He'd help save Alison, whether or not Marlo liked it. He had a score to settle.

Two scores, he conceded as he replayed the kiss in his mind yet another time and felt its arousing power all over again. One score to settle with those goons and their pistols, and another with Marlo—for turning him on and then turning him away, for being too damned principled to make love with a man she mistakenly thought was unavailable, for throwing his emotions into such a turmoil...for having those endless legs and that luscious mouth and those wide-set, infinitely dark eyes that turned his mind to jelly and his body to steel.

He had something to settle with her, all right. And he'd gladly settle it with her a thousand times, just for starters.

HE WAS ALREADY OUT in the parking lot when she emerged from her room at seven-fifteen the following morning, blinking like a mole in the glaring daylight. Not surprisingly, the previous night had proven far from restful, but it hadn't been a total waste. She'd gotten a lot of thinking done.

Mostly, she'd thought about the impossibility of having Jeremy with her for the rest of the trip. She knew how close they'd come to crossing the line last night; she knew exactly how eager she'd been to cross it. Even before she realized that Jeremy returned the feeling, she had been far too attracted to him. Giving in to temptation and acting on that attraction would lead to one result: disaster. Jeremy would break Alison's heart or he would break Marlo's, or both. She couldn't let it happen.

She had to get rid of him, that was all. She had to assuage his fears by explaining to him that Alison wasn't really in any danger, and then send him home.

She hated defying a client's wishes, and in telling Jeremy the truth about Alison's little fraud she would be defying Porter Havelock's. But she could see no other way to resolve this dilemma. Jeremy ought to have been set straight right at the start. He'd been the only true victim of this whole stupid affair. He'd already been hurt physically, and once he was informed of Alison's duplicity, he was going to be hurt emotionally. He deserved to know the facts.

If Havelock didn't like it, he could lump it. If he felt Marlo had acted unprofessionally in divulging the truth about his empty-headed daughter to his future son-in-law, he could refuse to pay her. She would rather forgo the money than continue to deceive Jeremy.

Besides, it wasn't as if she were broadcasting the news on the public airwaves. Jeremy was a business associate of Havelock's. He had enough sense to keep his mouth shut and protect his colleague's ego. Jeremy wasn't stupid; he struck her as a discreet sort. She doubted he would race off and trumpet the news to the media.

Hovering unnoticed in her room's doorway, she spied on him. He leaned against the hood of her car, his two-suiter balanced against the bumper. He had on the same clothing he'd been wearing last night—the leg-hugging jeans and the broadcloth oxford shirt with its sleeves cuffed to the elbow. He hadn't shaved since last night, however, and his cheeks were shadowed by an overnight growth of beard. The sunlight slanted into his face, making him squint. Except for the exquisite tailoring of his shirt, he looked less civilized than usual. Jeans suited him. So did wind-mussed hair. So did the stubble of beard and the half-mast eyelids and the hint of crow's feet at the corners of his eyes.

Spotting her at last, he shoved away from the car and curled his fingers around the handle of his bag. He didn't smile.

She swung her suitcase onto the sidewalk outside her room and heaved the door shut. Digging into the pocket of her slacks, she produced her car keys and approached him, focusing on his Adam's apple because it seemed safer than raising her eyes to his.

"We've got to talk," he said.

"Yeah." She moved past him, heading directly to the trunk and unlocking it.

Apparently he took her response as a brush-off. "I'm serious, Marlo. There's something we've got to straighten out—"

She ground her teeth together. Given his reliance on worn-out clichés last night, she could easily predict what he was likely to say today: "I respect you, Marlo. I admire your morals. I was secretly relieved when you brought things to a halt last night. I hold you in the highest esteem...." The sort of speech designed to soften her up and make her more receptive to his next seduction attempt.

Before he could launch into the expected soliloquy, she said, "We've got something to straighten out, all right, but I'm not going to do any straightening without a cup of coffee in my system, okay?"

He gazed intently at her. Daring to glance up, she saw the gray shadows underlining his eyes and the tightness around his mouth. His was not the expression of someone about to recite a well-oiled spiel about how highly he thought of her and how he hoped she took the pass he'd made at her as the compliment he'd intended. He appeared distinctly ill at ease.

Maybe he was experiencing major qualms. Maybe he was afraid she was going to run to Alison and tattle about his naughty behavior.

The possibility would have made her laugh if she weren't so troubled by him, by the understanding that she was about to breach a client's explicit instructions and by the equally devastating understanding that she'd brought this entire debacle down upon herself by allowing Jeremy to accompany her in the first place. That circumstances had brought her and Jeremy to this awkward place in time was nobody's fault but her own.

"Here," she said, handing him her room key. "Check us out. I'll drive around and pick you up at the office."

He nodded, turned and loped across the parking lot to the office. She busied herself arranging their bags in the trunk and locking it, then got into the car and cruised slowly to the office door. In less than a minute Jeremy emerged empty-handed.

They drove down the frontage road without speaking. Although the strip of fast-food joints hadn't exactly offered a pretty panorama last night, it looked even drabber in the morning, with all the neon off and the soot-stained walls of the buildings and the potholed lots surrounding them fully visible. Marlo swung into the closest restaurant's lot, pulled into the first empty space and shut off the engine.

Still without speaking, they went inside. The closest Jeremy came to an affectionate gesture was to hold the door open for Marlo. He made no move to take her hand or her elbow, to smile at her, to stand close to her. Just as she'd avoided letting her gaze meet his outside the motel, he evaded her gaze now.

After the morbid silence of their drive, the noisy bustle inside the restaurant jangled Marlo's nerves. She took a minute to adjust before moving to the counter and ordering a fried egg sandwich and coffee. Jeremy perused the wall menu in its entirety before requesting scrambled eggs, orange juice, hash brown potatoes and coffee. He looked somewhat unnerved when the energetic young clerk behind the counter placed a rectangular envelope on his tray. "What's that?" he asked suspiciously.

"Your hash browns, sir."

Jeremy's scowl deepened, but he pulled out his wallet and paid for his breakfast. He didn't offer to pay for Marlo's meal, which she took as a promising sign. Perhaps he wasn't going to butter her up in an attempt to make her more receptive to his overtures.

Pocketing her receipt, she wove among the tables until she reached a booth against a paned-glass wall overlooking the parking lot. As soon as she was seated she tackled her coffee, gingerly lifting the lid from the cup and taking a sip. It was too hot, but she was willing to scorch her tongue for a quick, desperately needed hit of caffeine.

Jeremy concentrated on his hash browns, peeling back the paper wrapper and prodding the solidified contents with the tines of his fork. "I think you're supposed to pick it up and eat it like a candy bar," Marlo advised him.

He curled his lip and turned to his eggs.

She would wager good money he never ate breakfast at fast-food places. Even in a rush, he would probably stop at a bakery for fresh-baked croissants and French-roast coffee before he'd sully himself by stepping inside an eatery favored by the peasant classes.

She took another sip of coffee, then unwrapped her egg sandwich. "Okay, Jeremy. Let's be frank," she said.

"Yes, let's," he agreed too quickly. Marlo shot him a dubious look, and he reached across the table and covered her left hand with his right. The contact sent an unwelcome warmth up her arm. She was horrified by her reaction. She didn't want to respond to him, but she couldn't help herself—and it annoyed the hell out of her.

"I know that when you hear the truth you aren't going to want me along with you." He pressed ahead, his eyes the pale, gentle color of fog but as clear and direct as a noon sun. "But I can't keep lying to you anymore, Marlo."

"Lying to *me?*" What was he talking about? *She* was the one misrepresenting the situation to *him*.

"I'm not engaged to Alison Havelock," he said.

She sank against the banquette, oddly disappointed. She had expected a juicier revelation than that. "I don't want to argue semantics with you," she muttered, trying unsuccessfully to slide her hand out from under his. "I understand the situation. You and Alison haven't made any formal announcements. That doesn't mean—"

"No, listen to me," he persisted. "There's nothing to announce. Alison and I aren't lovers. We've never been, and we'll never be. There's nothing of a passionate nature between us. I've never even kissed her."

This Marlo found hard to believe. Maybe they had made no specific commitment to each other, but never kissing? When Alison was so beautiful and Jeremy so gorgeous? How could they *not* kiss? Last night, Marlo had found it nearly unthinkable not to kiss him.

"Why haven't you ever kissed her?" she asked, making no effort to hide her skepticism.

As soon as she spoke, she realized that whatever did or did not occur between Jeremy and Alison was none of her business. But he answered anyway. "We aren't a couple. She's a child, Marlo. She's much too young for me. I don't love her." He shook his head, as if bewildered that anyone could believe otherwise. "I'm still not sure why Porter left you with the impression that we were in love, unless it's wishful thinking. Alison thinks he's trying to marry her off, and I guess I was a convenient man for him to marry her off to. But as far as she and I are concerned, we're just friends."

"We're just friends" was as trite a cliché as "It isn't what you think." Yet Marlo wanted to believe Jeremy. She had already decided that Jeremy and Alison were a lousy match, and she experienced a heady blend of validation and relief at his confession. The validation she could understand: she was pleased that her instincts in this instance had been on target. The relief was harder to justify, however. She was just a bit too happy to know that Jeremy wasn't a two-timing rat, that he wasn't simply stringing her along with slick moves and smooth patter, that he was unattached and available.

He might be available, but not to her. As wrong as he was for Alison, he was even more wrong for Marlo. He was from another society, another universe. He didn't even know how to eat fast-food hash browns.

His hand tightened slightly on hers, warm and snug and possessive. "I know you're going to think this means I no longer have any right to come to Maine with you," he continued, his tone low but resolute. "I know you only brought me along because you thought I was Alison's sweetheart. But Marlo—"

"No," she interrupted, abruptly recalling that she, too, had a deception to clear up, and that her purpose in clearing it up was to send Jeremy packing. With a resolute tug, she pulled her hand from his. As soon as it was free it began to turn icy, and she folded her hands together in her lap for warmth. "I mean, yes. I'm going to send you back to Connecticut."

"You can't," Jeremy declared with quiet force.

"Now, Jeremy," she said, her mind racing. Maybe she wouldn't have to betray her promise to Havelock, after all. Maybe she could get rid of Jeremy without going public with the news that Alison was an imbecile. "You've already told me about how if I say you can't come with me you'll follow me anyway and make it harder for me to do my work. But from what you've just revealed, you've got absolutely no reason to tag along. You aren't in love with Alison. You have no vested interest in her welfare."

"I have a vested interest in nailing the thugs who kidnapped her," he argued, his voice becoming gritty. "They hurt me, and right now they could be hurting her. She *is* my friend, and I'm not going to sit quietly on the sidelines while three creeps are doing God only knows what to her—"

"They're not doing anything to her," Marlo attempted to assure him.

"I don't happen to be as positive of that as you are."

"Jeremy, please." Marlo didn't want to beg him, but she couldn't keep the imploring undertone from her voice. She wasn't fighting for the right to do her job as she saw fit; she wasn't worried about Jeremy jeopardizing Alison's safety or his own in some ill-conceived act of vengeance. She wanted him gone so she could regain her equilibrium, so she could stop dreaming about his eyes and his broad chest and the way his mouth had felt on hers.

"You know as well as I do that Alison's in trouble," he persevered. "You know she's being held captive by three armed men. I can help, Marlo. I can make a difference. I want to rescue Alison from the guys who tried to crack my skull open—"

"The guys who tried to crack your skull open are Alison's classmates from Fairleigh Dickinson University," Marlo snapped, just to shut him up. If she didn't tell him the truth, he'd start foaming at the mouth, making Rambo-esque noises or sentimentalizing about damsels in distress. Marlo saw no other choice but to hit him with a heavy dose of reality.

His jaw fell open. He gaped at her incredulously. His hands fisted against the table, and he gulped in several ragged breaths and fought for control. Marlo watched him warily, noting the subtle changes in his expression and posture as shock gave way to confusion, and then to anger.

"I don't believe you," he finally said.

"It's the truth. They're Alison's friends. She set the whole thing up with them to get her father's goat."

"I don't believe you," he repeated.

"Jeremy..." She sighed, flipping through the pages of her memory, searching for evidence she could present to him in support of her statement. "There was a parking decal on the bumper of the van, remember? It was issued by Fairleigh Dickinson." He looked distinctly unimpressed. "You said she made lots of phone calls from your friends' house the night of the abduction, right? She was calling her buddies, working out the last-minute details, letting them know exactly when you'd be leaving so they could intercept you on that shoreline road."

"No."

"She's been telephoning them from Porter's house, too, setting up the whole stunt. They all know each other from school. Right now, they're hanging out at a vacation house. They're a bunch of spoiled brats on a tear."

"No." Just as she'd feared, Jeremy directed his anger at her for having told him things he didn't want to hear. His chin was thrust out pugnaciously and his eyes burned with outrage. "They couldn't be school kids. They had guns, damn it."

"So they had guns. I'm sure if the dean heard about it they'd get suspended. So what?"

"They hurt me, Marlo. They knocked me cold. They hurt me."

"Hey, they aren't on my list of nice people, either."

"I don't believe it. I *can't* believe it...." He drifted off, wrestling with his thoughts. He appeared astonished, flabbergasted and deeply, personally offended. That was it, of course: he *couldn't* believe what Marlo had told him. To believe it would mean believing that a young woman he considered a friend had tricked him, a woman he'd liked enough to bring to his friends' house for dinner had sacrificed his safety and very nearly his life in some sophomoric prank.

Marlo could believe it, of course. She could believe that people were capable of all sorts of malicious mischief. She'd spent years snaring errant husbands, straying wives, employees who ripped off their employers because they somehow couldn't make ends meet on the fifty thousand dollars a year they earned. Before that, she'd spent years running after kids who were strong and healthy and smart and gifted but whose only goal in life was to get high. She'd seen enough garbage in her life to believe anything.

And she could especially believe anything when the perpetrators were a group of bored, overindulged kids. She could believe they'd do anything for a giggle, even if a man wound up getting cracked in the head along the way.

Jeremy didn't want to believe it. But when he sagged in his seat, when his shoulders went slack in defeat and his gaze fell, she realized he did believe it. Even though, as it turned out, Alison wasn't his inamorata, what she'd done to him hurt. Badly.

Compassion welled up inside Marlo. "I'm sorry, Jeremy," she murmured.

He lifted his eyes to her, but they were blank, unseeing. He didn't speak.

She sighed and took a sip of her coffee, which had cooled off enough not to blister her tongue. Setting down the cup, she toyed with the plastic stirrer for a minute. She wanted to choose her words carefully, to avoid adding fresh bruises to his already battered self-esteem. "The only reason I let you come along was because I thought you were Alison's boyfriend. I thought it might be a good idea to have you with me, so that when she saw you maybe she'd suffer some remorse and come home without a fuss. But now you tell me you're only casual friends. And we already know she's not in any danger. So, I think the best thing would be—"

"Forget it," he said vehemently, springing back to life. His eyes lost their dazed, glazed look and sharpened on her, hard and metallic. "You aren't going to get rid of me now."

"There's no reason for you to come."

"There's every reason. Just because those animals are classmates of Alison's doesn't mean they're harmless."

"Granted, they banged you up. If you want to press assault charges—"

"It isn't me I'm worried about," he cut her off. "It's Alison. I *know* her, Marlo. Whether or not she planned to run away with them, she didn't plan for them to hit me. She wouldn't. I know it." His entire body seemed to hum with energy and determination. "I think she's still in trouble."

Marlo didn't want to agree, but she had to. It was her job to be prepared for every possibility. In this case, one possibility was that Alison had bitten off more than she could chew and her supposed pals from school were in

fact a bit more savage than she'd realized when she'd en-
listed their aid in her escape from Connecticut.

"And furthermore," Jeremy continued, leaning forward, "my ego is at stake."

"Your ego has nothing to do with—"

"My ego, while probably about half the size of yours,
is still very important to me. Maybe you're too professional to believe in getting even, but as far as I'm concerned, the stakes have just gone sky-high here. I'm not
disappearing now. I'm a part of this."

"Jeremy—"

"Think about it, Marlo: what are you going to do if
your car breaks down? You'll be stuck on the side of the
road in your broken-down wreck of a car, and I'll cruise
right by you in my rental car, heading north on a straight
line to Beresford. I'll wave to you as I go by." He gave her
a triumphant look, then consumed his orange juice in one
large swallow. He slammed the plastic cup onto the table
and bore down on her. "I'm coming with you, Marlo,"
he declared with resounding finality.

She closed her eyes. If only he were less sure of himself, less convincing, less compelling . . . less correct. She
couldn't argue with him, because he was right. She
wanted him along in case her car broke down again, and
he might do in a pinch if Alison's buddies turned out to
be psychopaths, and . . .

Oh, hell. No matter what her brain told her, her heart
insisted that she wasn't ready to say goodbye to him. Allowing him to remain with her was without a doubt a
stupid move. It wasn't professional, and it wasn't safe.
But since she could believe anything, she could believe
herself capable of a rare act of imprudence.

"All right," she heard herself say. "You're coming."

CHAPTER SEVEN

SHE WOULDN'T CRY. She wouldn't.

She felt light-headed, literally. That morning, when Ned awakened her with the announcement that he was going to drive her up to Bangor to buy some new underwear, she was thrilled—until he added, "I'm gonna cut your hair, first. That way you won't be as recognizable."

"Who's going to recognize me in Maine?" she balked. "Nobody around here has ever seen me before."

"Just in case," Ned argued, his eyes gleaming as if he thought this was real cool and criminal. The next thing she knew, he plunked her down on the upholstered stool in front of the vanity and went at her with scissors. Her hair, her beautiful, long wavy hair was hacked off in clumps and dropped into the garbage pail. She stared at the three-way mirror in horror, watching as Ned chopped off another thick lock and another, wondering how much Germaine would charge to repair the damage—if, in fact, it was repairable. By the time Ned was done Alison had her doubts.

"You look great," he said as he tossed down the scissors. Of course he was actually praising himself, his masterwork. As far as Alison could tell, she looked like a cross between Shirley MacLaine and Buster Brown, neither of whom she had ever wished to resemble. Her hair fell limp and straight to just below her ears, where it ended in a scraggly edge.

Her eyes burned with tears. She really, really wanted to cry. But she wouldn't. She wouldn't let Ned and the others know how bad she felt. They'd done all this for her, hadn't they? They'd brought her here because she'd wanted them to. Even if they'd done everything wrong, they'd done it in answer to her wishes. And Ned was going to take her shopping.

As soon as they were finished with breakfast—cold gummy corn muffins and instant coffee—Ned and Alison left the Olson house and drove to Bangor. With uncharacteristic tact, Ned had explained to the others that Alison needed to buy some personal items, and even with her brand-new hairstyle he'd just as soon keep her out of view in Beresford, so he was going to take her up north to civilization. When Dave had asked to come along, Ned had given him a meaningful look and said he and Alison wanted a little time alone.

They'd had all last night alone in that bedroom, and Ned had seemed to have himself a grand old time. Alison had been too tense to enjoy it, and she didn't have her pills with her so she was afraid to do it more than once. Ned had been pretty annoyed that she'd lacked the foresight to bring along her pills. But by this morning, he had worked it all out, telling her that after she went shopping for her undergarments he'd pay a visit to a well-stocked drug store.

He must love me, she told herself. Boys who loved their girlfriends protected them. Just because he didn't know the first thing about cutting hair didn't mean he didn't love her.

Bangor wasn't a particularly exciting town, but Alison was delighted by the fact that it *was* a town, practically a city, full of people and stores and restaurants. Ned wouldn't allow her to indulge in a leisurely stroll through the shopping district, though. He marched her directly into a department store, hovered on the outskirts of the lingerie department while she bought what she needed with the thirty dollars he gave her, and then marched her right back out again, refusing to let her browse in any of the other departments. "You haven't got any of your own money, remember?" he grumbled, steering her briskly through the store and outside.

He had her wait in the car while he ran into a pharmacy. When he emerged a couple of minutes later, holding a small paper bag, he had a cocky grin smeared across his face. It was the sort of smile she usually found sexy, but today she didn't. She reminded herself that he'd bought the contraceptives for her sake, not his own, but still, she didn't like the arrogant glint in his eye, the smug twist of his lips.

"All set," he said, climbing in behind the wheel and starting the engine.

"Can't we stay a little longer?" Alison asked. Sure, she didn't have any money to spend, but it was nice being out in public for a change. After spending so many hours under a blanket in the car yesterday, she deserved a spin around town in the morning sunshine.

Ned shook his head and navigated through the traffic toward the highway. "We've got business to attend to."

Alison eyed the paper bag he'd carried out of the pharmacy and grimaced. She hoped that wasn't the business he was referring to. She really wasn't in the mood. She felt too ugly at the moment, with her hair lopped off and no makeup on.

"What business?" she asked when he didn't elaborate.

"You've got to make a tape recording."

"What tape recording?"

"To daddy dear."

"To tell him I'm all right, you mean." She had almost forgotten that her father didn't know she was among friends. She hoped he was frantic, agonizing over her well-being, but she suspected he wasn't. "Why don't we let him sweat it out a little longer?" she suggested. That was the whole point of this exercise, wasn't it? To make him worry about her.

Ned shot her a quick look. "I'm up for letting him sweat," he confirmed. "As far as telling him you're all right, though…" He meditated for a moment, then raked his hand through his spiky black hair and chuckled. "No, princess. You're gonna tell him you *aren't* all right."

Alison frowned. "What do you mean?"

"We're gonna get some bucks out of the old man."

"Bucks?" She twisted on the seat to face Ned, whose eyes remained on the road ahead. "What are you talking about?"

"I'm talking about you haven't got any money, and I'm getting a little low on cash myself. We've run this play, Alison—we may as well get as much yardage out of it as we can."

What he was saying made no sense. This thing had never been about money. Sure, they didn't have much money with them, but how much did they need? They were only going to stay up in Maine for a few days. "What are you going to do, ask him to wire a hundred dollars through Western Union or something?"

"A hundred dollars?" Ned threw back his head and laughed. It was a harsh, derisive bark of a laugh, and it set Alison's nerves on edge. "Wake up, sweetheart. This is reality calling. I was thinking more along the lines of a million."

"A million?" The words came out in a faint rasp. She could hardly breathe, let alone talk. "A million dollars?"

"No, a million rubles. What's wrong with a million dollars? Ol' Porter Havelock the First could afford more. I'm going easy on him."

"Ned—" she swallowed and forced her voice louder "—this was never part of the plan."

"It's *my* plan, Alison, and I decide what's part of it."

"But...a million dollars? Ned, the whole point was to get back at my father for ignoring me."

"And your mother for marrying some dweeb fresh out of diapers. So what's the problem? Let's get back at them."

"Running away is getting back at them. Milking them for a million dollars is a whole different thing."

"What, you don't think you're worth it? You don't think they'd pay that much to get you back?"

Alison turned away and batted her eyes against the sting of fresh tears. This was supposed to be a gag, nothing more. Why couldn't Ned have kept it at that? First he had to bring guns into it, and then Dave had to hurt Jeremy, and now this: a ransom demand. This was really dangerous. Ned was frightening her.

She filled her lungs with air, then emptied them slowly and steadily. Ned wasn't the only one running this show. It was her life; if he truly loved her he'd show some respect. She wasn't going to let herself be cowed by him.

"I won't make a tape," she said.

He swerved off the road and skidded to a halt. Then he switched off the engine and turned to her. "Yes you will."

"I won't."

He made a face that seemed to convey that he was trying to be reasonable. "Why not?"

She gazed at him. His pale blue eyes reminded her of sharp splinters of tinted glass, and his lips curved in a surly smirk. She glanced briefly at the pharmacy bag, reminding herself of how much he cared for her. She wanted to please him. She couldn't afford to have him angry with her because if he stopped liking her she'd have no one at all.

But still, a million dollars? Extortion? She couldn't do it.

He seemed able to read her thoughts. When he spoke his voice was surprisingly gentle. "They don't care about you, Alison. That's really what this is all about, right? Sure, they'll shell out the money to get you back home, but they still won't really give a damn about you. So take them for what they're worth and run with it."

"Maybe they *do* give a damn," she argued feebly. "*That's* what it's about—making them give a damn. I don't want their money, Ned. All I want is for them to care."

"Speak for yourself," he countered, sounding his usual sarcastic self again. "That's all *you* want. I say, take the money and run. Get real, babe. They've never given a damn about you and they never will."

"That's not true!" she protested, mainly because she couldn't stand hearing her greatest fear put into words. The tears welled up, unstoppable, and she averted her face and closed her eyes so Ned wouldn't see.

They *did* care. They had to. If her father didn't care at least a little bit, he wouldn't have sent her presents over the years, and he wouldn't have signed her birthday cards, "Love, Dad." He wouldn't have told his housekeeper to help Alison in any way she could while she was staying with him, and to be nice to her because she was upset about her mother's remarriage, and he wouldn't have set her up with a man—a real gentleman—like Jeremy. He would have said, "You're on your own this summer, kid," and he wouldn't have minded if she'd spent every night hanging out with whoever she chose till all hours.

And her mother... She had always paid attention to Alison, at least until she'd fallen in love with Lucian. But that hadn't happened until Alison had started college, and by then Alison had been involved with her own social life, her own friends. She hadn't really minded that her mother was dating him—she hadn't been around enough to be bothered by it. It was only that they'd gone and gotten married, when he was so much younger than Alison's mother and probably a gold digger.

Like Ned, she thought, as his words echoed inside her skull. *Take the money and run.* What if he'd staged this thing not because he wanted to help her but only because he wanted to get at her father's money?

"Hey, come on, Alison," he said cajolingly. He touched her shoulder, but she recoiled so swiftly he let his hand drop. "Don't cry."

"I'm scared," she admitted, loathing herself for her weakness. "This wasn't supposed to be like a real crime."

"It was a real crime from the minute we thought of it."

"It was just for fun. I don't like my stepfather, that's all. I don't like that he and my mother went to the Riviera for the summer. I don't like my father working on weekends and talking about construction over dinner. That's all he ever talks about, and it's boring—but that doesn't mean we're supposed to steal money from him."

"It's not stealing."

"It *is* stealing." She sniffed and rummaged in her absurdly dressy evening purse for a tissue. She blotted her cheeks and blew her nose. "I won't do it, Ned. I won't make a tape demanding money from my father."

His eyes grew impossibly hard and cold. "You know he'd give you the money anyway, if you went home and behaved yourself. But if we get the money from him now, you'd never have to go home. Think about it, Alison. We could run away and be together and not have to deal with our folks ever again. I wouldn't have to be a lifeguard at my mother's country club, and you wouldn't have to listen to your father talk about construction over dinner. You wouldn't have to go back to school. We'd have each other and all that money to live off."

Alison's first thought was that, given the high style in which she liked to live, a million dollars might not last very long. Her second, more sobering thought was that if she took her father's money and ran off with Ned, there would be no coming back. The only thing she'd wanted was for her parents to pay attention to her, and if she did this thing with Ned, her parents would never forgive her when they found out the truth. They'd go on living their lives without her, and she'd never find her way back to them. It would be the end of everything she'd ever really wanted.

All she'd have was money and Ned. Money she could have either way, and Ned . . . Ned with his diamond stud earring and his sardonic smile, his aura of danger and his sexy body . . .

Maybe he didn't love her. Maybe he only wanted her money. Maybe nobody loved her at all, nobody.

Don't cry, she commanded herself, swallowing down the salty lump in her throat. She wouldn't be weak anymore. If it was true that nobody loved her, all she had was herself. And if that was the case, she was going to have to be tough.

Inhaling, she lifted her face and stared at Ned. "I won't do it," she said firmly. "I won't make the tape."

Ned's icy gaze held hers for a long moment. He studied her, deliberated, moved his lips as if mulling over his words.

Then he slapped her.

"HOW ARE YOU DOING?" Marlo called over to Jeremy.

He glanced up from the map, removed his eyeglasses and tossed her a brief smile. "I'm fine. Are you sure you don't want me to drive?"

"Positive." The thing about long-distance driving was that you never realized how uncomfortable you were until you stopped. As long as Marlo remained in the driver's seat, focused on the road ahead of her, she wouldn't notice the stiffness in her neck or the strain in her legs.

Even if she did, she wouldn't want Jeremy driving right now. Despite his scholarly perusal of the Maine road map, he seemed distracted, shaken to his soul by what Marlo had told him over breakfast an hour ago. His revelation had shaken her, too, but the only negative thing about it, as far as she was concerned, was that it deprived her of a convenient reason not to get involved with him. All the other reasons—his wealth and polish and social register pedigree—had a way of fading from her mind whenever she caught a glimpse of him, whenever she recalled the erotic warmth of his lips on hers. Whenever she remembered his stricken look when she'd told him the truth behind what had occurred on that abandoned shoreline road in Westport Saturday night.

That look had had the same impact on her as the anguish he'd revealed when he had described his nightmares about his convertible car. All he had to do was give off the merest whiff of vulnerability, expose a glimmer of the profound emotion lurking beneath his debonair facade, and she melted like an ice-cream cone on an August afternoon. Somehow, he seemed to have no trouble getting through to her, softening her up...suckering her.

"I really wouldn't mind taking a turn at the wheel," he persisted, meticulously folding the map along its original creases. "I'd hate for you to be exhausted by the time we get there."

"I won't be," she assured him. "Anyway, this car is kind of moody. Broken air conditioner, iffy muffler... I know its idiosyncrasies, but you don't."

"I'm good at reading cars," he said.

True enough. He, not she, had been the one to diagnose the broken muffler and tail pipe clamp. "How did you get to be so good at car repairs?" she asked.

"I used to work as an auto mechanic."

She looked at him in disbelief. Sure, she could imagine him tinkering with a precious British sports car like his MG. She could picture him in overpriced work clothes—designed by Ralph Lauren, no doubt—fooling around with a buddy's Jag or waxing poetic over a Lamborghini engine, but...an auto mechanic? "I thought you were an architect."

"I am now. When I was a teenager I worked summers as a grease monkey in the Hamptons."

Oh, of course, the Hamptons: one of the premiere summer addresses on the East Coast. He wouldn't be a grease monkey just anywhere. He had to be one in an exclusive community, where they probably only pumped deluxe-blend gasoline and where they cleaned up oil spills by sprinkling gold dust on them.

She arched her eyebrows, not minding if her skepticism showed. "Why do I have trouble picturing you as a grease monkey, Jeremy?"

"I have no idea." He leaned back in his seat, shutting his eyes against the warm breeze that gusted in through his open window. "I had a real knack for it. My parents owned a car, but we hardly ever used it in the city. We'd use it only when we went out to our house in Westhampton Beach. We'd pile into the car and pass through the Midtown Tunnel, and suddenly we'd be tearing along, cruising at seventy, surrounded by wide open spaces. Long Island isn't empty anymore, but twenty-five years ago it wasn't so clogged with traffic. And we'd just drive and drive, and my father would start unwinding and my mother would start laughing, and my brother and I would count Volkswagens and make peace signs at the other drivers. I loved it. It was like being let out of jail."

"Twenty-five years ago you were too young to be a teenage grease monkey."

"Even as a kid I used to fool around with my father's car. When we'd gas up he would always let me work the nozzle, and he'd let me check the air in the tires. He taught me how to read a dip stick, how to check the water level, how to tighten the fan belt. I loved seeing how everything fit together, how it all worked. It was like an incredibly complicated three-dimensional puzzle."

"How come you didn't grow up to be one of those rich playboy race-car drivers?"

He eyed her curiously, as if he couldn't understand why she would ask such a thing. "Driving is all right," he explained, "but fiddling with an engine is much more fun. I think I went into architecture for the same reason: designing a building is like working out a puzzle, fitting in everything you need under all sorts of constraints and

making it come out right aesthetically. An engine has to
fit into this much space, it has to propel this much weight,
it has to include these features. One small part gets out of
whack and the whole system collapses. It's a challenge to
get it to work."

"So, you parlayed this interest into a high school career," she said, sounding less sarcastic than simply be-
mused. She believed Jeremy, even though it was still
difficult for her to conceive of him holding down a genuine dirt-beneath-the-nails job like her male contempor-
aries in high school. Her classmates always complained
about their jobs, though. She found Jeremy's enthusiasm appealing.

"My mother and brother and I used to spend the
summers out at the house, and my dad would join us on
the weekends," he recollected. "I worked weekday af-
ternoons and the Saturday night shift. Nobody else
wanted it."

"That must have done wonders for your social life,"
Marlo remarked. "Working every Saturday night."

"Actually, it wasn't bad. I got to meet all the girls who
had wheels. I'd fill up their tanks and we'd flirt awhile,
and then maybe one of them would come back at closing time and take me to a party somewhere. It wasn't bad
at all."

Marlo ought to have been irked to hear that even as a
gas jockey Jeremy Kent had had the Midas touch, turning a dreary summer job into a glamorous way to meet
girls. But she wound up laughing instead. He sounded
like such a regular guy when he described his stint at the
gas station, almost like someone she could have known
in her youth.

Except, of course, that he'd been a regular guy in posh
Westhampton Beach and the boys she'd known had been

regular guys hanging out near the Barnum Museum or at the Crossroads Mall, trying to convince the girls they met to go parking with them down at Black Rock. She herself had worked after school and summers behind the counter at a doughnut shop, and the guys who flirted with her were coarse and blunt. The parties they invited her to—invitations she invariably refused—consisted of one boy, one girl, one automobile and at least one bottle of cheap wine.

Once, just before she'd graduated from high school, she'd been invited to a Gold-Coast party. Debby Szarek's older brother had met a girl from Darien at U Conn, and he'd offered to bring Debby and some of her friends along to his girlfriend's house for a party. The house had been a sprawling Sixties-modern ranch house on a couple of manicured acres. The party had been down in the basement, which had been finished and decorated with more elegance than Marlo's whole house—and had probably contained more square feet of space than the entire McGinnis house, as well. The floor had been covered with genuine slate tile, the walls paneled in birch, the lighting provided by ornate Tiffany-style hanging lamps and the air warmed by a floor-to-ceiling fieldstone fireplace. The beverage of choice, served at a built-in bar with brass fittings, had been a chilled Chardonnay. The boys had all worn loafers and looked like stockbrokers in the making. The girls—other than Marlo and her friends—had all had glowing peaches-and-cream complexions, and they'd worn Fair Isle sweaters and styled their hair like Farrah Fawcett's. Marlo had had the largest feet of all the girls there.

Jeremy would have been in his element at that party, she reflected—and then she corrected that misperception. If he'd spent his adolescence pumping gas, maybe he wouldn't have fit in so well, after all.

"Are you seeing anyone?" he asked.

Despite the casual way he'd tossed off the question, Marlo flinched, almost swerving out of her lane. She clutched the steering wheel and shot him a venomous look. Reminiscing about their adolescence was one thing; talking about the present was quite another. "None of your business," she snapped. "How much farther till we get to Brunswick?"

He ignored the question. "I don't mean to put you on the spot, Marlo, but you're a fantastic woman. I'm just wondering whether there's any one special person in your life."

Her hands still tight around the steering wheel, she gritted her teeth to keep herself from saying something she might regret. Jeremy had diplomatically refrained from specifically mentioning what had happened last night, and for that she supposed she ought to be grateful. But they were still miles from Brunswick, and many more miles from Beresford, and she didn't welcome the prospect of spending the next several hours examining her love life, or lack thereof, with Jeremy.

"At the risk of being redundant, it's none of your business."

He shifted in his seat, stretching his legs as best he could in the tight space under the dashboard. The wind raveled his hair as he regarded her, and his thumbnail made a faint scratching sound against his bristle of beard as he stroked his chin. "Is there some way I could make it my business?"

"Look, Jeremy..." She loathed him for goading her into it, but since she'd resolved to be honest with him about Alison, she felt she had no better alternative than to be honest with him about herself. "Last night was a mistake, okay? It shouldn't have happened."

"Even if it was the best thing that's happened since we met?"

"Speak for yourself," she mumbled, feeling like a coward as she beat a hasty retreat from the truth.

"All right. Speaking for myself, it was the best thing that's happened in a long time. I enjoyed it."

"Well, good for you," she snapped.

He appraised her for a minute, the corners of his mouth twitching upward in an enigmatic smile. "You enjoyed it, too."

"Fine. I have a pulse. I'm not dead. I enjoyed it. Big deal."

"You're so fearless when it comes to chasing kidnappers—and fake kidnappers," he pressed her. "Why are you afraid of talking about last night?"

"I'm not afraid," she said testily. "I just don't happen to find it especially entertaining as a topic of conversation."

He continued to study her, his eyes attempting to penetrate her, his smile remaining mysteriously ironic. She considered asking him to trade places with her and drive for a while, just so he would be forced to stare at the road instead of her. She fumbled for a new topic, drew a blank and resorted to turning on the radio. Set at no local station, it broadcast static.

Jeremy reached for the dial and clicked it off. "Are you nursing a broken heart or something?" he asked.

"No, are you?"

"No."

Now there was a successful diversionary tactic—turning his questions back on him. "Involved with anyone?" Marlo asked.

His smile slowly expanded as he realized what she was doing. "No."

"How come? A man of your age ought to be bouncing the next generation of Kents on his knee."

"I'm not that old," he told her.

"Not old enough to father a child?"

"Not old enough to feel any pressure to," he clarified.

"But you'd like to have children someday," she guessed.

"Definitely."

"So, what are you waiting for?"

He chuckled. "Call me old-fashioned, but I'd prefer to be married to the mother first."

Marlo grinned. Discussing such personal subjects could be a great deal of fun if the focus was on Jeremy instead of herself. "You're thirty-three years old," she said, "and usually, by that age—"

"How do you know how old I am?" he asked, apparently surprised.

"It was on the report you filed with the police. Anyway, by that age, if a man is unmarried and unattached it's generally for one of three reasons: A—he's divorced, B—he's gay, or C—he's a compulsive womanizer who can't sit still long enough to get serious with anyone." She allowed herself a quick glimpse of him and found him smiling with open amusement. "Divorced?" she hazarded.

"No."

She wrinkled her nose. "Well, you obviously aren't gay."

"You don't seem pleased."

"I'm not pleased to think you fall into the third category. That's the worst one, Jeremy."

Laughing softly, he shook his head. "How about D—none of the above?"

"Care to elaborate?"

"I've gotten close to marriage a couple of times," he explained, evidently not the least bit offended by her prying. "The first time was when I moved back to New York after taking my degree in architecture. She and I were together for three years. She was an actress, trying to get her career off the ground in New York. It's a tough field to break into, though, and her frustration was compounded by the fact that my career was soaring. She finally decided to move to Los Angeles and test the waters there. She loved me, but she felt like a failure professionally. I couldn't hold her back. She needed to see how far she could go."

An actress. In spite of what he'd just told her about his sweetheart's struggles and thwarted aspirations, Marlo automatically envisioned a glamorous starlet. "Did she become a big success out in Hollywood?"

Jeremy shook his head again, this time sadly. "Afraid not. Last I heard, she met someone out there, got married and obtained a real estate license."

"How about the other time you got close to marriage?" Marlo asked.

"It didn't work out."

"Why not?"

He ruminated for a moment. "It was one of those things," he explained vaguely. "We *should* have been good together. We had so much in common—a similar background, excellent schooling. We met through work—she was an interior designer, very talented. She played squash, like me. She liked sailing." He paused, remembering. When he next spoke, he sounded wistful, oddly bewildered. "I really don't know why it didn't work out. We both tried hard. It all seemed so right on the surface. But that was it—after a couple of years we came to realize that it was all surface, that we just weren't connecting on a deeper level. So we parted ways."

Marlo was amazed that he would confess such intimate things to her—amazed and flattered. If she'd thought about it, she would have suspected him of ulterior motives, but she was too touched by his candor to throw her guard up. Once more he had offered a teasing glimpse of his soul, and once more she had fallen for it. Not until he smiled, tapped his fingertips together, gave her a cool, challenging stare and said, "I've told you mine, now you tell me yours," did she realize that he'd suckered her again.

He responded to her scathing look with a laugh. "There's nothing to tell," she muttered.

"Fair is fair," he chided. "Having not had the advantage of reading a police report on you, I don't even know how old you are."

"I'm thirty," she informed him, a vain attempt to prove she had nothing to hide.

"Thirty," he repeated, reassessing her with this knowledge. "All right, you're thirty. You're very attractive. You're bright, you're knowledgeable and mature. I'm not going to believe nobody's ever fallen head over heels in love with you."

A strangled sound caught in her throat, half a cough and half a guffaw. "I hate to disappoint you, Jeremy, but no, I don't think anyone's ever fallen head over heels in love with me."

"Why not? Are you A—divorced, B—gay, or C—a nymphomaniac?"

She deserved that, and she relented with a feeble smile. "D," she answered, then decided that, just as she'd demanded more of him, he deserved more of her. "You may not know this, but as a rule police officers make lousy partners, romantically speaking."

"Why is that?"

She shrugged. "They're always strung out, tense, looking over their shoulders. It's such a high-wire life, you can't be focused on anyone but yourself."

He nodded at the reasonability of her explanation. "You're not on the police force anymore," he reminded her.

In his own courteous way, she acknowledged, he was as stubborn as she was. He wasn't going to let her off the hook with the pat reply she'd tossed him. She pretended to be absorbed in the task of passing a sluggish flatbed truck piled high with lumber, but once that was accomplished she became uncomfortably aware that Jeremy was still waiting for a reply.

What to say? That she, too, had gotten close to men a couple of times in her life, that both times she'd believed it was love, that in each case the man was basically decent, well-meaning, attractive and willing to reciprocate, but that ultimately, when things began to intensify, she felt compelled to run for cover? That whenever she thought about happily-ever-after she wound up thinking about how ever-after sometimes walked right up and hit you in the gut, and that whenever she thought about till-death-do-us-part she wound up thinking about the death and the parting—and the inevitable grief? That she'd seen what love and marriage and interdependency had done to her father when his wife was taken from him? That as frightening as it had been to stare down a street kid with a Saturday night special, Marlo found it infinitely more frightening to stare down the pain that could come of loving someone and then losing him?

She had spent her professional life learning about self-defense, learning how to stay out of harm's way, how to avoid tragedy. She knew the difference between courage and recklessness. As brave as she tried to be in relationships, she couldn't allow herself to get reckless. It just wasn't in her.

"I guess Mr. Right just hasn't come along yet," she mumbled, recognizing that she had to tell Jeremy something.

"Oh, of course," he mocked her. "You're the meek, retiring kind of woman who prefers to sit tight and wait for someone to come along. That's what I like about you, Marlo—your utter passivity."

"Hey, I'm doing other things with my life right now, okay?" she protested. "I don't have time to run around looking for true love. It's not my top priority. There's the Brunswick exit. Should we stay on the highway or take Route 1?"

Jeremy reluctantly followed her hint and abandoned his interrogation of her for the more immediate task of navigating them to Beresford. He pulled out the map and unfolded it across his lap. "Stay on the interstate," he advised. "It may be more miles if we go through Bangor and then south, but they'll be easier miles."

She nodded. The highway was the more sensible choice. Route 1 would parallel the ragged coast line, passing through hamlets and quaint seaside villages. It would be more picturesque, more exotic, but less pragmatic. She didn't want to take the time and risk missing Alison and her friends at Beresford.

Never take unnecessary risks, her instructors at the academy had drilled into her.

So why had she taken the unnecessary risk of letting Jeremy stay with her? Why had she taken the risk of letting him kiss her?

Why did some small, insane part of her wish she were brave enough—or reckless enough—to take that risk again?

CHAPTER EIGHT

"HELLO, DADDY, this is Alison..."

"Alison!" Porter bellowed into the telephone. "Damn it, where are you?"

"...is a tape," her voice continued in an even recitation. As soon as she'd identified herself, Stan had switched on the recording function on Porter's answering machine. Porter had been upset that Stan had insisted on recording any and all calls from Alison—as he'd said, it shouldn't be necessary if the kidnapping was merely a hoax—but Stan believed in doing a thorough job. In addition to taping calls from Alison and her cohorts, he'd arranged for his friend Angie at the phone company to trace all calls coming in to either of Porter's two home numbers, as well as his office number. Too frazzled—and too hung over—to go to the construction site at the North Stamford office complex, Porter had remained at home on Monday and entrusted his secretary to stay at the construction site trailer so she could answer any calls he might receive there.

This call, the first since that one brief communication from New Hampshire the previous day, had come to Porter's home, and Stan was ready for it. At the first ring, he'd set down the corned beef on rye Dolores had sent into the study for him and crossed the room to Porter's desk. By the time Alison's voice emerged through the answering machine's speaker, the tape was spinning, preserving the call.

"I'm okay, Daddy. Nobody's hurt me...."

"We already know that," Porter grumbled, waving his hand impatiently in the direction of the answering machine as if encouraging Alison to speed things up and get to the point.

"...Anyway, they want five hundred thousand dollars. Well, that's not really true—they want a million dollars, but I sort of bargained them down. I mean, I think a half a million dollars is plenty enough, and I told them I refused to ask you for any more than that..."

"Good for her. That took guts," Porter murmured proudly, as if he'd forgotten Alison was a party to this scheme and not a victim.

"...So anyway, they haven't worked out yet where they want you to send the money, so I guess we'll be in touch again soon. I'm sorry if this is a problem, Daddy—really. Okay? I'm really sorry."

There was a click as the tape ended, and another as the connection was severed. Stan reached across the desk to turn off the machine and rewind the tape. Then he called the phone company. Angie told him she had to go through the computer to trace the call but she'd get back to him as soon as she could. If this had been a real kidnapping, with the police and the FBI involved, the phone company would have had an instantaneous trace mechanism already in place. But since it wasn't, Angie had to comb through the regional computer logs in search of a call that connected to Porter Havelock's home number at exactly 12:03 p.m. It would take a while.

Porter sprang out of his chair and paced in a wide circle around the paneled room, intoning an assortment of expletives under his breath. Stan replayed the tape, but

Porter seemed too agitated to listen. At the conclusion of the tape, he said, "I don't like it."

Stan turned off the machine and straightened up. "What don't you like?"

"If this is a gag, why is she asking for money?"

For the same reason any daughter would ask her rich father for money, Stan almost replied. *Because she wants the bucks.* He refrained from saying so, however, and chose instead to analyze Porter's suspicions. "What are you getting at?"

"What I'm getting at is, maybe it's not a gag. Maybe it's for real."

Stan shook his head and returned to his sandwich. Dolores had slathered on an abundance of mustard, and his nostrils filled with the spicy aroma as he settled on the sofa and lifted his plate back onto his lap. "It's not for real," he declared. "If it was, she wouldn't be saying she was sorry. And she wouldn't have been able to negotiate her alleged kidnappers down in price."

"How do you know she really did talk them down? Maybe she was just saying that to keep me from getting angry."

"If she wasn't in on it, they would have been asking for more than a million, not less. They would know what you're worth, Porter, and they'd ask for plenty more than five hundred grand. And she wouldn't have cared whether or not you got angry." He took a hungry bite, chewed and swallowed.

"I still don't like it," Porter complained. He moved in another circuit around the room, then hesitated by the bar. Stan cleared his throat disapprovingly, and Porter continued past the liquor bottles—not before casting them a longing look. In collusion with Dolores, Stan had managed to keep Porter sober since yesterday afternoon, but it was a chore that required constant vigilance. "Why hasn't Marlo found her already?" he griped. "What's taking her so long?"

"I told you," Stan answered, as patient as Porter was frantic. "She had car trouble and got held up overnight in New Hampshire. She called me from a motel in Portsmouth."

"Car trouble," Porter huffed. "What kind of investigator is she, driving off to Maine in a jalopy?"

"She's the kind of investigator who can't afford a new car loan at the moment," Stan said with a wry smile.

"I'd give her a car loan if she wanted one."

"Fine. I'll pass the word along."

"She should have been there by now," Porter railed, completing yet another circuit that brought him back to his liquor supply. "And what about Alison's school chums? Why haven't we figured them out?"

"There's nothing to figure out," Stan explained for the umpteenth time. "I've told you: Marlo already spoke with the Sawyer kid's mother and got the names of the other two kids. I've tracked down Peter Olson's home number and given it a ring, but a housekeeper there said the family's on Martha's Vineyard for the week. The third punk is this Ned Whitelaw character. His mother's remarried; I haven't been able to learn her new name yet. If you want, I'll go back to my office and do some more digging on the kid. That would mean you'll be all alone here with Dolores, and she's about ready to pour the contents of those bottles down the drain."

Porter glanced at the bar one last time, then sighed and resolutely turned his back on them, evidently believing that it was better to forgo a drink right now than to risk losing his entire liquor supply. "What I want," he said testily, "is to have Alison back. I want her here, locked up in her room so she can't cause me any more grief."

"Oh, right," Stan responded. "Lock her up in her room, Porter. That'll solve everything."

Porter glowered at Stan. His flinty eyes narrowed, his chin trembled with suppressed rage and his forehead contracted in parallel creases of anger as he absorbed Stan's sarcasm. Then, slowly, he relaxed his brow, his jaw, his body. He trudged across the room to the sofa and slumped onto it, sending Stan a doleful look. "Tell me what to do," he implored.

Helpless. Helpless and thoughtless, but at least Porter Havelock wasn't heartless. Stan honestly pitied him. It was strange, being put in the position of family therapist for the man paying his fee. He was used to giving Porter advice on safety and security issues: arranging office buildings to allow the security guards an unobstructed view of the parking lots, designing indoor and outdoor lighting for maximum effectiveness, performing adequate background checks on Havelock employees working in sensitive areas and the like.

But to counsel him on his relationship with his child... Stan was no professional when it came to that. Whatever he knew he'd learned from experience.

Judging by the results, he knew a hell of a lot more than Porter. "Tell me what you want," he demanded in a gentle tone, "and then maybe I can tell you what to do."

Porter sighed and studied his hands, the surfaces of his palms with their webbing of lines and then his thick knuckles and buffed nails. Given that he was significantly smaller than Stan, he fit more comfortably on the stiff, undersized cushions of the couch. "I want Alison back, for starters," he said.

"You'll have her back," Stan assured him. "But if you lock her in her room you're going to lose her again, real fast and probably for good."

Porter gave him a sidelong glance. "What did you used to do to Marlo when she broke the rules?"

"When she was a teenager, you mean? I...well, I grounded her."

"In other words, you locked her in her room."

But it wasn't the same thing, Stan almost protested; Porter couldn't compare the two situations. First off, the times Stan had grounded Marlo she'd been younger, still fully in his care. By the time she'd reached Alison's age she'd been enrolled in the police academy, responsible and self-supporting, well on her way professionally. She'd lived with Stan to save money, but essentially she'd been on her own.

Also, she and Stan had had a relationship. Porter and Alison didn't.

He couldn't very well put that distinction into words, not without hurting Porter's feelings. Porter was Stan's boss. While Stan wanted to help him, the need for diplomacy limited how candidly he could speak.

"Do you want to ship Alison back to her mother?" he asked.

"I don't know. No," Porter decided. "No. It was her mother's stupid marriage that precipitated everything. I can't send Alison back to that." He paused, still examining his hands, lacing his fingers together and then pulling them apart. "Why is she asking for money?" he groaned, trying to hide how distraught he was and not succeeding. "She didn't have to pull this stunt if all she wanted was money."

Money wasn't all she wanted, not by a long shot. But once again Stan opted for tact and didn't mention that obvious truth. "I wouldn't worry about that phony ransom demand," he said.

"But what she said . . ." Porter gestured vaguely in the direction of his telephone. "Why would she be asking for it if she didn't want it?"

"They're going through the motions," Stan explained. "It's like a performance, a theater piece. They're playing let's-pretend."

"It's not that I haven't got the cash," Porter continued, his voice gruff with contained emotion. "It's not like I couldn't raise it in a minute if I had to. But . . ." He sighed and gave his head a forlorn shake. "It's one thing to run off and make believe it's a kidnapping, Stan, and it's another to extort money from your own father. I mean . . . I just don't believe Alison could do such a thing. She may be an airhead, but she isn't venal. She might want to scare me, but I can't see her going for my jugular, you know? I just don't think it's in her to do something like that."

"Meaning you suspect something's gone haywire with this gig?"

"It just doesn't smell right to me. I know she's with friends, but even so . . . something smells fishy."

Stan wasn't convinced, but he sympathized with Porter. That the man was so worried about his daughter was a good sign; maybe he was ready to stop griping about how personally humiliating Alison's behavior was to him, and instead direct his concern toward Alison herself. Maybe he was ready to look past his own nose.

"I'll tell you what—let me see if I can raise Marlo on her car phone," he suggested. "I'll find out how close to Beresford she is and pass along the word about Alison's message. Okay?"

"Okay," Porter said, evidently relieved that steps, however trivial, were being taken. "Give her a call. Tell her the morons who nearly cracked Jeremy Kent's skull in two are now trying to milk me dry. Tell her about what these harmless kids are up to."

BERESFORD, MAINE, could have been a set for a saccharine Hollywood movie; it looked much too charmingly picturesque to be real. The winding road that descended through the hilly outskirts of town was bordered by rolling meadows where cows grazed randomly and groves of sugar maple and pine trees stood, where wildflowers bloomed and grass grew knee-high. The houses past which Marlo drove were scattered, some a half mile from their nearest neighbors, and each one was large and white, with even clapboards, a wide front porch, a peaked roof and at least one redbrick chimney climbing up a side wall. Every barn was dark red with white trim. Glimpses of an impossibly blue harbor could be seen to the south. Not a single human being was in sight.

It was all so pure, so pristine, so uniformly lovely Marlo couldn't decide whether to laugh or cry. If she laughed it would be out of cynicism, an inherent disbelief that any place on earth could be this beautiful. If she cried it would be because she'd lived thirty years of her life ignorant of such beauty, excluded from it. If she had been driving farther north and inland, where tough Maine natives pieced hardscrabble lives out of the rocky soil and the brutal climate, she would have felt at home. Here, though, in this lush, healthy environment of bright colors and cloudless skies, she felt like an outsider.

No wonder. She *was* an outsider. Jeremy, on the other hand, looked as if he'd fit right in. Indeed, he seemed less than overwhelmed by the splendid scenery. He scrutinized each house as they approached with a critical eye, as if searching for a clue that Alison and her buddies were somewhere inside. Marlo sensed in him no appreciation of the breathtaking scenery.

"We'll drive into town," she told him, "and get the address for the Olson house."

"Sounds good," he agreed, although he didn't stop inspecting the houses for clues.

The road continued to twist through the hills, losing altitude as it coursed southward. The houses here stood closer together, and barns were used as garages and storage sheds. At last the road leveled out. Tree-shaded sidewalks edged the street, which cut through a three-block-long commercial district—also as ideally pretty as a Hollywood set. No supermarket, Marlo noted, no hardware store or drug store. Quaint downtown Beresford featured a general store and an apothecary. She spotted an ice-cream shoppe, complete with the extra P and E painted on the weathered oak sign, and a souvenir shop, the windows of which were filled with scrimshaw, old bottles, and blown-glass balls in trawling nets draped like hammocks. A clothing store, a sandwich shop, a bank, a church, a combination town hall and post office, and a sporting goods store completed the Norman Rockwell picture.

Marlo took the first parking space she could find and shut off the engine. Once she was out of the car, she filled her lungs with the crisp, pine-scented air. Jeremy got out of the car, too, but he didn't seem the least bit awed by his surroundings. He strode directly to the parking meter, fished in his pocket for a coin and inserted it.

"Let's find a phone book," Marlo suggested, surveying the row of stores lining the block and figuring the sandwich shop was the place most likely to have a public telephone booth with a directory.

She'd figured correctly. Ignoring the curious stares of the luncheon customers, she wove among the tables to a narrow hall at the rear of the room, where she spotted a pay phone on the back wall just past the rest room doors. The county directory chained to the wall by the phone was barely a half inch thick, but it contained several dozen listings under "Olson." Marlo ran her thumb down the list until she found "Olson, Lewis." When she'd contacted her father from the motel in Portsmouth, he'd supplied her with Peter's father's name.

The address to the right of Lewis Olson's name was "Box 69, Beresford." "Well, that's real useful," Marlo muttered under her breath.

"What does it say?" Jeremy asked.

Rotating, she found him standing within inches of her. In the dimly lit hallway he seemed much too close, his tall body shielding her view of the tables and his face cast into shadow as the midday sun flooded the dining room behind him'. She listened to the clink of china and silverware, the low babble of voices in conversation. The restaurant was redolent with the aromas of toast and fresh-brewed coffee, but Jeremy smelled of herbal shampoo and clean male warmth, and that was the smell she responded to, experiencing not hunger for a good, wholesome lunch but hunger of a perilously different kind.

This was neither the time nor the place to be responding to Jeremy's nearness, the silhouetted proportions of his tall, lean body and the understated grace of his hands. She had more important things to be thinking about than the way his mouth had felt on hers last night and the way he'd insisted, earlier that morning, that he wanted to make her social life his business. If only he took a step back, her nervous system would stop pulsing with awareness. His face would become visible and she'd take in his polished features and realize how well he belonged in this carefully staged enclave of upper-class privilege, and then he wouldn't appeal to her quite so much.

He seemed to have no intention of backing up, however. "What does it say?" he repeated, motioning with his head toward the phone book.

"The only address is a post office box," she answered, pleased by the cool authority of her voice. She took a step forward and he moved aside to let her pass.

"What do we do, then? Go to the post office?"

"They won't give out the address," she said. "We'll have to ask around." She scanned the small dining area and sized up the woman seated at a cash register behind a counter near the door as a potential target.

Jeremy trailed her through the room to the counter. She offered the cashier a pleasant smile, which was not returned. "Hi," she said brightly. "I'm wondering if you can help us out. We're trying to find Lewis Olson's house."

The woman behind the counter blinked. She wore a deceptively plain shirtwaist dress with Liz Claiborne buttons down the front, and her silver-streaked hair fell in a neat pageboy around her lantern-jaw chin. She stared at Marlo, then at Jeremy, blinked again and remained silent.

"Do you think you could help us out?" Marlo asked.

"Lewis Olson's house," the woman finally said.

"That's right."

"Nope, don't think I can help you."

Marlo dropped her sunny smile. No sense wasting it on such an unfriendly person. "Thanks," she muttered, then turned and gave the front door a shove. The cheerful tinkle of a bell as it swung open made her want to gag.

Outside, she gave her eyes a minute to adjust to the glaring sunlight, then skimmed the street with her gaze. "How about the sporting goods store?" Jeremy suggested.

With a shrug, she crossed the street and entered the narrow shop. A counter ran the length of the room; behind it stood an arsenal of hunting rifles large enough to keep a third-world country at war for a year. Below the scarred wooden countertop was a glass display case filled with knives: pocket knives, sheathed knives, knives for filleting fish, knives for whittling toothpicks and knives for purposes Marlo hadn't given much thought to since her days on the Bridgeport force. If this was really a sporting goods store, she had to conclude that sport was a fairly gruesome business in Maine.

A beefy gray-haired fellow in a red-and-black checked shirt lumbered from the rear of the store and positioned himself across the counter from Marlo and Jeremy. "What can I do for you folks?" he asked pleasantly.

Still irked by the frosty demeanor of the cashier at the restaurant, Marlo wasn't about to be gulled by this man's cracker-barrel congeniality. "We're trying to find Lewis Olson's house," she said.

"Lewis Olson," the man repeated, smiling benignly. "That'd be Lewis Olson from down New Jersey somewhere?"

"Yes, that's right," she said, taking heart.

The man stroked his chin thoughtfully. "Say, Herman!" he shouted toward the rear of the store. Marlo turned to discover a thin elderly man arranging fishing rods vertically against a wall stand. He glanced up from his chore, nodded at Marlo and Jeremy, and then turned to his colleague behind the counter. "Yeah?"

"You know that Lewis Olson from New Jersey?"

"Yeah."

"You know where he lives?"

"New Jersey."

"No, Herman. I mean, up here. Where he lives here."

"He don't live here," said Herman. "He lives down in New Jersey."

The man behind the counter turned back to Marlo and shrugged helplessly. "Looks like we can't help you out, ma'am," he said, infusing his voice with contrition even though his eyes were bright with mocking laughter.

Marlo understood the two men were ridiculing her. She didn't even bother to mumble a thank-you as she stalked to the door and yanked it open. She heard Jeremy cover for her, thanking the men for their time before he chased her outside. "That was rude," he reproached after joining her on the sidewalk.

"*They* were rude. They were making fun of us, Jeremy."

He mulled over her words, eyeing the store thoughtfully. "I should have shaved this morning," he muttered.

"Your appearance has nothing to do with it," she argued, assessing him in a sweeping glance. With his sun-streaked blond hair, his clean, evenly faded jeans, his chiseled features and deep-set eyes, his appearance could not possibly have offended anyone in this town. The faint stubble darkening his jaw only enhanced his looks, reducing his prep school sheen just enough to lend the impression that he knew how to use most of the knives in the sporting goods store's showcase. "It's because we're outsiders," she explained, "and they're tight-lipped Yankees."

"We ought to think up a better strategy," he suggested. "Coming right out and asking people isn't working."

"Have you got any ideas?"

He meditated for a minute more, then shrugged. "Let's try the town hall."

"I don't have any legal leverage here," she reminded him, falling into step next to him as he started down the sidewalk toward the square redbrick building with an American flag snapping above it in the wind. "I can't get into the municipal records or anything. I'm not an officer of the law with extradition documents. I'm just a P.I. investigating a non-crime."

"We can't do worse there than we've done so far," Jeremy observed. "Maybe the town employees consider it their civic duty not to make fun of visitors."

Marlo doubted it. However, she lacked a better idea. Her purse slung by its strap over her shoulder and her hands in her pockets, she kept pace with Jeremy, wondering if he in fact did have a strategy, whether it would succeed and whether she'd resent him if it did. He had already proven himself indispensable once on this trip. If he proved himself indispensable again, she would never forgive him.

They climbed the three granite steps to the front door and entered the building. The long, fluorescent-lit corridor was lined with doors with frosted-glass windows built into them. The door to their right had "Post Office" painted on the glass in gold letters; to their left, the door was labeled "Town Clerk." Jeremy opened that door and stepped inside.

A woman—presumably the town clerk—glanced up from her desk behind a waist-high room divider. "Yes? May I help you?" she asked, stabbing the pencil she'd been using through the topknot into which her snow-white hair was pinned.

"I sure hope so," Jeremy replied, giving her a sheepish grin. "My name's Jeremy Kent. I'm an architect, and I'm kind of lost."

The clerk peered at Marlo over the rims of her reading glasses, then turned back to Jeremy. "If you're lost, Mr. Kent, I can tell you you're in Beresford, Maine. Says so right on the front of the building: Beresford Town Hall."

"Oh, I know that," Jeremy said, allowing his grin to widen while somehow looking even more sheepish. "A fellow named Lewis Olson hired us to do some renovations on his summer house here in town. Well, I packed everything into my portfolio—blueprints, sketches, exteriors, interiors. . . . And when we got up here, I discovered the one thing I forgot to pack was the piece of paper with Mr. Olson's address on it. Now, there was a house on that road that comes into town from the north—"

"Route 46," the clerk said helpfully.

"That's right, 46. Anyway, there was a house on that road that looked a little like the photographs Mr. Olson sent me, but it had cows in the pasture out back. Mr. Olson never mentioned he was a farmer."

"He's not," the clerk confirmed. "Must've been someone else's house you were looking at. The Olson place is up on Old Meadow Road—not far from where 46 comes into town. Hasn't got a number, but you'll know it when you see it."

"From the piled stone fence," Jeremy improvised.

"That, and the wagon wheel. And the flowers, of course. You aren't going to do anything to mess up those flowers, are you?"

"I wouldn't dream of it," Jeremy vowed. "Now, how do I get to Old Meadow Road?"

Astounded and unabashedly annoyed by Jeremy's success, Marlo listened as the clerk rattled off the directions. As soon as the clerk wound down, Jeremy thanked her copiously and ushered Marlo out. She braced herself for the expected gloating and strutting, but Jeremy wasn't even smiling as they crossed the street and retraced their steps to the car.

"I didn't know you were such a good liar," she muttered.

"Neither did I," he said with a dry laugh. He seemed grateful rather than boastful. "Come on, let's go find the house with the wagon wheel and the flowers."

She almost wished he *would* gloat. If he did she would be justified in despising him. Recalling the ingratiating smile he'd worn for the clerk, she realized that it wasn't his lie that had done the trick so much as his charm. The clerk had opened up to him for no other reason than that he had dimples and dazzling gray eyes.

That, plus the fact that he fit in in a town like Beresford and Marlo didn't. The clerk had undoubtedly viewed him as one of their own.

Trying to keep her resentment contained, she got back into the car and turned on the engine. She glanced at Jeremy as he arranged himself in the passenger seat, but again failed to discern any smugness about him. Even so, she thought it best to clear the air before her resentment started to fester. "Look," she said quietly, "you happened to get lucky in there. But don't let it go to your head."

"I won't," he promised.

She waited for him to elaborate, to attach a few riders to the deal, to do something to give her an excuse to loathe him. All he did was adjust his seat belt and roll down his window.

She pressed her lips into a straight line and tore away from the curb. She knew she shouldn't say anything further, but she couldn't help herself. "The lady was obviously smitten with you, that's all," she said.

"Who? The town clerk?" He let out a laugh, obviously finding the notion preposterous. "That woman was old enough to be my mother."

"So what? She took one look at you and spilled her guts. That's not the way things usually work."

"I see." He cast her a sidelong glance and smiled. "Don't you sometimes have to use your looks to seduce information from people?"

She ground her molars together, then forced herself to relax. "I've never resorted to that tactic, no," she said, not bothering to add that a woman with her unremarkable looks would be wasting her time if she tried.

They had left the heart of town, and Jeremy told her to turn right. She might have needed him to wrangle the directions out of the clerk, but she didn't need him to repeat them to her. She had memorized them as the clerk had recited them.

Within ten minutes they reached the meandering Old Meadow Road. Half a mile along it they spotted the riotous colors of wildflowers dappling the generous front yard of an enormous white farmhouse with a wide front porch. An old wagon wheel stood balanced against the corner support beam of the porch, its spokes artfully overgrown with flowering ivy. The loose-gravel driveway was empty.

The wagon wheel looked trite, Marlo decided. The flowers were too gaudy. The porch was too wide, the house too spacious, the stone wall bordering the property too deliberately pastoral, the curtains fluttering in the open windows too lacy.

She'd give her eyeteeth to live in a house like it.

"It looks like no one's home," Jeremy observed as she slowed the car at the entrance to the driveway.

"So it does." She veered onto the driveway and rolled the car to a halt. Pulling the key from the ignition, she caught a glimpse of Jeremy as he stared at the house. He looked upset. "Hey, don't worry," she placated him. "They're out for a while, that's all."

"What if it's not just for a while?"

"They left two front windows open. They might be stupid, but I don't know if they're so stupid they'd take off for good without shutting the windows. Unless, of course, they aren't thinking that far ahead." After pocketing her key, she opened her door and got out. The air, though warm, was bracing, the flowers lending it a tangy fragrance. In the distance to the south, she could see the harbor.

God, it was beautiful. If Marlo could live in a place like this, live here and belong here and know it was hers...

If she could do that, she'd be a fat cat, a rich, snooty upper-crust snob. No way. She belonged on the grimy streets of Bridgeport and she wasn't ashamed to admit it. "Let's go in," she said brusquely.

Jeremy eyed her askance. "But no one's here."

"We are," she pointed out, jogging up the slate walk to the porch. She knocked on the door, waited, heard no response from within. Then, shifting a whitewashed Adirondack chair out of her way, she bent down near one of the open windows to peek inside. The house did, indeed, appear vacant.

Behind her came the thump of Jeremy's footsteps as he joined her on the porch. "What are we going to do?" he asked. "Wait for someone to come home?"

She allowed herself a private smile. Jeremy Kent might have been a whiz at seducing information from Beresford's town clerk, but when it came to the nitty-gritty he was totally at sea. She searched the room for confirmation that this was, indeed, the house they were looking for, and let out a silent cheer when she spotted an L. L. Bean catalogue lying on an end table. The address sticker was upside-down to her view, but it definitely said Olson.

"We're going to let ourselves inside," she told Jeremy.

"Break in, you mean?" He sounded both concerned and intrigued.

"That's the general idea." She tested the screen window's frame; there was no play in it. Just as well—Marlo preferred walking into a house to climbing in through a window.

She straightened up, groped in her purse and pulled from a zippered inner pocket her lock-picking tools. Jeremy's eyes grew round. "Is this legal?"

"Don't sweat it."

"I'm not sweating it. I just want to know if I'm going to end up in jail for this."

Marlo laughed, inserted a slender steel rod into the keyhole and jiggled it around, listening for the catch. "Don't worry about jail," she said, angling the rod up and down until she felt the bolt give. "You can plead temporary insanity."

"Wonderful," he groaned. "What a relief to know I'll be sentenced to an insane asylum instead of a prison." But despite his complaints, he eagerly followed her into the house once the lock gave way and the door opened.

The inside of the house was as lovely as the outside, and Marlo steeled herself against the sudden rush of covetousness that enveloped her. She honestly didn't want to admire the colorful rugs, the cozy furnishings, the rustic fireplace, the atmosphere of prosperity and comfy indulgence. She didn't want to stand motionless, gaping at a room in which the value of a few casually placed knickknacks was higher than the entire contents of Marlo's apartment—and where the living room alone seemed as large as her living room, bedroom and kitchenette put together. She didn't want to find herself amid such luxury, feeling impoverished and deprived. She didn't want to hate Alison and her friends for having things Marlo had never had and would never have.

She wanted to hate Alison and her friends for a legitimate reason: because they'd run away. Because they'd injured Jeremy. Because hating them made it easier for Marlo to do her job.

As soon as she recovered sufficiently from her bout of envy, she began to inventory the room with a professional eye. The sculpted ceramic ashtray on the end table contained a cigarette butt and a pale gray mound of ashes, implying that the cigarette had been smoked recently. A glass on another table held a watery brown liquid and slivers of ice—another indication that people had been here not long ago. Marlo lifted the glass and sniffed: cola.

She moved further into the house, down the hall to a kitchen. The countertops were cluttered with traces of junk food—crumbs of what appeared to be corn muffins, a broken pretzel, a half-empty bag of taco chips, a crushed box from a frozen pizza, a crust of wheat bread. Dirty dishes filled the deep-basin sink. A road map was wedged between the sections of a Bangor newspaper on the sturdy pine table.

Marlo pulled out the map and unfolded it. It featured the province of New Brunswick, although the northern half of Maine appeared on the page, as well. A line had been drawn with a ballpoint along Interstate 95 from Bangor to the border crossing at Houlton, and on into Canada. A comically large dollar sign had been inked at the end of the line, followed by an exclamation point.

She stared at the line, noticing the way the paper was dented at Houlton as if whoever drew the line had paused there and dug the point of the pen into the paper. She stared at the way the line continued past the dent. She stared at the dollar sign.

She cursed.

"What is it?" Jeremy asked.

Turning from the table, she discovered him hovering in the doorway, watching her. "They may be contemplating a trip to Canada."

"What?"

"Canada," she said, crossing the room in long, rapid strides. Jeremy reflexively stepped out of her path as she raced from the room, then trailed her down the hall, through the living room and out the front door. She didn't slow down until she reached her car, where she tugged open the door and dove across the driver seat for her cellular phone. She punched her office phone number. Ida answered.

"Ida, it's Marlo. Can I talk to my father?"

The agency's trusty secretary let out a snort. "Where have you been?" she scolded. "Your father and I have been trying to reach you since a little past noon."

"I've been in and out of the car," Marlo told her. "Mostly out. Could you put my father on, please?"

"He's at Porter Havelock's house," Ida told her. "Porter's being very cantankerous. He doesn't want to be left alone."

Marlo rolled her eyes. When Porter didn't want to be left alone, Stan couldn't leave him alone. "All right, I'll call him there," she grumbled. "What's the number?"

Ida recited it and Marlo instantly memorized it. "Thanks, Ida."

"Don't leave your car for such long stretches," Ida said by way of farewell. As if Marlo could get her job done by sitting in her car all day, waiting for the telephone to ring—but she didn't bother mentioning that.

She pushed the buttons for Porter's home number, waited, and heard a click after the second ring. "Yes?" came Porter's voice, hard and breathless.

"Porter, it's Marlo McGinnis."

"Oh." She heard him mumble, "Here, it's Marlo," and then the muffled rattle of the phone changing hands.

"Hi, Marlo," her father said. "I've been trying to reach you."

"Ida told me. Listen, I'm at the Olson house and nobody's here, though they've obviously been here within the past hour or so. The place appears very lived in."

"You've been inside," he said knowingly.

"Just to look around. Why have you been trying to reach me? Ida sounded pretty worked up about it."

"These kids," her father grumbled. "I sure hope they get tired of this game soon. They phoned in a tape of Alison asking her father for ransom money."

"Ransom money?"

"Half a million dollars."

Marlo cursed again. "I don't know, Dad, but I've got a hunch they might be thinking of heading on up to Canada."

"Canada?" Her father sounded nonplussed. "I had Angie Russo over at the phone company trace the ransom demand call and it came from somewhere south of Beresford, not north. Southwest, actually—a town on the Belfast exchange. If they were heading to Canada, wouldn't they have made the call somewhere along the way?"

That would have been the logical choice. On the other hand, if they were heading straight to Canada, they might not have left the house messy and the windows open. "Maybe they called from there to throw us off."

"You think they're that clever?" her father asked. His skeptical tone conveyed that he didn't.

"Maybe they're just winging it, I don't know. But this map I found... I tell you what, Dad—I'm going to go back into the house and check the place out some more. Maybe Canada's just an idea floating around in their heads right now. I'll see what I can find."

"Okay. And keep in touch, Marlo."

"I'll check in when I can," she said, then hung up the phone and climbed out of the car.

Jeremy closed the door for her. She started to walk past him, heading back to the house, but he clasped his hand over her shoulder and held her in place. As soon as she stopped his fingers relaxed against her.

She looked at where he was touching her, where his palm molded around the ridge of her shoulder, where his thumb came to rest on the edge of her collarbone. For a fleeting instant she believed he was about to pull her to himself, to kiss her again. It was a crazy notion, and much as it galled her, she understood that it arose not from anything Jeremy had done but from her own outlandish preoccupation with him.

"What's going on?" he asked. "Does your father think they're going to Canada, too?"

She lifted her gaze to his face, willing herself to ignore the gentle pressure of his hand on her, the warmth he ignited in her with a single meaningless touch. "He says they've called Porter and asked for money," she informed him, her voice sounding strangely distant.

"Money to take to Canada with them?" Jeremy guessed.

"Maybe. I think we should go back inside and scope it out some more. I may be completely wrong about this Canada business."

"You haven't been wrong about any of it, yet," he noted.

Oh, yes she had. She'd been wrong about not wanting to bring Jeremy with her. She'd been wrong to think he would slow her down or tie her up. If she hadn't had him with her she would never have found this house. She would never even have gotten to Beresford, given her broken muffler.

So far, the only thing she'd been right about was her prediction that the more time she spent with Jeremy the more desirable she would find him. As his fingers molded snugly to her shoulder and his gaze wandered over her face, probing and intense, she found herself experiencing a deep, visceral awareness of his hand on her, of his body so close to hers she could reach up and run her fingers over his stubble of beard. She wanted to do that, to say, "The hell with Alison," and to walk with him, arm in arm, back to that gorgeous white farmhouse with its glut of wildflowers and its corny wagon wheel. She wanted to pretend she could belong in a house like that, with a man like Jeremy Kent.

And that was about as wrong as she could get.

CHAPTER NINE

STANDING UNNOTICED in the bedroom doorway, Jeremy watched Marlo pick up the pearls.

He had been following her through the house, observing her at work. He didn't share her conviction that Alison and her friends were headed for Canada—one mislaid map with some scribbles on it wasn't exactly unimpeachable proof—but Marlo was the expert here, and he let her go about her business without interfering. In a sense, he hoped Alison and crew *were* on their way to Canada, because if they weren't they might return here and catch him and Marlo snooping through the house.

Marlo seemed to suffer no qualms about the questionable legality of what they were doing. She prowled from room to room, mentally recording each scene, saying little. In the first-floor lavatory she discovered that a hand towel was still damp; on the stairs she noticed some carelessly flicked cigarette ashes. The second floor contained six bedrooms, three of which had apparently not been used during the previous night. Their beds were freshly made and the tops of their dressers were devoid of personal articles. In the bedroom above the kitchen, the bed linens were rumpled and a collection of travel brochures lay scattered across the dresser. Marlo picked through them: a trail guide to Baxter State Park; a pamphlet about Acadia National Park; glossy tourist flyers describing Kennebunk, Deer Island and "Freeport,

Home of L. L. Bean''; a schedule of the ferry service between Bar Harbor and Yarmouth, Nova Scotia; a guide to provincial parks and campgrounds on the Bay of Fundy. "Well," she opined, flipping through the schedule, "I guess they aren't planning to leave the country by boat. If they were, they would have brought this with them."

"They wouldn't take a ferry," Jeremy confirmed. "Alison gets seasick." He had learned this after inviting her to go sailing with him and some friends a few weekends ago. "If they were planning to go to Canada," he went on, pointing to the toiletry items that shared the dresser top with the brochures, "they *would* bring their hairbrushes along, wouldn't they?"

Marlo dismissed the toiletries with a shrug. "For half a million dollars, they can buy themselves new hairbrushes."

"Half a million dollars?" The sum staggered Jeremy, not so much because he was squeamish about large amounts of money as because hearing the actual number made the situation seem more real to him somehow. Half a million dollars. Was Alison truly capable of extorting that kind of money out of her father? Jeremy had been listening to her pathetic laments about Porter for a month. Was she hard-hearted enough to calculate the monetary value of a father's love and demand reimbursement?

She was hard-hearted enough to have her schoolmates knock Jeremy unconscious and abandon him at the side of a road. Alison was apparently not the sweet, innocent, misunderstood young lady he'd assumed.

Marlo crossed to the bathroom door, vanished inside for a moment and then reemerged. She opened a dresser drawer, took note of the ample stores of clothing inside and slid it shut. "This must be Peter Olson's room," she concluded. "He's the only one likely to leave stuff behind—his parents own the house."

She swept out of the room in search of more evidence. Remaining behind, Jeremy returned to the dresser to examine the brochure about the Bay of Fundy. If Alison and the others were going to Canada, wouldn't they have brought this information along with them?

If they were going to Canada with a half million dollars in their pockets, they would be planning to stay in ritzy hotels, not campgrounds. Belatedly he realized what Marlo had already figured out: on the dresser were the brochures they didn't need. They'd taken with them only the relevant brochures, the ones concerning deluxe accommodations in Fredericton or Saint John or wherever the hell they were planning to spend the night.

He left the bedroom and walked down the hall, peering around the open doors of two unused but nicely decorated bedrooms. At the third door he spotted Marlo and halted.

She stood before a mirrored vanity table, one hand cupped around the triple-strand necklace of freshwater pearls Alison had worn the night of the phony abduction. Marlo lifted the pearls, trailed her fingertips over their uneven, lustrous surfaces, let them spill across her palm, then raised them to the window and admired their delicate iridescence in the afternoon light.

Ignoring the necklace, Jeremy looked only at Marlo, at the artless emotion in her face, the wistful curve of her lips and the radiance of her eyes. It occurred to him from the way she fondled the pearls, the way she gazed at them and played their cool, slippery surfaces through her fingers, that she didn't get this close to pearls on a regular basis. Her yearning was almost palpable.

He entered the room and approached her, his foot-steps muffled by the rug. She must have discerned his movement in the mirror, because she hastily tossed the necklace back onto the vanity and spun around, her cheeks flushed and her eyes wide with panic. She looked mortified, as if he'd caught her in the act of some hei-nous crime.

He knew she hadn't been planning to filch the pearls; this was a woman who refused to doctor her expense ac-count so Porter would pay for her car repair. She was extremely ethical. Why did she look so guilty?

"I didn't mean to startle you," he apologized.

Her cheeks still blazing with color, she averted her eyes. "It's all right. Never mind."

He gestured toward the necklace. "It's pretty, isn't it."

"It's okay," she mumbled, a patent understatement. "If you like that kind of thing."

It was obvious that *she* liked that kind of thing. From the way she'd held the necklace, the way she'd examined it with breathless delight, Jeremy knew she did. Why should she deny it? Taking pleasure in a beautiful piece of jewelry was nothing to be ashamed of.

He scooped up the necklace and untangled its strands. "It would look terrific on you," he said, nudging her down onto the stool and rotating her so she faced the mirror. "Here." He reached forward from behind her and draped the necklace around her throat.

She stared at her reflection as if stunned. The neck-lace looked better than terrific on her. The glossy cream-colored pearls flattered her graceful throat and comple-mented her tawny complexion in a magnificent way. Jer-emy fastened the gold clasp at the nape of her neck, then slid his hands to her shoulders and helped her to her feet, turning her so he could view her.

"I shouldn't do this," she said, though she made no move to undo the clasp.

"Where's the harm in it?"

"It's not mine." She lifted her hand to her throat, but instead of removing the pearls she only stroked them, experiencing in a tactile way what she'd already studied in the mirror.

"You're only trying it on. Alison wouldn't care. They're just freshwater pearls—it's not like they're worth a fortune or anything."

"That depends on your definition of a fortune," Marlo argued. Her voice was hushed, though, not caustic but laced with longing. She caressed the necklace for one more second, then snapped out of her reverie and reached beneath her hair for the clasp. "This is stupid," she said, her tone brimming with remorse and self-reproach. "I shouldn't want things like this."

"Why not?" It bothered him that Marlo believed there was something wrong in a woman's wanting to adorn herself with pretty jewels. It bothered him that she behaved as if she didn't think she deserved such luxuries. Apparently she couldn't afford them, but that didn't mean it was a sin to want them.

He grasped her hands before she could remove the necklace. His initial intention was to let her wear the pearls for a moment longer. But the minute his hands closed around hers, other thoughts superceded, other desires. His fingers relaxed as she let him draw her arms to her sides. He skimmed his hands up to her shoulders and urged her to himself, sensing no resistance from her. When he bowed to her, her lips met his eagerly, soft and warm and yielding.

He struggled to remember what he'd done last night, how he'd blundered, what had driven her to break from him and run away. As she timidly lifted her hands to his sides, though, he stopped trying to remember, stopped thinking altogether and gave himself over to the pleasure of kissing her, tasting her, drinking her in. He forgot about the necklace, the ransom demand, Alison's possible flight to Canada. As his tongue claimed possession of Marlo's mouth and his body surged with its own heated longing to possess her, he abandoned all pretense of rationality. After this kiss they would get back to business. After this kiss.

Her mouth was welcoming, all darkness and texture, her teeth smoother and whiter than the pearls and her inner lips velvet-soft. Her tongue tantalized, teased, lured him deeper. He ran his hands down her back to her hips and held her tight against him, allowing her to feel his arousal. She moaned slightly and fit her hips to his, leaning into him, swaying against him, letting him know she wanted him as much as he wanted her. Then, abruptly, she turned her head, breaking her mouth from his. She hid her face against his shoulder and shuddered.

It was all he could do to keep from shuddering, too. His body ached in a wonderful way, every nerve strung taut, every sense attuned to her, every beat of his heart sending fire into his muscles. He lifted his hands to her waist and hugged her consolingly.

"I have work to do," she murmured, her breath warm and uneven against his neck.

"I know. This isn't the right time. It's just..." He glided his hand up her back and into the dense black waves of her hair. "You're so beautiful, Marlo."

She issued a short, dry laugh and he realized that she'd regained her poise—a lot quicker than he had. "Any woman can be beautiful if you hang enough pearls around her neck," she said, brushing his hands out of her way so she could unfasten the clasp of the necklace. Turning from him, she dropped the pearls onto the vanity table. Only someone observing her with an almost obsessive curiosity, as Jeremy was, would have noticed that her hand was trembling.

If she was trembling due to an overloaded nervous system, he would accept it without question. But he suspected that her edginess had less to do with any lingering sense of arousal than with something else, something deep within her, the same internal confusion that filled her with chagrin at having admired the pearls in the first place. He'd seen it in her before: when they'd first arrived at the Olson house and she'd gaped with blatant astonishment at its size and its gloriously unruly garden. When she'd referred to Alison and her comrades as spoiled brats. When she'd grumbled about having to pay half the money in her checking account—less than two hundred forty dollars, if Jeremy remembered correctly—for the muffler repair. When she'd said, just a few minutes ago, "That depends on your definition of a fortune."

It was more than simply that she was a hardworking woman of modest means, more than simply that she couldn't afford to throw away money on freshwater pearls. He recalled the flicker of shame in her eyes when he'd first caught her handling the pearls, practically worshipping them.

His physical desire for Marlo was abruptly supplanted by a desire much stronger and more significant: to unravel her mind, to make sense of the emotions that seemed to be warring deep inside her. He had thought she was afraid of confronting their mutual attraction, but now he knew she wasn't. He knew from the way she had opened to his kiss, from the way she'd held him and moved with him and melted in his arms that she was brave enough to face their passion. Jeremy didn't frighten her.

But something about him did. And he was dying to figure out what it was. More than anything else, he wanted to solve the mystery of Marlo McGinnis.

The search for Alison Havelock would have to take precedence for the time being. He put his own personal puzzle aside and followed Marlo as she moved about the room, inspecting the unmade bed, poking her head inside the empty closet, opening a dresser drawer and discovering some department store tags. "Maidenform," she read. "Three-fifty. She must have bought new underwear."

"Alison is a happy shopper."

"I'm glad she's having fun." Marlo opened another drawer, found it empty and shut it. "There are four tags, but I don't see any new undies—any clothes at all, for that matter. She must have taken everything with her."

Jeremy eyed the vanity and scowled. "I really don't think she and the others could be on their way to Canada. They must be coming back here. You said it yourself—they left the windows open downstairs."

"Maybe they're stupider than I thought. If they were coming back here, Alison would have left her underwear someplace."

"It doesn't make sense that she would take her underwear and not her pearls."

"It makes perfect sense," Marlo snapped. "She's a careless twit. Underwear is a necessity, so she'd make a point of remembering it. A little thing like pearls, though—to someone like Alison, they're negligible. They must have just slipped her mind. I mean, pearls! Who could be bothered?"

Jeremy detected the bitterness creeping into her voice and he decided not to contradict her. Instead, he wandered to the bathroom and opened the door. Hanging from an enamel hook on the back of it was the silk jumpsuit Alison had worn Saturday evening. As with the pearls, his immediate thought was that Alison wouldn't have been so thoughtless as to leave behind a designer outfit worth several hundred dollars. But if he voiced his opinion to Marlo, she'd reply that Alison was precisely that thoughtless.

Maybe Marlo was right. To someone like Alison, whose father was always ready to hand over a blank check in compensation for his neglect, designer silk garments and jewelry weren't anywhere near as important as underwear.

Turning from the door, he glimpsed the garbage pail beside the sink. Something inside the pail caught his attention, and he moved closer. He squatted down, reached in and pulled out a lock of reddish-brown hair. "Oh my God."

Marlo materialized in the doorway. "What?"

He held up the hair for her to see, then dug deeper into the pail and pulled out some more. "It's Alison's," he said, his heart pounding crazily as the ramifications of his discovery sank in.

Marlo didn't seem anywhere near as concerned as he felt. She entered the white-tiled room, knelt down next to Jeremy and rummaged through the contents of the garbage pail. She examined some of the hair, then shrugged. "If it's any consolation, it looks like the job was done with scissors."

"As opposed to what? A hatchet?"

"Relax," she said. "Alison's got a new look. She's hanging out with a bunch of punks right now. Maybe she wants to look like a punk, too."

"You told me this is what professional kidnappers do—they cut off their victim's hair."

"They cut off a lock of it and send it to the victim's family," Marlo reminded him, "to prove they've got her. This isn't a single lock—it's a haircut. And the ransom demand was made by Alison in her own voice. Porter doesn't need to see a sample of her hair to know she's with these jerks." She tilted the garbage pail, apparently hunting for more interesting contents, then set it back in place beside the sink. Standing, she brushed off her hands and gave Jeremy a long, probing stare. "Can I ask you something personal?"

"What?"

"You aren't..." She pondered her words for a moment, weighing each one carefully. "You aren't *involved* with Alison, are you?"

After all he'd told her, after the way he'd kissed her, did she have to ask? Just because he was alarmed at the sight of a woman's shorn hair didn't mean he was in love with her. He found it annoying that Marlo felt she had to interrogate him on the subject at this point. "No," he said tersely. "I'm not."

Marlo seemed to sense his irritation, because she quickly explained, "I'm asking only because I think she's sleeping with one of the kidnappers."

Her revelation shouldn't have shocked Jeremy, but it did. Alison was about to begin her senior year in college, and many college women—the daughters of Jeremy's business associates included—were sexually active. But to be having sex with a thug, a crook, the sort of man who brandished a gun at innocent people in a convertible sports car—

No. Alison wasn't an innocent person. If she could plot such a stunt with her friends—if she could *act* so innocent while it occurred and then run away, hack off her hair, soak her father for an exorbitant sum of money and flee the country, heedlessly leaving valuables behind... Sure, Alison could be sleeping with a creep.

"Are you okay?" Marlo asked.

He checked himself in the mirror above the sink and realized he looked stricken, his eyes glassy and his jaw stiff with tension. "I'm fine," he managed. "It's—it's strange having to readjust my entire concept of Alison, that's all."

Marlo scrutinized him. "You thought she was a virgin?"

"I thought she was basically a decent human being," he said brusquely, then moved past Marlo and out of the bathroom, suddenly anxious to get away from the trash pail full of hair. He studied the rumpled bed, seeing what Marlo had already noticed: each of the two pillows bore the rounded impression of a head. Two people had slept in this room last night, and given the pearls on the vanity table and the jumpsuit in the bathroom, he knew that one of them was Alison.

Marlo hovered in the bathroom doorway, tactfully refusing to crowd him. "You're taking this too much to heart, Jeremy," she said.

"I feel..." He sank onto the edge of the bed and shook his head. Staring at his hands in his lap, he struggled to put his thoughts into words. "I feel like a fool, Marlo. I cared about Alison. I worried about her. I wanted to cheer her up. I felt sorry for her."

"And meanwhile, she was having a hot time between the sheets with Ned Whitelaw. That's just a guess," she added when he shot her a surprised look, "but we've already established that the Olson kid was staying in the bedroom above the kitchen. As for the Sawyer kid, I saw some photographs of him at his mother's house, and to be totally honest, he was kind of clunky, you know? Given how gorgeous Alison is, she wouldn't be likely to hook up with an out-of-shape clod like him."

"All right. Fine. She's been getting her kicks with Ned Whitelaw. Who cares which one it was?"

"That's what I was about to ask you," Marlo said quietly. "Who cares?"

Her insinuation provoked him to a fresh burst of anger, not at Alison for having hoodwinked him but at Marlo for questioning his motives and affections. "Of course I care!" he erupted. "Why shouldn't I care? I looked out for Alison. Ever since she arrived at Porter's house a month and a half ago, I took better care of her than he did. I devoted my free time to keeping her busy and happy. I was the only friend she had in Connecticut."

"And after all you did for her, she never invited you inside her lacy little Maidenforms."

He sprang to his feet and stormed across the room to confront Marlo. "I never had the urge," he retorted, his voice a growl of rage. "I like my women tall and strong and tough. I like them to be as old as me and as smart as me. I like them to know all the good Eagles songs. I like them to be on an equal footing with me." For emphasis, he grabbed her by the shoulders, yanked her away from the door and gave her a hard, fierce kiss on the lips. Then he pulled back, his fury spent. "Are we clear on this?" he asked, his tone muted.

Her gaze skipped away, careering from the vanity table to the rug, from the window to the pearl necklace. "It's just..." She ran her tongue nervously over her lips. "You seemed so stunned when I suggested Alison didn't sleep alone last night."

"I am stunned," he acknowledged. "I'm stunned by the realization that I was a sap. I took Alison under my wing, and all the while she was scheming with her lover to beat my brains out and run away. Yes. I'm stunned."

Marlo considered his words and smiled crookedly. "Great. Maybe when you're done breaking the guys' noses you can break Alison's."

He couldn't deny the appeal of her facetious suggestion. Not that he would ever follow it. He might be in shock, dumbfounded by the extent of Alison's duplicity, appalled by his failure as a judge of character. But he wouldn't take out his anger on Alison; he'd save his vengeance for the three thugs.

He let out a long sigh. The hell with Alison and her foolish games. The hell with her criminal friends. The hell with vengeance. Jeremy had just kissed Marlo, not from affection or sexual desire but from the raging need to establish something with her. Whatever her misgivings about him, whatever mysteries lurked within her clever, complicated mind, she hadn't refuted him. She hadn't said, "No, we're not clear on anything; no, I don't know what you're talking about; no, I still believe you and Alison are lovers." She had appeared as stunned as he'd felt, but she hadn't backed away.

She was clear on this, as clear as he was. They had an understanding. Jeremy didn't need fantasies of revenge to leaven his mood. He and Marlo had an understanding, and he was suddenly, wonderfully elated.

MARLO PULLED INTO an empty parking space outside the coffee shop and turned off the engine. It was not quite four o'clock and downtown Beresford looked uncrowded and serene, the sidewalks cooled by the shade of the broad-leafed elms and maple trees that stood along the sides of the street. "The restaurant's open," she said. "You remember where the phone is, right?"

Jeremy nodded. They'd driven back to town because he wanted to touch base with his secretary at Pace & Hartley. Had he remained in Connecticut, he'd told Marlo, he would have spent most of the day in and around Porter Havelock's construction trailer in North Stamford, so the fact that he hadn't spoken with anyone at his office all day wouldn't have caused his secretary undue alarm. However, he felt he ought to contact her to collect his messages and let her know he'd be incommunicado for a while longer.

"Tell her you'll probably be home some time tomorrow," Marlo advised him.

He gave her an incredulous look. "If we have to go up to Canada—"

"We won't have to," Marlo assured him. "They couldn't have left for the border more than a couple of hours ago, which means they've got a way to go. We can intercept them before they leave the U.S."

"We can?"

"Sure. I'll have my father call the border guards at Houlton and ask them to notify the other border crossing stations. I hope you don't mind making your calls from the pay phone. After I call my father, I want to leave the car line free in case he has to call me back." Besides, she added silently, if her father tried to reach her on the car phone and got a busy signal, she wouldn't be able to explain afterward that Jeremy Kent had tied up the line. Her father still didn't know Jeremy was with her, and that was how she wanted it.

As soon as he was out of the car, she phoned her father and filled him in on everything she'd discovered at the Olson house: that Alison had cut her hair, that she wouldn't take a ferry to Canada, that she'd left her necklace behind. Her father told her Porter had heard nothing further from Alison and crew but, not surprisingly, he wanted them prevented from crossing into Canada.

"Do you want me to chase them up to Houlton?" Marlo asked.

"Too risky. You might drive up there and miss them. They might head for a different border crossing, or change course and go back to Beresford. Don't forget, these are crazy kids."

"I know."

"They're bound to chicken out sooner or later. I have the feeling they're going to run out of steam soon. What do you think?"

Marlo allowed that she shared his suspicion. Fun was fun, but Alison was sure to start missing her Chanel No. 5 soon.

"I think it would be best if you stay put in Beresford until we can track them down," her father said.

"Okay."

"They might return to the house. You never know."

"Right. I'll stake it out."

After promising to contact the border patrol, Marlo's father issued his usual warnings to drive carefully, stay in touch and take care of herself, then signed off. She returned the phone to its cradle and gazed through the windshield at the restaurant. It appeared relatively empty in the late afternoon; a couple of older women sat sipping from tall tumblers of iced tea at a table adjacent to the window, but the other window tables were vacant.

She couldn't see Jeremy, of course. He was at the rear of the dining room, in the unlit alcove near the rest rooms. Perhaps he was leaning against the wall, the phone tucked between his unshaven jaw and his shoulder, his lanky body arranged in a pose of casual alertness. Perhaps he was lying to his secretary about where he was and what he was doing. She tried to imagine what excuse he would cook up: "I know this is really unexpected, but I took off to spend a few days in Maine with an incredible woman. Call it love, call it madness, but here I am."

Who was she kidding? Whatever Jeremy was doing here in Maine with her, it was more likely madness than anything even remotely resembling love. The closest she'd ever come to the description "incredible" was when she'd wrapped those incredible pearls around her neck. When she'd wrapped them around her neck and wrapped her arms around Jeremy and felt him full and hard against her, seeking her warmth....

If anyone was incredible it was Jeremy.

She recalled the first kiss he'd given her in the Olson house. It had been slow, loving, luscious. Then she recalled his second kiss: hard and brutal. His words echoed inside her skull: *Are we clear on this?* As if that one adamant, angry kiss clarified everything.

In a way, it did. She had to admit it—that kiss had brought her mind into focus as her interrogation of him hadn't. That kiss had told her that he wasn't fooling around, that even without strings of pearls around her neck he wanted her, that he harbored nothing romantic toward Alison or anyone else, that when it came to Marlo he meant business.

From the first moment she'd laid eyes on him, when he'd stood in the front doorway of his house wearing nothing but a pair of sweatpants, she had known he could turn her on. She hadn't planned on giving him the opportunity, but she had known. Now, like so many of her hunches, this one was bearing out.

She shouldn't want pearls or fancy vacation houses or all the luxuries money could buy, and she shouldn't want Jeremy Kent. Why was it that, when she thought logically about the situation, she had no difficulty telling herself she could do without the luxuries, yet she couldn't seem to convince herself that she could do without Jeremy? She didn't want to want him. He could wind up costing her a hell of a lot more than any necklace.

The door to the restaurant swung open and he emerged into the late afternoon light. She tried futilely not to respond to his inherent grace as he strode to the car. She tried not to admit she was delighted by his return.

"What did your secretary say?" she asked, her subtle way of finding out the story he'd concocted to explain his absence.

"She said a design I submitted for a hospital extension survived the hospital board's first cut, and one of the other secretaries announced she's pregnant."

"Congratulations," Marlo said, referring to his successful design.

He misunderstood her. "Don't congratulate me—I'm not the father."

"No—I meant about the hospital extension."

His low laugh implied that he'd known all along what she meant. "It's a bit premature for congratulations, Marlo. If I told you how many times I made the first cut only to lose in the final round I'd get depressed."

"And what did you tell your secretary?"

His smile grew enigmatic. "That a personal matter had called me out of town for a few days."

A personal matter. Not quite as romantic as love or madness, especially since the personal matter undoubtedly referred to Alison and the thugs rather than to Marlo. But still, she had to be at least part of the reason why he hadn't been at his office today and wouldn't be tomorrow. She might permit herself some tiny measure of satisfaction that whatever Jeremy was doing with her fell under the heading of "personal."

"Where are we going?" he asked as she turned the key in the ignition.

"Ultimately, we're going back to the Olson house to wait for the prodigal idiots to return. First, if it's all right with you, I think we ought to pick up something to eat while we're waiting. I'm starving."

"I am, too." He glanced left and right as she backed out of the parking space. "Is there a supermarket in town?"

"Just the general store." She drove down the block and pulled in to the curb near the entry to the general store. "I hope we don't have to put up with any more of that homespun Maine congeniality," she muttered as she climbed out of the car.

As it turned out, once the clerks realized they were in the store for no other reason than to spend money, they couldn't have been more helpful. The selection of prepared foods was limited, but Marlo and Jeremy filled their basket with a loaf of wheat bread, sliced Swiss cheese and turkey breast, chilled cans of soda, potato chips, two Granny Smith apples and a couple of dark, moist, ostensibly homemade brownies. Jeremy made some noises about paying for the groceries when they reached the cashier, but Marlo insisted that she needed receipts to submit to Porter or he wouldn't believe she'd really been in Maine.

They got back into the car and headed out of town, navigating over the winding route that carried them north toward Old Meadow Road. Although it wasn't quite evening, the sun was flirting with the mountains to the west, glazing the sky with a layer of amber. Marlo cruised past the Olson house, which was still dark. "They aren't back yet," she said.

"What makes you so sure they'll return?" Jeremy asked.

"I'm not sure," she admitted. "But there's no reliable way to track them up to Canada. We're going to stay here until we get word from my father that they've been spotted by a border guard."

"Would a border guard have the legal right to stop them from crossing?"

Marlo U-turned to face the house and found a secluded place to park on the grassy shoulder of the road, partially concealed by a stately oak tree. She shut off the engine. "They could come up with something, I'm sure," she said. "Transporting guns, maybe. Or entering the country with insufficient cash. Canadians will sometimes deny entry if they think someone's going to settle in the country and take a job that should be going to a Canadian citizen. At least they could stall them for a while, do a drug search or something, until we got up there." She shrugged. "Truth is, my father and I are both of the opinion that Alison is going to chicken out before she reaches the border. So we'll just wait here and keep an eye on the house."

He glanced at the house, and then at Marlo, his eyes growing round. "This is a stakeout, isn't it."

"You guessed."

"I'm on a stakeout," he said to himself, obviously awed. "This is exciting."

"Actually," she warned him, "it's going to be boring. Pass me some food, please. I'm famished."

Chuckling, Jeremy contorted himself to pull the shopping bag from the back seat. He brought it forward, stood it on the floor between his legs and pulled out the bread, cheese and turkey. "We should have bought some napkins," he said as he broke open the bread package.

"Not to worry." Marlo reached across his lap and opened the glove compartment, inside of which was stashed a wide assortment of napkins from fast-food emporiums. Her elbow brushed against his leg as she groped for the napkins, and she hastily withdrew, embarrassed by the contact and even more embarrassed by how keenly aware she was of the lean surface of his thigh. Given the way they'd kissed earlier, given that everything was supposed to be "clear" between them, she had no reason to be disconcerted, but she was.

He evidently didn't share her embarrassment. "Look at all these napkins," he exclaimed, sorting through the colorful logos printed on them. "Good lord, Marlo—you've got every take-out joint in New England represented here! I can't believe you could have all these napkins in your car and not a wire hanger for doing patch-up repairs. What's this?" he asked, smoothing out the wrinkles of a napkin with bright red letters slanting across it. "I never heard of that one."

"It's a restaurant with outlets on the Mass Pike," she explained laconically.

"You really eat this stuff a lot," he concluded.

He probably wasn't being judgmental, but Marlo felt abashed, anyway. Jeremy Kent was apparently used to a different sort of dining. "Well," she joked, "I tried to filch some napkins from the Quilted Giraffe last time I was in Manhattan, but I struck out."

He gave her an inquisitive look, and she realized that he was trying to interpret her uneasiness. His perceptive gray eyes remained on her as he unfolded a napkin across his knee and balanced two slices of bread on it. He looked away only to center a portion of cheese and turkey on the bread, then closed the sandwich and handed it to her.

"Thanks," she said.

"What is it, really?" he asked as he fixed a sandwich for himself.

"What is *what*, really?"

He dug in the shopping bag for the two cans of soda and pulled them out. He popped them open and handed one to her. "It has to do with money, doesn't it?" he said.

"What has to do with money?" she mumbled, knowing full well that pretending she didn't know what he was talking about wasn't going to work for long.

He took a drink of soda, then propped his can on top of the dashboard and settled his large body as best he could on the seat. "You seem uncomfortable about—I shouldn't say money. It's more wealth. Is it a class thing, Marlo?"

She absolutely did not want to have this discussion with Jeremy right now. Just because he thought things were clear between them didn't mean she liked being transparent to him. If she harbored class resentments that was her prerogative. Jeremy had no right to go poking around in her psyche.

Well, she amended, maybe he did have a right. Kissing her as soundly and convincingly as he did gave him certain rights. Yet if he poked around he would discover her biases and recognize how close to him they slanted.

She stalled by taking a bite of her sandwich, chewing, swallowing and sipping some soda, all the while spying on the Olson house through the windshield. Jeremy ate as well, but he watched her.

"It is a class thing, isn't it?" he said.

"I don't know what you're talking about," she claimed disingenuously.

"I'm talking about how easily embarrassed you are by things like fast-food napkins, or getting caught admiring Alison's pearls—"

"If I was embarrassed about the pearls it was because you might have thought I was planning to steal them or something. And as for the napkins," she continued, unable to keep her defensiveness from her voice, "it's because there were so many of them jammed into the glove compartment, all crumpled up."

"That's not it at all," he charged, his tone gentle but firm. "Tell me the truth, Marlo. I can't help but think maybe I'm a part of it."

"You are," she said, dreading the direction this conversation was taking yet accepting the inevitability of it.

Her blunt statement silenced him for a minute. He twisted in his seat so he was angled toward her, leaning his back against the door and extending his legs toward the radio and the dysfunctional air conditioner. As he ate he scrutinized her, apparently trying to decide what to do now that she'd uttered the unpleasant truth. "Have I done something wrong?" he finally asked.

"Other than forcing your way onto this trip?" She sighed, trying to decide how much honesty he could take—how much *she* could take. If she told him the truth she would destroy any chance of a relationship between them, and when she remembered the way she'd felt in his arms she could scarcely stand the possibility of that happening. But it would be for the best—not only for her to be honest, but for her to put an end to this relationship before it began. It was doomed, anyway. She and Jeremy could never build anything lasting, and Marlo couldn't imagine herself enjoying something transient with him and then walking away unscathed.

"It's nothing specific," she explained. "And it's nothing you did personally. I just...I don't trust rich people."

He could have ridiculed her. He could have accused her of being a Communist or some such thing. All he said, however, was, "Why not?"

"They're out of touch with reality."

"Now that's what I call a sweeping condemnation," he remarked, his eyes sparkling with amusement.

"I know I'm prejudiced," she admitted before he could say it. "But if I am it's based on experience. I work for rich people, Jeremy. Poor people don't hire private investigators. I see how rich folks screw up their lives. They think they can fix all their problems by spending lots of money—and they have so much money to spend." She took a bite of her sandwich, then continued. "A typical case—the adulterer. He's fooling around behind his wife's back, and she gets suspicious because he starts spending guilt money on her. She realizes her marriage is in trouble, so she spends money to have me shadow her husband. I find out the truth, she pays me off, her husband buys her a two-carat diamond, and they still haven't got any idea of how to make their marriage work. If they donated their money to the Red Cross and spent their time talking to each other, trying to make each other's lives a little happier, the world would be a better place."

"No argument there," Jeremy conceded. "But not all rich people are adulterers."

"No." She stared through the windshield at the Olson house and issued a mirthless laugh. "Sometimes they bang people on the head and run off and try to squeeze money from their fathers, all for a bit of attention. Think of the waste, Jeremy! Your time, my time, my father's time, your skull, her pearls..."

"It's income for your agency," Jeremy pointed out.

"I know. But there are other things I could do with my life. This is where my talent lies, and I'm good at it, but if I could pay my rent with air I'd be using my skills to help poor people. I'd be solving *real* crimes, not this kind of garbage."

Jeremy lapsed into thought. "The Havelocks may have more money than most people," he observed, "but it doesn't mean they haven't got genuine problems."

"Right. I'd trade problems with them in a minute," Marlo retorted.

"Would you really?"

She contemplated the question, then relented with a small sigh. "Well, maybe not. But the thing is, they brought their problems on themselves. Most people in this world—and I know this may be news to someone like you, Jeremy—most people in this world don't have to deal with such crises as what to do now that mother dear has married some young stud and romped off to the Riviera. Most people in this world are busy worrying about whether the electricity is going to get turned off because they're two months in arrears."

"I think you're wrong," he disputed her. "I think poor people are just as worried about affairs of the heart as they are about affairs of the pocketbook."

"But it's a matter of proportion. Poor people worry about their love lives but they worry just as much about how to keep their kids in sneakers. Rich people can buy all the hundred-dollar sneakers they want. They can call the shots because they've got the bucks. Rich people finance politicians, so they get to decide how the country is run. Rich people shut themselves up inside their affluent communities and throw some money at the Bridgeport Police Department and say, 'Here's our tax dollars. Now you keep those troublemakers far away from us, down in the city where they belong.' They buy private education for their kids so they don't have to think about what sort of education everyone else is getting. They buy the best medical care, the best legal advice, the best everything, and they don't give a damn what's left for the rest of us."

She hadn't meant to rant and rave, and when she paused for a breath she glimpsed Jeremy's bewildered expression and bit her lip. "I see we've moved beyond sweeping condemnation," he murmured, appraising her thoughtfully. "We seem to have graduated to blanket indictment." He raised his soda can to his mouth and drank, then lowered it, his eyes never leaving her. The car had gotten darker as the sun began its slow descent below the White Mountains. The encroaching dusk threw intriguing shadows across Jeremy's face, adding dimension and complexity to his features. "Have I personally done any of these things?" he asked quietly, sounding not indignant so much as simply curious.

Exhausted by her tirade, she wilted in her seat, rolling her head back against the headrest and gazing at him from beneath lowered lids. One part of her was contrite—she shouldn't have lumped Jeremy with all the selfish, greedy rich people she'd had occasion to work

for. Another part of her was rueful—what she had said
had irrefutably spelled out why she and Jeremy could
never pursue a relationship, never follow up on what
they'd begun last night outside the motel in New Hampshire. She had known that truth from the start, but
whenever she looked at Jeremy, whenever her eyes met
his, or her lips, she'd wanted to ignore it, to pretend they
could breach the class barrier and become friends, inti-
mates, lovers.

But now the truth had been spoken, and she couldn't
retract her words or deny her sentiments. "I don't know
if you have," she conceded, running her finger around
the rim of her soda can while her gaze strayed back to the
Olson house. "I don't know you very well."

"So you might as well assume the worst about me," he
said.

She sent him a brief glance and found him smiling
tenuously. He didn't seem particularly offended. "Actually, I've assumed the best about you so far," she said,
returning his nebulous smile. "If I hadn't you wouldn't
be here now."

"And you've made quite clear that you think my
presence is a mistake." He drained his soda can. When
he lowered it his smile was gone. "What *really* happened, Marlo? You don't seem like a bitter person.
Where did all this anger come from?"

She didn't want to discuss it. It was her life, her privacy—hers and her father's. But she'd already told Jeremy everything; all he was asking for were the specifics,
the details, the facts to support the theory.

"Have you ever heard of the Greenwich Horticultural
Association?" she asked.

If he was startled by the apparent non sequitur, he
didn't let on. "No," he answered.

"It's a philanthropic organization devoted to the beautification of Greenwich. They raise money to plant flowers along the public roadways. You know, those little planters at intersections and shopping centers, with peonies and geraniums inside them? And strips of tulips in different colors outside public buildings, and stuff like that."

Jeremy nodded slightly.

"Well, the association used to be run by this woman in Greenwich. Maybe it still is, I don't know. But anyway—this was eighteen years ago—she was always throwing fund-raising benefits and parties to pay for the flowers. She was a ditz—one hell of a great lady, even though she didn't know how to use a telephone directory or glue a stamp on an envelope. My mother used to do that for her."

"I see."

"For a salary of around eight thousand dollars a year, my mother did everything for this woman. She organized the benefits, called the caterers, arranged for the invitations to be printed and mailed and on and on. She never attended any of the benefits, of course—it cost five hundred dollars to attend—but her boss would be there, accepting all the applause and all the adulation, accepting plaques from the mayor's office and being written up in the society columns for her good works. I'll tell you, thanks to my mother's labors, that lady raised a lot of money for flowers, bless her soul." Marlo paused, trying to rid her voice of rancor. "When I was thirteen, my mother discovered a lump in her breast."

Jeremy winced. "Oh. How is she now?"

"She's dead."

Jeremy studied her, his jaw flexing slightly as he considered his words. Marlo prayed that he wouldn't resort

to some trite expression of condolence. She wasn't telling him this because she wanted him to pity her or her
father. She was telling him because she wanted to open
his eyes to the way rich people treated working-class
people.

To her relief, he didn't say anything. He simply reached
across the seat and captured her right hand in his left. He
held it loosely, leaving her the option of pulling away, but
she didn't. Her hand felt good within his. As the sky grew
darker and Jeremy's face became less and less visible, she
liked having this contact with him.

"My mother went through the whole routine," she
went on, her voice deeper and softer. "Surgery, radia-
tion, chemo. She lost her hair, she lost weight. She was
ravaged, Jeremy." His hand tightened on hers, barely
perceptibly, just enough to convey his sympathy. "But
the thing was, there was this benefit scheduled to raise
money for plantings for a park. We're not talking about
something as trivial as life and death, you know, nothing silly like cancer research or anything. We're talking
about something very, very important—daffodils for a
town park. And the benefit couldn't be done without my
mother there to put the whole thing together. Her boss
was hysterical. My mother simply had to come back to
work."

"She didn't have to," Jeremy argued gently. "She
could have refused."

"We needed the money," Marlo countered. "It was a
private employment—she couldn't collect disability pay-
ments. My father had started the agency a couple of years
before my mother took ill. He'd worked for another
agency, but his boss retired and the agency was dissolved, and so my father decided to start his own. We
were broke, Jeremy. My mother didn't want me to go to

school without shoes on my feet and breakfast in my stomach. Mothers have such weird priorities...." Her eyes suddenly filled with tears, tears she hadn't cried since she was fifteen, standing beside a freshly dug grave.

This was no time to fall apart. She was supposed to be in charge here, the competent investigator on the job. To weep—especially in front of Jeremy—would be demoralizing.

She slid her hand from his and surreptitiously dabbed at the dampness forming along her lashes. When she next spoke her voice was husky but steady. "I'm not saying she wouldn't have died if she hadn't gone back to work. But maybe, just maybe, she would have lived a little longer. Or at least—if we'd had enough money to hire a nurse or to pay for better care—she might have been more comfortable at the end. She shouldn't have had to spend her last months of life helping some egocentric queen in Greenwich raise money for daffodils."

"No," he agreed. "She shouldn't have." He arched his arm around Marlo's shoulders and drew her across the gear stick, urging her head against his shoulder. "Your mother must have been a special woman. I wish I could have known her."

Marlo craned her neck to peer up at him. Why wasn't he mouthing the expected platitudes? Why wasn't he saying how awful it must have been, and how sorry he was for Marlo? Why wasn't he protesting that, no matter how tragic her mother's final years were, it wasn't his fault and Marlo shouldn't hold it against him?

"I shouldn't have told you all this," Marlo mumbled, wishing his shoulder didn't feel so strong, his neck didn't smell so good, his arm didn't fit around her quite so naturally.

He played his fingers through her hair. "No, you should have. I'm glad you did."

She sighed, nestling her head against the firm muscle of his shoulder. She ought to have been uncomfortable stretched between the bucket seats, and she ought to resist the solace Jeremy was offering. But she wasn't uncomfortable, and she did want the shelter of his arm for a few minutes.

To her amazement, his gentle embrace seemed to have a healing effect on her. For the first time in fifteen years—the first time since she'd last shed tears over her mother—she was tired of carrying her constant burden of grief and anger. She was immeasurably grateful to Jeremy for lifting it from her.

They sat that way, Marlo cuddled within the curve of his arm, as the sun dipped lower, as the sky faded from gold to pink to lavender to mauve. They sat, gazing out at the evening, at the winding country road, at the spacious six-bedroom farmhouse, at the resplendent wildflowers surrounding it, flowers no charitable horticultural society had had to plant. They gazed at the pickup truck bumping along the road, its headlights darting past Marlo's car as it slowed near the Olson house.

The truck stopped, its engine idling noisily as two silhouetted figures leaped down over the tailgate. Through the open window of Marlo's car a young man's voice was heard thanking the driver of the truck, who shifted into gear and continued on down the road. The two silhouetted figures watched it vanish around a bend, then headed up the gravel driveway to the dark farmhouse.

"That's them," Jeremy whispered, whipping his arm from around Marlo and leaning forward, gripping the dashboard with tense fingers. "The guys with the guns, the ones who hurt me. That's them."

CHAPTER TEN

"DON'T," MARLO whispered, lunging across Jeremy's lap to prevent him from opening the car door.

He was willing to accept that she was the expert here, that she knew better than he did how to go about this sort of thing. But the sight of those two men—the beasts who had violated his MG and his psyche and forced him to contend with his fragile mortality—caused his heart to drum in overtime, pumping adrenaline through him, making him want to run them down hard, fast, now.

"You open that door," she explained, still whispering, "and the interior light's going to go on, and then they'll see us."

She was right. Of course she was right. Seething with frustration, he took a deep breath and removed his fingers from the chrome handle.

He watched through the windshield as the two men climbed onto the porch, unlocked the farmhouse door and went inside. What if they escaped out the back door before Marlo and Jeremy reached the house? What if they were right this minute loading their guns and girding for battle? "They're going to get away," he predicted glumly.

"How? They haven't got a vehicle. They hitchhiked here."

True enough. "Where's their car?" he asked.

"Where's Alison and Pinhead Number Three?" Marlo shot back. "Obviously there are a few things we've got to find out."

"How are we going to find out anything sitting in this car?"

Marlo turned to Jeremy. The tender emotions she'd given vent to just minutes ago were nowhere in evidence now. Her eyes were steely, her jaw set, her spine resolutely straight. "Listen to me, Jeremy, and listen good. Either you do this thing my way or I do it myself. I'm running the show. You do as I say or I'm going to lock you in the trunk until it's over. I won't have you going off half-cocked and screwing everything up. Is that understood?"

"Understood," he grumbled.

"No heroics."

"No heroics."

She gave him an assessing look, as if searching for the merest hint that his swift capitulation was anything but sincere, then relented and slid the strap of her purse onto her shoulder. Her gaze remained riveted to the house for a full minute, during which the living room windows blazed into two bright rectangles of light as the lamps inside were lit. Neither man came back out of the house.

"Okay," she said, her voice low and steady. "We're going to get out of the car now, slowly and quietly. Don't slam your door, and don't lock it. We're going to walk across the street by the stone wall there, and then crouch down and approach from behind the wall. Understand?"

It took all his willpower not to respond, "Roger, over and out." Honestly, she didn't have to lecture him as if he were a mischievous toddler. He'd been the one to find out where the Olson house was, after all. He'd been the one to fix Marlo's muffler and navigate her up here. She would never have gotten this far without him.

Wisely, he kept his sentiments to himself. Nodding to inform her that he would obey her instructions, he opened his door. He slid out, shut the door as quietly as he could, and then raced across the road with Marlo.

They moved stealthily toward the farmhouse. Crickets chirped in the evening gloom; an owl hooted in the distance. Fortunately, the Olsons' nearest neighbor was situated well down the road, a good quarter of a mile away; equally fortunate was the absence of traffic on the road. The only sounds were those provided by Mother Nature: the insects, the toads, the breeze rustling the unmown grass and whistling through the pine trees. The only lights were the waning three-quarter moon in the sky and the diffuse amber glow spilling from the living room windows of the Olson house.

A gap in the stone wall marked the entrance to the driveway. Marlo halted there, extending her arm like a crossing guard to block Jeremy before he could proceed onto the property.

Her caution rankled. No matter how many times he told himself to respect her experience, he couldn't stifle the urge to charge the house with fists flying, to kick in the door and then kick in the teeth of his two assailants. Hovering at the juncture of the driveway and the road, hiding behind the three-foot-high stone wall, not moving, not taking any action, strained his patience as nothing ever had before.

After another minute or so, Marlo waved her hand to indicate they were going to advance on the house. She touched her index finger to her lip to remind him not to talk, a reminder he didn't need.

He tried to keep his resentment focused on the men in the house, but it was difficult. Just minutes ago Marlo had been snuggled up to him, baring her soul and welcoming his comfort. He'd felt so protective of her then, so eager to take care of her. Now, all of a sudden, he was her subordinate, not taking care but taking orders. It undermined his self-esteem. He'd given her his word that he would obey her. She was running the show, and when he considered the situation rationally he knew she was much better suited to run it than he was. But some things, like male pride and the lust for vengeance, defied rationality.

No heroics. The warning echoed inside his skull, first in her voice and then in his. He'd promised: no heroics. He begrudgingly placed his machismo in storage for the time being.

He and Marlo tiptoed around the edge of the stone wall to the flower-choked front yard and inched forward toward the house. Near the porch Marlo motioned to him to stop and kneel down. She rose slightly to peek at the illuminated window. Shrugging, she gestured that he could stand, as well. "Stay with me," she mouthed before ascending the steps to the porch.

He stayed with her. His heart began to pound faster again, energizing him. The moment of truth was about to arrive, the ultimate test. He was about to face down the creeps who had not only threatened him with death but, perhaps worse, duped him. He was about to get even.

Quietly, of course. Unheroically. In compliance with the edicts of his self-appointed boss, Marlo McGinnis.

To his amazement, she walked right to the door, her head held high and her purse tucked under her arm, and knocked.

The thinner of the two men opened the door. Jeremy saw the huskier one lurking behind him, squinting out into the night. "Yeah?" the thin one asked.

"Hi," said Marlo with astounding aplomb. "My name is Marlo McGinnis, and I'd like—"

The husky one's eyes adjusted to the darkness first. His gaze narrowed on Jeremy and he let out a yell. "Peter—"

At that instant Peter recognized Jeremy, cursed and started to slam the door. Marlo deftly blocked the door with her foot, reached inside her purse and produced a small black pistol that she aimed at the two young men. The husky one let out another cry. The one named Peter stumbled back a step, then pivoted as if ready to make a break for it.

Jeremy himself was frozen in place, not afraid so much as dumbfounded by the comprehension that Marlo was holding a gun—that she'd been in possession of a gun all along. When she'd pulled a pad and pencil from her purse outside the Sawyer house in Montclair, Jeremy had inquired about whether she had a gun and she'd wise-cracked a response.

She hadn't said no, he recalled. She hadn't denied that she was carrying a firearm. She'd made a joke, and he'd reached the wrong conclusion.

For some reason, he wanted to laugh. Marlo had a gun. She really was a detective. This was really happening.

Unlike the two nitwits currently quaking in their shoes on the other side of the threshold, Marlo looked as if she knew what to do with a firearm. Her fingers were still, her hand steady, her eyes targeted on her quarry, her posture firm and her respiration slow and deep. She ap-

peared confident and competent and—he couldn't ignore it—unbelievably sexy.

Before Peter could run very far Marlo had her hand
clamped around his upper arm. She dragged him across
the room and shoved him against a wall, where she pro-
ceeded to frisk him. He gave her a smirk as she ran her
hands over his hips and legs, patting him down. "Enjoying yourself?" he sneered.

"Yeah, as a matter of fact, I am," she answered once
she'd satisfied herself that he didn't have any concealed
weapons on him. "You feel so nice and soft." She aimed
her gun at the husky one, whose eyes grew round with
panic.

"Hey, lady, we aren't armed," he swore.

"You were armed on Saturday night," she said as she
patted him down with brisk efficiency. "Come in and
close the door, Jeremy. These turkeys are harmless."

The husky one turned to Jeremy and gave him an en-
treating look. "Hey, look—I'm really sorry about what
happened, man. I mean, it was Ned's idea. The whole
thing. Even the guns. It was all Ned's show."

"Where are the guns now?" Marlo asked, angling her
head toward the couch.

The two young men eyed each other, then yielded to
her unspoken command and dropped, side by side, onto
the overstuffed cushions. Marlo herself didn't sit; Jeremy remained standing, too. He liked looming above his
foes and watching them squirm and gawk at Marlo's
pistol. It wasn't quite as cathartic as beating them to a
pulp would be, but it wasn't bad.

"Ned's got the guns," said Peter.

"They were his all along," said the husky one.

"I could really use a drink," said Peter, assuming the role of host and starting to his feet. "Would you folks like something?"

"We didn't drop by for cocktails," Marlo said, silencing him. She conveyed with a few meaningful waves of the gun that he should resume his seat. "Where's Alison?"

"She's with Ned," said the husky one. "I swear. This whole thing was their idea, right from the start—"

"Shut up, Sawyer," said Peter.

Dave Sawyer appeared to be on the verge of blubbering. "It's their show, man. We're just their friends. They asked for some help, that's all. We were only helping."

"What a pair of altruists, eh, Jeremy?" Marlo asked, although her eyes never left the men on the sofa. "Only helping. Such generosity. I'm moved to tears." Her voice had lost all traces of sarcasm when she next spoke. "All right, so are they going through Houlton or what?"

The men exchanged another look, this one filled with awe at her perspicacity. "Who are you, anyway?" Peter asked.

"Marlo McGinnis. I'm a private investigator." Without lowering her gun or shifting her gaze, she removed her identification from her purse and flashed it before them. "I was hired by Alison's father to find her and bring her home. Now, if you guys really want to be helpful, you'll tell me where she is and how to get her back to daddy in one piece, and maybe we won't have to drag the cops into it."

"The cops?" Dave Sawyer was definitely blubbering. "Alison promised there wouldn't be any cops."

"Not exactly a promise she's in a position to keep," Marlo observed. "However, *I'm* in a position to keep the cops out of this—me and Jeremy here. Of course, he's still got the option of bringing an assault charge against you.''

"Hey, no! Please! I'm sorry, man! I'm sorry I hit you—''

"Shut up, Sawyer." Jeremy said it this time, with great relish.

"I need a drink," Peter complained.

"You'll live. Are they going through Houlton or what?''

"That's what they were planning," Peter conceded, glowering impotently at her.

"Whose car is it?''

"Mine.''

"How come you aren't with them?''

He glanced at Dave Sawyer. "Ned kicked us out.''

"Kicked you out of what?''

"The show. The money. The whole gig.''

"And you let him take your car?''

"He sort of helped himself to it," Peter explained vaguely.

"You handed over the registration?''

Peter looked momentarily startled. Then a slow grin spread across his face. "Uh-uh," he answered. "He forgot about the registration. I've still got it in my wallet.''

"Great. Let me have it," Marlo demanded.

Apparently seeing no alternative, he removed his wallet from the hip pocket of his designer jeans and handed it to her. She flipped through it until she found the registration card, which she pulled out before tossing the wallet back to him. She presented the gun to Jeremy and said, "Keep an eye on these guys. I've got to make a phone call." Then she stalked down the hall into the kitchen, letting the door swing shut behind her.

Jeremy closed his hand around the butt of the pistol. Despite its compact size, it was heavy. His fingers doubled up on themselves after circling the petite handle of the weapon. If he ever owned a gun, he'd prefer something larger.

If he ever owned a gun? Again he suppressed the urge to laugh. He didn't know the first thing about guns. He didn't know whether this one was loaded or not, whether the safety catch was on or off, whether if he sneezed he would accidentally give Dave Sawyer a second navel. He would never reveal his ignorance to the men on the couch, however. He simply aimed the gun in their direction and felt its power permeate him.

"Who's she calling?" Peter asked.

Jeremy had no idea. "None of your business," he said.

"What's she going to do to us?"

"The hell with her," Dave muttered, his frantic eyes never leaving Jeremy. "What are *you* going to do to us?"

He gazed coolly at Dave, then at Peter. "Castrate you," he said. Although they had to know he was kidding, they flinched in unison.

After a long silence, Peter thought to mention, "We aren't getting any of the money, you know. I mean, we had nothing to do with that. It's all Alison's and Ned's trip. I just want that straight."

"All right," Jeremy said agreeably. "It's straight."

"I mean, bottom line: we got nothing out of this. Zilch. As it is I'm out of a car."

"Ah, the irony of it."

"I mean, you think you got a bum deal?" Peter continued, his tone pleading. "Well, so did we. Even Alison isn't getting what she wants out of this thing."

"And what does she want?"

Peter looked for assistance to Dave, who shrugged. "Hey, Peter, this guy's tight with her old man. I don't know that we ought to be discussing this with him."

"Discussing what with me?" Jeremy inquired.

They stared blankly at him. Figuring he ought not to waste what he'd been given, he made a tentative motion with the gun, shuttling its barrel back and forth between the two youths. Much to Jeremy's gratification, they both flinched again.

"Look, bud," Peter remarked, "Alison said you were all right. She said you were a good guy and we shouldn't have popped you. Well, if you're such a good guy then you probably already know what she wants. She wants her old man to pay attention to her, you know? She wants him to miss her."

"Of course he misses her," Jeremy mumbled, wishing he were as certain as he sounded.

"I mean, she's mad at him, and I can't say as I blame her. He ignores her, he throws money at her and tells her to get out of his face. He treats her like dirt, you know?"

"That's between him and her," Jeremy noted.

"And we're her friends. You're supposed to be her friend, too. So look at it from her point of view. Think of how she feels."

"Feeling bad about her father is no excuse to go around beating up innocent people, extorting money, stealing cars—"

"Let's hear it for stolen cars," Marlo declared cheerfully as she emerged from the kitchen. She strode down the hall to the living room and plucked the gun from Jeremy's hand. "The border guards at all the crossings are going to be notified that a certain white Volvo sedan with New Jersey plates has been reported stolen by the owner. That'll give the guards an excuse to detain Ned and Alison if they try to cross into Canada.''

"But—" Jeremy scowled. "I thought Porter wanted to avoid that kind of official involvement."

"No problem. They'll detain Ned and Alison until someone—yours truly—can bring the automobile's owner up to Houlton or wherever, and he can say, 'Oh, I'm sorry, it was all just a big misunderstanding. I gave this fine gentleman permission to borrow my car. It wasn't really stolen.' And then we'll get the car and Alison and go home.''

Jeremy expected her to exhibit some arrogance about how neatly she'd finessed Alison and her pals. Marlo looked pleased but not particularly smug. Solving this case was apparently all in a day's work for her.

He himself believed a bit of noisy celebration was called for. Following her example, however, he remained sedate. "What are we going to do with these jerks in the meantime?" he asked Marlo.

"That's been taken care of, too," she explained. "Ray Kimball, my father's old boss—the one who retired— well, he retired to Deer Island, maybe a half hour from here. We'll run them down to Ray's cabin. He's got a nice cellar they can spend the night in."

"A cellar!" Dave wailed.

"It's a *nice* cellar," she emphasized. "Ray says it never floods much in the summer. Anyway, somebody's got to keep an eye on you, and it's not going to be me. I may have to drive up to Houlton later tonight; I can't baby-sit for you two. I'll run you down to Ray's place and you'll get a safe night's rest, out of reach. And once we get Alison back, you can take your fancy white Volvo and go home. It's the best deal I've got, boys, so I suggest you take it.''

Peter and Dave exchanged another look and sighed in resignation. "We'll take it," Peter said.

"Great. Let's go." She issued one of her tacit gun-gesture directives, and the two young men rose to their feet and plodded to the door, Marlo keeping her revolver trained on them as they passed in front of her. Before she followed them onto the porch she sent Jeremy a quick, breathtakingly lovely look and murmured, "Thanks."

Thanks. He hadn't really done much of anything. He'd held her gun and stood guard for a few minutes, but that had been a minor responsibility. Marlo—levelheaded and skillful, calm and proficient—had succeeded. All Jeremy had done was be there.

Maybe simply being there was worth something. Maybe his presence had helped. Maybe, just maybe, this wouldn't have worked out quite as well without him.

Marlo's thanks gratified him as much as nabbing the two creeps did. With a private smile, he followed them out of the house.

IT WAS DARK, IT WAS LATE, and Alison was despondent. Nothing Ned could do would make things better any more. All she wanted was to go home.

"Listen, babe," he was saying. His voice was all jazzed up, and he punctuated each phrase with a puff of his cigarette. "We'll get married. Would you like that?"

At one time, she would have been ecstatic about it. At one time she thought Ned Whitelaw was the sexiest, wildest, most outrageous man alive. At one time she would have done just about anything for him: run away, cut her hair, even milk money from her father.

But that was before Ned had hit her.

Nobody ever hit her. Well, maybe her father had when she was a kid, before the divorce. Maybe she'd gotten a spanking once or twice for doing something naughty. Probably not, though. If she did naughty things as a child her father probably wouldn't have been around to witness them, and her mother would never spank her. Her mother was big on explaining things. "You mustn't play with mommy's Joy," she'd say, pulling the crystal bottle from Alison's grubby hands. "This is the most expensive perfume in the world. You mustn't fool with it," or "No dress up in Mommy's tennis bracelet. Those are real diamonds, sweetie. You wait till you're a grown-up, and then you'll get your own tennis bracelet," or, when she got older, "No, honey, you mustn't date boys like that. They're ethnic," or "You mustn't go to parties where they have drugs. Our lawyers wouldn't be able to fix it if you got caught."

But nobody hit her. Nobody until Ned. When he'd smacked her cheek, the impact jarred everything loose inside her brain, making her realize quite suddenly that anything had to be better than staying with a guy who hit you. Even going back to her father had to be better than that.

Going back to him had been the whole purpose of this thing, anyway, going back home and having him apologize for neglecting her. It had nothing to do with ransom money or leaving the country. Why had Ned twisted the whole thing around?

The highway was dark; nobody seemed to be driving this far north this late. She thought wistfully of Dave and Peter, wondering whether they'd made it safely back to Beresford. Apparently they had thought Ned was just joking when he and Alison had gotten back from Bangor and he'd announced that they should pack their bags.

They'd seen nothing wrong with Alison's making that stupid tape, and then, when they'd all driven down to Belfast to place the call to her father, they'd been in a party mood. Then they'd driven around some more, west to Augusta and then up to Waterville for something to eat, and then back toward Bangor. When Ned failed to take the Beresford exit, though, they'd started getting antsy.

"Hey, come on Ned—let's go home," Peter had said.

"Enough is enough," Dave had added.

"We're talking big bucks," Ned had reminded them. "If I were you guys I'd sit tight and come along for the ride."

"I'm sick of the ride," Dave had retorted. "Turn around, Ned. Let's go back to the house."

"I'm not turning around," Ned had declared. "This car's going to Canada."

"This car is mine," Peter had reminded him. "I may be letting you drive it, Whitelaw, but it's mine."

"He who drives it owns it," Ned had snapped. "That makes it mine. So get the hell out."

"You're crazy, Whitelaw." The laughter in Peter's voice had sounded an awful lot like sheer panic.

"No," Ned had drawled, "I'm smart." He'd swerved onto the side of the road, got out of the car, yanked open Peter's door and hauled him out. "You missed your chance, buddy," he'd growled, shoving him toward the bumper. "You, too," he'd shouted in to Dave, whose face had turned pasty white as he'd scrambled out of the car after Peter. "Nice knowing you losers," Ned had snarled as he'd climbed back in behind the wheel, practically slamming the door on Peter's fingers when Peter had tried to stop him. He'd revved the engine and sped away, leaving them at the side of the road.

Alison should have gotten out with them. But she'd been too scared. Ned was always bossy, but he was pushing it to a new level. He'd never let her get out of the car now. He needed her to get the money from her father, and he needed her because this was all supposed to be for her. He'd schemed it all because she'd asked him to help her get back at her father, and if she walked out on him after everything he'd done he'd probably go berserk—if he wasn't berserk already.

"I don't want to get married," she told him now. He'd parked on the shoulder of the highway just a few miles from Houlton. The clock on the dashboard said ten-thirty. She was tired and worn out, but she struggled to stay alert. If she dozed off Ned might cross the border, and she wouldn't be able to stop him.

"Why not? You, me and half a mil. Ain't a bad way to start out in life."

"Who says my father is going to pay you the money?" she argued. "If he did, it would only be to get me back."

"You don't think he wants you back badly enough to pay it?" Ned asked, giving voice to her worst fear.

"That's not the point, Ned. The point is, if he *does* pay it, he's going to expect you to send me home. You can't go back on your end of the deal."

"Why not?" He used the glowing coal of his cigarette butt to light a fresh smoke, then tossed the butt out the open window. "He's a successful businessman, which in my book translates to he's used to double-crossing his adversaries. So what's wrong with our double-crossing him? I mean, there's a certain poetry in it, don't you think?"

Her fear mounted. There was something particularly sinister about the way Ned could rationalize everything. "What do you know about poetry?" she countered petulantly. "You want to get married? Forget it. I won't marry you."

"Why not?"

Closing her eyes for a moment, she attempted to revive her love for Ned. She tried to recall her fantasies about the blue-eyed babies they would create, the house they would make their home, the life they would live. All she felt inside was cold. "You hit me," she said.

He seemed irritated. "So what? Big deal. It's not like I gave you a black eye or anything."

She stared across the car seat at him, at his glacial eyes and his gaunt cheeks, his conceited grin, his practiced roguishness. He was a man who could hit her again. She knew it.

He might hit her right now, if she resisted crossing into Canada with him. Yet she couldn't cross the border. It was more than just a political line drawn between two friendly nations. In her heart, leaving the United States would imply leaving everything, everything she'd been trying so hard to attain, everything she'd been hoping for when this whole crazy scheme first began to take shape. If she left now, it would be for good, forever.

Bracing herself for the worst, she took a deep breath and said, "I won't go to Canada with you, Ned. I won't marry you and I won't go to Canada."

"I can make you."

"You try to force me and I'll scream to the border patrol that you kidnapped me."

He smoked for a few minutes, saying nothing, simply staring at her and blowing thick streams of smelly smoke at her. At last he said, "You could get out here. I could leave you all by your lonesome on the side of the road."

She thought of the horrible fates that befell young women foolish enough to hitchhike alone at night. None of them seemed quite as bad as staying with Ned. "Fine," she said, jerking the lever on her door and pushing it open.

In a flash, he reached across her seat and yanked her back inside. "What are you, crazy?"

"Look who's talking!"

He raised a hand threateningly. "Don't mess with me, Alison."

He might hit her, right now. He might beat her up and leave her on the side of the road, the way he'd left Jeremy. Jeremy had been so brave, though. He hadn't cried, and if he'd pleaded it had only been on her behalf, not his own. She wasn't going to plead with Ned, either. And she wasn't going to cry, even though she felt tears accumulating along her eyelids.

"Go ahead," she dared him. "Be a real man. Hit me."

He wavered. Slowly he let his hand drop. "Come on, baby," he wheedled, reaching across the seat to take her hand. "Who loves you better than I do?"

Nobody, probably, she answered silently. She stared at her lap, hating the way his fingers looked wrapped around hers.

"We're in this together," he murmured. "Don't back out on me now. I need you."

You need a straitjacket, she almost said.

"You wanna wait a while before we cross the border?" he suggested. "That's cool, babe. We'll just sit here and think about what we really want, okay? No hurry. We'll give your daddy a few more hours to get the bucks together, and then we'll roll. Meantime, we'll just sit here and think about how much we love each other."

Not much, Alison thought to herself. But sitting here was better than driving on. As long as they stayed in

Maine she still had a chance to escape. Ned hadn't hit her. She was all right, at least for now.

It amazed her to think she'd scored a victory—a tiny one, but as long as the engine remained off she counted it as a win for her side. "Okay," she said. "Let's sit here a while."

"WHY DIDN'T YOU TELL ME you were armed?" Jeremy asked as he and Marlo walked back to the car after dropping Dave and Peter off at Ray Kimball's rustic cabin for the night. The two boys had been extremely pale and compliant by the time Marlo and Jeremy had delivered them into the burly old man's custody. "I'm doing you a favor," she'd informed them during the drive to Deer Island. "Your friend Mr. Whitelaw is cruising around Maine with a couple of guns. I can't think of a better place for you to be than someplace where he'll never be able to find you."

"But he said he wasn't coming back to Beresford."

"He's driving a stolen vehicle," she'd reminded Peter. "Sooner or later it's going to dawn on him that he needs the registration to get out of the country. He'll be back. And the safest place for you to be when he comes back is far away."

Evidently, Peter had bought her explanation, because he'd been remarkably diffident when Marlo had handed him and Dave over to Ray. "Hey, listen," Peter had said as Marlo and Jeremy were about to leave. "Are you guys going to get my car for me if Ned comes back to Beresford?"

"It's on the agenda," Marlo had assured him.

"Where are you going to stay?"

She herself had given that question some thought. Beresford didn't contain any motels, and even if it did, staying at a motel wouldn't enable her to keep an eye on the Olson house. "I imagine Jeremy and I are going to take turns staking out your parents' house," she said.

Jeremy had winced. "You mean, we're spending the night in your car?"

"That was the general idea."

"Listen, man," Peter had intervened. "Why don't you stay inside the house? It's okay with me. I mean, I'd like you to. There's plenty of room, and you'd be doing me a favor if you could get my car back."

Not wanting to give him the opportunity to retract the offer, Marlo had accepted immediately. Peter had pressed his house key into her hand—she'd thought it best not to mention that she'd already gained entrance to the place without a key—and she had exchanged some small talk with Ray before she and Jeremy took their leave.

Before she'd gotten the car started Jeremy turned on her. "Have you been carrying that gun around all this time?"

His voice was intense, his stare relentless. To her, the gun was just a prop, a means to an end. Obviously, to him it was a strange, unnerving instrument of terror.

She backed down the gravel drive and started down the street. "Yes," she confessed, "I've been carrying it around with me all this time."

"Why didn't you tell me?"

"Why should I tell you? A doctor doesn't tell you he's got a stethoscope in his pocket. A carpenter doesn't tell you he's carrying a ruler. This is a tool of the trade for me."

Jeremy digested her bland explanation and shook his head. "Stethoscopes and rulers aren't deadly weapons," he pointed out.

"God willing, my revolver will never be a deadly weapon, either. I have never once had to fire it in my work, and that's a record I'd like to keep."

"You mean . . . you've never shot anyone?"

"Never." She steered toward the causeway back to the mainland. "I keep in shape with regular target practice and I've got to admit I'm a damned good shot. But it's a skill I hope I'll never have to use in real life. Just showing people the gun is usually enough to get them to do what I want."

"It's licensed?" he asked.

She tossed him a quick look and laughed. "Of course it's licensed."

"And loaded?"

She nodded.

Jeremy swallowed. "In other words, I could have shot those kids." At her shrug of response, he sank into a deep, troubled silence.

"The safety latch was on," she told him. "It wasn't like you would have inadvertently blown their heads off or anything."

"I'm embarrassed to admit this, Marlo, but . . ." He sighed. "I like your gun."

"That sounds perverted."

He chuckled. "It's not . . ." He paused, searching for the right words. "It's not the sort of thing I would have expected. I don't—I don't usually find myself in these situations. Crime is something I read about in the newspapers. Guns are for drug runners and hunters and maniacs on the California freeways. And for police officers. I just . . . it's all a bit alien to me. I never held a gun before tonight."

Marlo allowed herself a brief glimpse at him, then turned her gaze back to the road. His expression was candid, his eyes alive with excitement. He was so different from her in so many ways. His concept of the world was so naive. How was it possible that a man with so much could know so little?

Nonsense. He knew plenty. He was smart, well-educated and sophisticated. The only things he knew little about were nasty things, the violent, sordid, rotten parts of life. He existed on an elevated plane, well above the squalor. How lucky he was to have lived so long without ever having to come in contact with guns.

They didn't discuss the gun anymore during the drive back to Beresford. The road was dark and empty, the sky sprayed with stars. Marlo told Jeremy a little about Ray, about what a fanatic fisherman he was, about how her father kept in regular touch with Ray and spent several long weekends with him on Deer Island every year, during which they did a little fishing and a lot of poker-playing. It had been her father's idea to deliver the punks to Ray, and he'd contacted Ray personally to make the request. She herself didn't know the man well enough to ask such a huge favor of him, and he still tended to look upon her as Stan's little girl. Tonight, in front of Jeremy and Tweedledum and Tweedledee, however, Ray had treated her with respect.

"Here we are," she said, turning onto the gravel driveway. She drove to its end and then onto the grass and around to the rear of the house. "If I leave the car in view, it might scare Ned and Alison away," she explained.

Jeremy nodded. He was still studying her, but his expression had become more contemplative. His eyes had softened into that gentle pussy willow color and his smile appeared tentative, questioning.

"What?" she prompted, turning in her seat to face him.

He ran his fingers through his hair. "I feel like we've been through so much this evening."

She felt that way, too. They'd been through so much since she'd rung his doorbell Sunday morning and the door had swung open to reveal him, bleary-eyed and shirtless and spectacularly handsome.

Abruptly she felt as unsure of herself as he looked. She lowered her gaze to her hands where they came to rest on the arc of the steering wheel an inch above her lap. "Jeremy?"

"Yes."

"All that stuff I told you before, about my mother and all..."

He reached across the seat to lift a stray lock of her hair from her cheek. His finger grazed her chin, kindling a remote response, a tug of longing deep inside her.

"I shouldn't have told you all that," she murmured.

He said nothing. He only brushed his hand across her cheek and through her hair again, even though no errant strands had fallen across her face. Perhaps he'd intended the gesture to be reassuring, but it only provoked another deep, dark pang of yearning in her soul.

Sitting in the silent shadows of the car behind the Olson house, she suddenly felt unprotected, susceptible, robbed of her defenses. Just as she'd handed her gun to Jeremy earlier that evening, so her intimate confessions about her past had provided him with a psychic weapon—one he could use against her. He'd seen her not only at her strongest but at her weakest. What he knew about her was potentially just as lethal as a revolver.

"How are we going to work this thing?" he asked.

Her stomach clenched. What thing was he referring to?

"I know we've got to wait up in case Ned and Alison come back, but it seems silly for us both to stay awake."

She nodded. "We'll take turns sleeping."

"You can go first," he offered. "You look awfully tired."

Actually, she was less tired than scared, scared to enter the house with him, to be alone inside with him. She desired him, and he knew she did, and just like the pearl necklace, he was something she couldn't afford and shouldn't want. Desiring what could never truly be yours only led to heartache.

He pulled her key from the ignition and left the car. When she heard him unlocking the trunk she got out, slowly and anxiously. By the time she reached the rear of the car he had both suitcases out of the trunk. "There's a back door," he noted, pointing at the house.

"I don't know if this key will work in it," she said as she dug Peter's key from her pocket. She scaled the steps to the small back porch, then inserted the key, twisted it and heard the lock give. The door opened into a mudroom off the kitchen.

Marlo entered the kitchen and looked around. The room was as disorderly now as it had been the first time she'd seen it, with food and dirty dishes scattered about. Yet entering the house through the back door gave her the odd feeling that the house was hers. There was something informal and proprietary about coming in through the back way. She could almost hear her mother's voice: "The front door is for company, Marlo. Children with muddy shoes use the back door."

Her family's kitchen had been about half the size of this one, but immaculate. The kitchen in Marlo's current apartment was one of those built-into-the-wall efficiency spaces, not much larger than a bathroom. To own a kitchen like this, big and airy and light, with hard-wood floors and varnished pine cabinets...

She resolutely banished the notion from her mind. She had wasted too much time today wallowing in envy. This house, the wildflowers, Alison's necklace, Jeremy... none of it would ever be part of her reality. She was just a tourist here.

Still, as she roamed through the kitchen to the hall, as she wandered into the living room and gazed at the fine, cozy furnishings, she couldn't keep herself from pretending this was hers, all of it, the rugs and knickknacks and solid mahogany tables. Who else but the lady of the house would stroll about, extinguishing the lights before heading upstairs to bed?

It was a dangerous fantasy—dangerous because it felt so lovely. She'd spent her entire life condemning wealth and the things it bought, and here she was, making believe she owned it all.

"Are you hungry?" Jeremy asked. "All you had was that one sandwich."

Turning, she found him standing at the foot of the stairs, still toting the suitcases. She shook her head. "I'm going to check in with my father," she said, "and then I'll try to get some rest. Who knows when Ned and Alison might return?"

Jeremy nodded and started up the stairs with the bags. She detoured back to the kitchen to telephone her father with an update, then headed for the stairs, as well. There were six bedrooms on the second floor, she recalled, three of them unused and all of them beautifully furnished. That she could choose which room she wanted seemed almost decadent.

Jeremy was waiting for her at the top of the stairs, allowing her to select a bedroom first. She peeked inside two of the unused bedrooms before entering the third. It was the smallest, but it had a charming brass bed made up with a fluffy white comforter and two plump down-filled pillows. An antique-looking dresser stood against one wall; the curtains at the window featured a trim of eyelet lace. "I'll take this one," she said, turning back to Jeremy to take her bag from him.

Instead of handing it to her he set it down on the thick area rug, and then set his own bag down beside it. He searched her face, and once again she sensed the question in his eyes, understood it and felt an answer echoing inside her. She shouldn't want this, she shouldn't want any of it—not the pretty room, not the man. She shouldn't want what could never be hers.

But just for now, for this night, she could pretend. Just for this moment, as Jeremy moved closer, as his arms reached around her and drew her to himself, as his lips found hers and graced them with a gentle kiss, and then a less gentle one, and then a deep, consuming one...

Just this once, she would make believe she could have it all.

CHAPTER ELEVEN

SHE CLOSED HER ARMS around him, flattening her hands against his back as she molded her mouth to his. If only his body didn't feel so good, if only his tongue didn't seduce hers with such tantalizing aggression, if only his shirt wasn't so smooth and soft against her fingertips, and his back so smooth and hard, and his eyes so radiant as he pulled back to view her...

Radiant yet perceptive. A faint line creased his brow as he studied her flushed face. "Is this wrong?" he asked, his voice gravelly and his breathing labored.

She met his unwavering gaze, noticing for the first time that his fog-gray irises were accented with nearly imperceptible flecks of silver. He made no move to release her. One of his hands remained on her hip, the other on her shoulder, and his chest was mere inches from hers. She could feel his breath on her cheeks and throat.

She wanted him so much it hurt.

"I think so," she managed to answer. What was wrong with it was that Jeremy was who he was and she was who she was, but she couldn't come right out and say that to him. "This isn't our house," she said instead.

"It is, tonight," he said, putting her fantasy into words.

"And Alison and Ned could barge in—"

"We have until they do." He brushed his lips against her forehead. "Tell me to stop and I will," he whispered, then dropped another light kiss between her eyebrows. "I don't want to but I will."

He was forcing her to decide. Earlier, when they'd snuck up on Dave and Peter, she had been keenly aware that Jeremy resented her authority, but now he was welcoming it. What happened next was entirely up to her. She could choose to act rationally and send him off to one of the other bedrooms for the night, or she could choose to abandon logic, toss aside her defenses and be reckless. All her training spoke against that choice; all her experience warned her to protect herself, to avoid opening herself to injury, to abstain from heroics and emerge from every encounter in the same condition she'd gone into it.

But tonight this house was hers and Jeremy's. Tonight was magic. Tonight wasn't the time to play it safe.

Lifting her hands to his head, she plowed her fingers into the tawny silk of his hair and guided his mouth to hers. She'd made her decision.

He groaned, a barely audible sound of satisfaction as his tongue found hers. And then she was spinning, levitating, floating within Jeremy's strong embrace until the world tilted and soft white clouds of linen billowed up to meet her shoulders. Gasping, she opened her eyes to find herself lying on the bed. Jeremy lay half beside her and half on top of her, gazing down at her and tracing the edge of her jaw with his knuckle. She was much too heavy for him to carry. She must have flown across the room to the bed.

Tonight was definitely magic.

She perused his face, delighting in its cleanly sculpted lines, in the unadulterated pleasure illuminating his eyes as he continued to stroke her. He trailed his fingertips along her cheekbones, down the straight line of her nose, over her parted lips to her chin, down further to her throat, to the delicate hollow at her collarbone. "You," he murmured, "are the most exciting woman I've ever met."

"You're just turned on by my gun," she teased.

His grin widened. "It's quite a gun." His hand flirted with the neckline of her sweater, then skimmed down to her waist and under the ribbed edge. His eyes remained locked onto hers as his fingers danced across her belly to the sharp rise of her ribs, to the satin trim of her bra. His smile faded slightly as his fingers inched higher, scaling the small mound of her breast until he found her inflamed nipple.

Closing her eyes, she centered her consciousness on his caresses, on the provocative motions of his thumb against the swollen bud, on the throbbing heat that burned from her chest down to her hips, making her eager for more, for the feel of his hand directly upon her skin, for the feel of his lips on her. She tugged at the hem of her sweater and Jeremy stopped caressing her long enough to help her to remove it. He unclasped her bra, tossed it away and then fulfilled her unexpressed wish, running his fingers in circles over her flesh, and then his lips and tongue.

She moaned at the thrilling friction of his day-old beard against her skin, at the gentle tugging of his teeth as he suckled first one breast and then the other. She groped for his shirt, and again he understood her unspoken need and stopped what he was doing long enough to answer it. He tore at the buttons, shrugged the cotton broadcloth from his shoulders and flung the shirt over the side of the bed.

Seeing his naked chest reminded her of how often since the morning she'd met him she had pictured it in her imagination. It looked as wonderful now as it had then—

and it felt even better than it looked. She let her hands journey over the magnificent contours of his torso, the limber muscles and warm skin and curling golden wisps of hair, the flat plain of his abdomen and the sexy indentation of his navel. She descended as far as the edge of his jeans before returning to his chest. She combed her fingers through the arrow-shaped mat of hair and scraped her nails across his flat brown nipples until they stiffened. Feeling a tremor ripple through him in response to her erotic exploration, she lifted her hands to his shoulders and pulled him completely on top of her.

His body crushed down on hers, all lean muscle and urgent desire. His mouth found hers, and his hips, his hard, unyielding flesh pressing against her. Her arousal matched his. She shifted beneath him, trying to align her body with his, and when he fit himself between her thighs she let out a faint cry of yearning. Her hands moved frantically on his naked back, following the slope from his shoulders to his waist and then down to his buttocks, holding him tightly to her.

He stopped breathing for a moment, then exhaled with a small shudder. "Marlo," he whispered, his voice a mere rasp. He propped himself up on rigid arms and she drew her hands forward to the snap of his jeans. He covered her hands with one of his, halting her. "Marlo—are we safe doing this?"

Given her dazed, delirious state, it took her several long seconds to comprehend that he wasn't questioning her about the Olson house or Alison and Ned. As understanding dawned, she stared up at him in astonishment. Men weren't supposed to bother asking about such things. Men—the sort of men Marlo knew, anyway—assumed it was the woman's responsibility, and if she didn't take that responsibility the consequences were her problem. Most men didn't seem to care.

Jeremy cared.

Tears filled her eyes. She shouldn't become sentimental over something so trivial—but it wasn't trivial. That Jeremy cared enough to ask meant the world to her.

He obviously misinterpreted her weepiness. "Hey, it's not so bad," he murmured, running his thumb gingerly along her cheek to wipe away a stray tear. "You didn't know this was going to happen. I didn't bring anything with me, either. So what? We can be creative."

"No, I'm fine." Swallowing, she gathered his hand in hers and lifted his palm to her lips for a kiss. "I mean, I'm protected. It was—it was just nice of you to ask."

"Nice?" He chuckled at the insipid adjective, then bowed and planted a light kiss on her lips. "I happen to be a hell of a nice guy."

"I noticed."

He kissed her again, a longer, hungrier kiss. His tongue forged deep into her mouth and his hips rocked against her in a slow, insinuating rhythm. She arched to him, wanting more, needing more, longing for the last of their clothing to vanish.

Once again he complied with her silent wish, pulling back far enough to get at the button of her slacks. He unfastened it, worked the zipper down and then slipped his hand inside, fingering the thin cotton of her panties. Her thighs clenched, driving her against his hand as he teased her through the fabric. She was burning, anxious, aching with want.

"Jeremy…" she pleaded, attempting to wriggle out of what remained of her clothes. Her knee rose between his legs and he clamped them around her, holding her within an inch of his aroused flesh.

He opened his jeans. His smile was gone, his gaze relentless, his chest pumping as he struggled to regulate his breathing. Marlo peeled down his slacks and underwear and he peeled down hers. Then his hand returned to her, gliding through the dark, downy triangle of hair, touching, invading, conquering.

The ache within her built to an unbearable pitch. She moaned in pain and pleasure, in impatience and anticipation. Her body flexed around his finger, flooding her with sensations, with emotions, with that same, inexcusable yearning she'd suffered earlier that day—the longing to possess, to take, to own. To have Jeremy.

She brought her hand down between their bodies and curled her fingers around him. As she ran her palm along his steel-hard length his hips lurched, his breath caught and the muscles in his abdomen tensed. He cupped his hands around her bottom and lifted her to himself, thrusting deep. Still the want was there, more imperative, more desperate than ever.

He withdrew and thrust again, filling her completely. His hands tightened on her hips as he surged inside her, angling her to him, increasing the contact of their bodies, stoking the fire that raged within her. She felt greedy, insatiable. He was giving her everything and it wasn't enough, she wanted more....

Abruptly, miraculously, she felt herself enveloped in a dark, lush spasm of ecstasy, the ultimate joy, a heaven where there was nothing more to want, nothing more than the knowledge that Jeremy was there with her. With a blissful cry, she drew him in, absorbing the tremors that racked his body as he met her in paradise, as relief swept through him in a fierce final rush.

His breath harsh and erratic, he sank down onto her. She wrapped her arms around him and sketched an abstract line along the perspiration-damp skin of his back. His head came to rest on her shoulder and he brushed his lips against the curve of her neck. "I suppose you'd call that 'nice,' " he whispered, nuzzling her throat.

His kiss ignited an echoing spasm in the cradle of her hips, and she issued a shaky sigh. *Nice* didn't even begin to approach what she had just experienced—what she was still experiencing in the sweet, ebbing pulses of their lovemaking. "What would you call it?" she asked, her voice as ragged as his.

"Phenomenal," he proposed. He nipped the underside of her jaw, setting off yet another remote spasm inside her. "Monumental. Extraordinary." He raised his head to view her. "Sensational."

Even those words seemed to fall short. What she had just shared with Jeremy defied description. She admired his attempt, though. "What a vocabulary," she murmured, staring up into his profoundly beautiful eyes.

"What a woman," he countered, brushing her hair back from her face with his hand. "I've never known anyone like you before."

She could have told him that she'd known more than a few men like him. She'd known men with fancy careers and bulging bank accounts, men who considered her a problem solver worth so many dollars a day to smooth out the universe's rough edges. She'd known men who welcomed her into their world for as long as it took to find out which employee was bleeding them or which country club pro was fooling around with their wife, and then wrote a check and sent her on her way, back to the other side of the tracks where she belonged.

But she couldn't say that, not to Jeremy. For this one enchanted night they had transcended their differences. She could forget that she was a P.I. and former cop from

Bridgeport and he was a hotshot architect from the Gold Coast, and they could be just what they were now: lovers, their naked limbs intertwined on these fresh-smelling linens in this provincial Maine farmhouse, their hearts beating in unison.

With obvious reluctance, Jeremy rolled off her and drew the comforter up over them. He nestled into the pillow next to her, urging her onto her side so she faced him. He appraised her for a minute and frowned. "I should have shaved," he said apologetically.

"I don't mind."

"I've left marks on your skin," he said, touching the underside of her chin first with his index finger and then with his lips.

She didn't even want to consider the marks he'd left on her heart, on her soul. "We should probably try to get some rest," she said.

"We should probably make love again. Did you know you yell when you come?"

"I do not!" she objected, blushing.

"Well, not yell," he hastened to reassure her. "It's more like a husky groan, deep in your throat."

Embarrassed, she lowered her eyes to the decorative stitching on the comforter. So, he'd never known anyone like her before. Ladies from the Gold Coast probably didn't make any noise at all. They probably didn't even sweat. They probably just lay there, with every impeccably coiffed hair in place, while pleasure automatically coursed through them. They probably assumed that pleasure in bed was their due.

"Marlo, look at me." Evidently aware of her discomfort, he cupped his hand under her chin and drew her gaze back to him. "I love listening to you groan. Just thinking about it..." He sighed. "It makes me want you again." His free hand found hers and steered it under the blanket to his aroused flesh. "It's incredible, the effect you have on me."

"It's *nice*," she said, attempting a joke.

He smiled and pressed into her hand. "Very nice," he whispered. "Very, very nice." He covered her mouth with his and gathered her into his arms, and her self-consciousness evanesced as the night wrapped them in its magic once more.

STAN MCGINNIS UNLOCKED the back door of the modest shingled row house that had been his home for twenty-five years. Entering, he flicked the light switch and locked the door behind him. The round fluorescent ceiling fixture glared its light off the linoleum floor tiles, causing him to squint for a moment. Then he took a deep breath and smiled at the familiar aroma of old coffee and smoke.

It was after ten and he was beat. Porter could tire anyone with his incessant demands. Sighing, Stan pulled a cigar from the box on the counter, tore off the cellophane wrapper and lit it. He'd given up cigars for Catherine and he never smoked them around Marlo, but at his age, he deserved this one small vice. If cigars killed him, as Marlo was always nagging that they would, so be it. He wasn't getting any younger.

He tossed his mail unopened on the kitchen table, pulled a beer from the fridge and trudged into the living room to watch television. The Sox were playing the A's; he could catch the last couple of innings. He settled his large frame comfortably in the oversized easy chair and let the lights from the screen flicker over his face, the babble from the audio wash around him. He puffed on his cigar and meditated.

Marlo was awfully close to tying up this case. Damn, but she was good. He doubted he could have worked things out so neatly—the Olson and Sawyer kids in Ray Kimball's custody, Alison and Ned facing an impossible situation at the Canadian border, and for Marlo, a comfy stakeout in some rich vacation hideaway. Not bad. All Stan had done was keep Porter company throughout the ordeal—hold his hand and prevent him from getting drunk. Marlo had done the rest. It was gratifying to think he could retire and leave the agency in her capable hands. If these cigars ever got him, he could die with the satisfaction of knowing she'd be okay.

If only...

He tried to chase away the thought by concentrating on a televised replay of a stolen base, but it came back to haunt him: if only Marlo could find herself a man and settle down. If only she could find a partner, a mate, a lover. Stan wasn't too old-fashioned—he'd prefer a proper church wedding for her, but he'd settle for a strong, solid relationship with a man she could trust, someone who would appreciate her and treat her right.

No doubt her experiences stalking adulterous husbands had jaded her some, but still, there had to be a few decent men around. On those rare occasions when Stan broached the subject with her she always got defensive, said guys didn't like women who were taller than they were, or hard-edged, or independent. That fellow she'd dated while she was on the Bridgeport force—well, Stan could have seen a mile away that that one wasn't going to work out. The guy didn't like the work she did, and she would never give up her work.

But there had to be other men out there. Stan recognized that Marlo was intentionally keeping her distance from them.

He rolled a cloud of acrid smoke around his mouth and expelled it in a series of perfectly shaped rings. It was late and he was tired. He ought to dump the beer, extinguish the cigar and go to bed. But if he did he wouldn't fall asleep. Ever since Catherine died he couldn't just go to bed and nod off. He had to wear himself down to the point where he was too exhausted to notice that she wasn't with him.

Times like these, he worried that it was his own fault Marlo was still single. She had seen what happened when you became too dependent on someone else—so dependent that more than fifteen years later you still had trouble getting into bed by yourself.

It wasn't as if he wanted to be alone. He dated women; sometimes he spent the night in a bed that wasn't his own. But whenever he brought a woman back to his house it felt like a desecration. This was Catherine's home, the home they'd made together. He couldn't stop loving her. He couldn't stop missing her. He had a good life and a terrific daughter, but there was always that vacuum, that empty place inside himself. He would never be complete again. That was what happened when you loved somebody so much. And Marlo knew it.

He used to pride himself on the fact that he'd taught Marlo everything she knew. But now, as he was getting on in years and watching her come into her own, he wished there was a way to unteach her the one lesson she'd learned too well.

HE OUGHT TO GET some sleep, but he couldn't bring himself to wake Marlo up. He couldn't stop gazing at her. She had insisted that they both get dressed before either of them fell asleep, so they'd be ready to spring into action if they had to. But even though they were fully clothed and stretched out on top of the blanket, Jeremy couldn't rid himself of erotic thoughts.

In all honesty, he didn't want to.

She appeared angelic in repose, her features visible in the diaphanous silver moonlight filtering through the curtains. Her lashes looked long and dark against her delicately shaped cheeks. Her lips were innocently pursed, her bent knees brushed his thighs and her hand rested against his chest.

The irony, of course, was that if any term didn't apply to Marlo it was angelic. She was not only unbelievably sensual, she was down-to-earth, sharp-minded and hardheaded. She didn't flitter above reality, strumming a figurative harp and seeing only the goodness in others. She wasn't ethereal or perfect or dreamy. Rather, she seemed the embodiment of the phrase "one tough cookie."

Tough, but oh, so tasty. So sweet. He leaned toward her, careful not to awaken her, and pressed his lips to the crown of her head. In her sleep she made a contented purring sound and her long, sleek legs moved against his.

It was bad form, but Jeremy found himself comparing Marlo to other women he'd known. He thought of Brenda, his most recent companion. He recalled her polish and élan, her innate elegance.... The way she always sat in the passenger seat of the MG, waiting for Jeremy to open the door for her. The way she walked, each step precise and solid despite the two-and-a-half inch elevation of her heels. The way she held her chin high, and the way she smiled without creating wrinkles at the outer corners of her eyes. Sarcasm was alien to her. Guns were something her eccentric great-uncle had used on safaris as a young man in the Thirties. On entering this house, she would not have gaped at the burnished antiques and the expansive proportions of the rooms, as Marlo had. Instead, her cunning mind would have immediately set about rearranging the furniture, visualizing a more suitable color scheme and engineering the maximal use of natural light.

That was what she'd done with Jeremy's house. She'd advised him on furniture, plants, textiles and textures. She'd put together an excellent living environment. But it was all so...so detached from reality, somehow. It was just a bit too flawless.

Marlo wasn't flawless, not by a long shot. She was bigoted and occasionally patronizing, too sure of herself in some areas and not sure enough of herself in others. Yet all she had to do was move her leg again or exhale a soft breath against his shoulder and his nervous system went wild. Even now, decorously dressed and sound asleep, she aroused him in an amazing way.

He heard the wind whipping up outside, and then a vague tapping sound as a branch bounced off the roof. Marlo's eyes shot open instantly. He'd been positive she was fast asleep; how could such a slight noise rouse her?

Before he could speak she passed her hand against his mouth. Her eyes sharpened as they met his, and he realized that she was, if anything, more awake than he was. *Don't talk,* she mouthed, and although he felt she was grossly overreacting to a windblown branch he nodded to indicate he understood.

She lifted her hand from his mouth and sat up, turning her gaze toward the door. In a lissome movement she sprang out of bed and glided across the room. She pressed her ear to the door and listened.

He lifted his wristwatch from the decorative brass knob on the bed's frame and squinted at it until he could decipher the position of the hands. Three-thirty.

Glancing toward Marlo, he suddenly heard another tap, a scraping sound and then a man's voice, distorted by the distance it traveled to reach their room. "Okay, so are you happy?" the man growled, sounding not the least bit happy himself. "Are you happy now?"

Then a woman's voice: "Don't yell at me. It's your own fault. I hate you!"

Alison. Jeremy bolted out of bed and opened his mouth to shout the news that Alison was here. One swift, stern look from Marlo froze his words in his throat.

"You're the only fault I've got, babe," said the growling man. "And you're in heap big trouble if I can't find Olson."

"I don't want to hear about it. This whole thing—it's such a disaster. I've had it, Ned. I've had it with you and your stupid plans. I want to go home."

"I'm the only home you've got, toots."

Marlo moved silently through the room, searching in the dark for her shoes. Following her lead, Jeremy straightened out his clothing. He wished he was as alert as Marlo. He had dozed only intermittently through the night. Every time he fell asleep he would dream of her and his overheated body would wake him up.

Sitting on the edge of the bed, he fumbled with his shoes, wondering whether Alison was going to come upstairs. He and Marlo had to be ready before Alison and Ned arrived on the second floor. Glancing at Marlo, he marveled at her ability to function in the dark at this ungodly hour. After running her fingers briskly through her hair, she shot him a quick look, then returned to her post by the door and noiselessly opened it a crack.

Alison's and Ned's voices sounded much clearer through the opening. Someone was stomping from room to room downstairs—probably Ned, since the footsteps were heavy and loud. At the bottom of the stairs he stopped and hollered, "Olson? Get your butt down here!"

"Ned," Alison implored, "let them sleep. We aren't going anywhere tonight."

"Oh, yeah? Who died and made you boss?"

"I don't want to go!"

Jeremy heard more footsteps, Alison's and Ned's both, as if they were tussling. He raced to the door, but Marlo blocked him and shook her head vehemently.

"Stop it, Ned," Alison demanded. "I'm done with this. I'm telling you—"

"You want to go back? What the hell have you got to go back to?"

"I don't care, as long as you're not a part of it."

"Bitch," Ned snarled. More tussling sounds.

Jeremy couldn't stand it. He couldn't stand the picture those sounds conjured up in his mind: Ned hitting Alison, hurting her, brutalizing her. Perhaps Marlo could be calm and professional, perhaps she could stand behind a door and listen while a young woman was being roughed up one floor below. But Jeremy couldn't. He wouldn't.

Before Marlo could stop him, he shoved her aside, wrenched the door all the way open and charged out into the hall, barely hearing Marlo's sotto voce curse. If she was angry, tough luck. If she resented his taking action, too bad. Jeremy was going to get the creep who'd gotten him and Alison. He was going to get his revenge.

He stormed down the stairs and into the kitchen, where a light was on. Alison, wearing jeans, a T-shirt and a weird punk haircut, was cowering behind a chair, using it as a shield. Ned—the fellow Jeremy had witnessed hoisting her into the van Saturday night, the fellow with the malevolent blue eyes, the fellow with the diamond stud in his ear and the indolent smirk twisting his lips— was swinging wildly at her head. One swing missed; one landed against the chair's ladder-back slats. One connected, glancing off the side of her head. Alison let out a screech, even though the light cuff seemed more to have startled her than caused real injury.

"Stop it!" Jeremy roared, causing them both to jump and turn to him.

With a tremulous cry, Alison threw down the chair and hurled herself into Jeremy's arms. Ned simultaneously hurled himself toward the back door.

Jeremy had to stop Ned, but he couldn't, not with Alison clinging to him, her arms wrapped around his neck, her head buried against his shoulder and the air resonating with her full-throated sobs. "Alison..." he murmured, following with his gaze Ned's departure out the door.

Inconsolable, she tightened her arms on him with the strength of a boa constrictor. He tried without success to peel her off him, all the while chanting inane words of comfort.

Suddenly Marlo appeared, a blur of energy darting from the hallway, across the room and out the door after Ned. Once again Jeremy tried to remove Alison from his neck. Ned could hurt Marlo; Jeremy ought to be outside helping her. Alison was hysterical but basically unharmed. Marlo needed him.

Alison wouldn't let go, however. Half carrying her and half dragging her along, Jeremy made his way to the open back door. Peering outside, he discerned two shadowy figures wrestling on the ground not far from Marlo's Honda. He turned on the back porch light, which illuminated the yard and the figures.

Actually, only Ned was on the ground, prone, his face pressed into the grass. Marlo straddled his back and was busy pinning his arms behind him. She scarcely seemed out of breath.

"I know you, don't I?" Alison called to Marlo from within the protective shelter of Jeremy's arms. "You look familiar."

"My father works for your father," Marlo told her with enviable composure. "I'm Marlo McGinnis, and you—" she reacted to Ned's attempt to wiggle out from under her by jamming her knee into his ribs "—are going home. You, too," she snapped at Ned. "Stop squirming."

"My shirt's gonna get grass stains on it," he complained. "This is Georges Marciano, man."

"Nice meeting you, George." With a minimum of movement, she pulled a pair of handcuffs from the waistband of her slacks and slapped them onto Ned's wrists. Jeremy shook his head in awe. Where had the handcuffs come from? First a gun and then those. It dawned on him that Marlo truly was an ex-cop, with a cop's training, a cop's agility, a cop's arsenal of equipment.

She was incredible.

She glanced over her shoulder at Jeremy. He wanted to apologize for having acted precipitously and risking the loss of Ned, but her stony stare silenced him. "Take her back inside, would you?" she said with a nod toward Alison. "Give her father a call. I don't think he'll mind being awakened."

"He will," Alison moaned. "He doesn't care anything about me."

"He cared enough to hire me to come up after you," Marlo pointed out. "Go on inside."

"Do...do you need any help?" Jeremy inquired. He could see she didn't, yet some vestigial chivalry on his part compelled him to ask.

Her reply consisted of a withering look.

All right. He deserved her anger. He'd jumped the gun, behaved hotheadedly, taken a chance and nearly blown everything. But he *hadn't* blown it. They had Alison, they had Ned, everyone was safe and Marlo didn't even have to brandish her gun this time.

Good lord—maybe his rash actions had forced her to sprint downstairs without arming herself first. Ned could be carrying a gun right now. What if the minute Jeremy ushered Alison back indoors Ned managed to break free of the handcuffs and shoot Marlo?

"Where's your gun?" he asked. He would fetch it for her before telephoning Porter.

Ned issued a strangled groan and grumbled something about being too young to die. Ignoring him, she gave Jeremy a menacing stare. "Don't worry about it," she said through gritted teeth.

She had it with her, then. She had it with her, well hidden—and she hadn't wanted Ned to know. Jeremy had only meant to help, yet with every well-intended thing he did he was making her job more and more difficult.

Exhaling, wondering whether Marlo would ever forgive his ineptitude, he reached for the back door and opened it. "I'll take care of Alison," he said quietly.

"You do that, Jeremy," Marlo muttered. "You take care of her." Her tone left him with the distinct understanding that the past few hours didn't count for much in her current assessment of him, that the ecstasy he'd shared with her earlier that night couldn't protect him from her contempt right now. He'd gone for revenge and aimed for heroics, and in her view he'd made an absolute fool of himself.

CHAPTER TWELVE

"I'M BURNING UP IN HERE," Ned complained. "Can't you turn the air conditioner on?"

Marlo sent a quick glance toward the young man seated beside her. She wanted him in the front seat so she could keep an eye on him, but every time she peeked at him she glimpsed the diamond adorning his earlobe and tasted bile. She had nothing in particular against men wearing earrings; it was Ned Whitelaw wearing a diamond that she objected to.

"The air conditioner doesn't work," she said. Even if it did, she wouldn't turn it on. He didn't deserve it.

"When are you gonna take these things off?" he asked, raising his cuffed hands.

"I don't know. Maybe never."

"Yeah? I'll bring you up on charges, lady. You aren't a cop. You're probably not even allowed to have these things."

"I've got a license for them," she said calmly.

The morning sun glared through the windshield as she cruised south on the interstate. This, she decided, was exactly what she needed: a long, uncomfortable drive home with a snotty, slippery post-pubescent goon to keep her occupied. If she were alone, she would wind up thinking about Jeremy, reliving the few precious hours they'd shared overnight, the fantasy of it. She would wind up mooning and pining for him, trying to convince

herself that it wasn't a fantasy at all, trying to pretend
that when she arrived back in the real world Jeremy
would be there, waiting for her, and they could pick up
right where they left off.

If Jeremy were in the car with her, she would probably never bother going back to the real world at all.
She'd drive off the road to the nearest motel—even that
seedy joint on the New Hampshire border would suf-
fice—and lock herself up in a room with him and refuse
ever to leave.

But Jeremy wasn't in the car. Porter Havelock, although bewildered by the news that Jeremy had partici-
pated in the big rescue, had requested that he bring
Alison home on the first commuter flight out of Bangor,
and Jeremy had reluctantly complied.

In a strange way, Marlo had been glad to see him go.
She was still furious about his crazed-avenger routine at
the farmhouse. He should have listened to her. Porter
Havelock he would obey, but Marlo McGinnis could be
ignored. What did she know, anyway? She was just a
working stiff from Bridgeport.

It wasn't fair to judge Jeremy so critically. But if she
didn't think harshly of Jeremy, she would think lovingly
of him. She would think of the way he had kissed her and
touched her, the way he had felt inside her. She would
think of the respect he'd shown her in bed. So what if
he'd been disrespectful of her afterward?

At least he'd had enough humility to look sheepish
once he'd realized how close he'd come to botching
everything. He'd seemed to be on the verge of apologizing, but Marlo had been distinctly unreceptive to apolo-
gies at the time. Her anger had been justified. If Ned had
been armed, Jeremy's stupid actions could have cost her
her life—and perhaps his own.

Anyway, she'd been too busy to entertain peace offerings from him. There had been phone calls to make—to Porter, to her father, to the airport, to Ray Kimball down on Deer Island. There had been a pot of coffee to brew and drink, then a drive to Bangor to drop Jeremy and Alison off at the airport. Alison, with her overdeveloped pout and her bizarre hairdo, had strode regally into the terminal and Jeremy had trailed behind. Before disappearing inside, he'd turned to stare at Marlo, who had remained in the car with Ned. His eyes had glowed with wistfulness and his smile had been cryptic. He hadn't said anything. He'd only seared her with that one parting look, then turned and entered the building.

From the airport, Marlo had driven directly to Deer Island to fetch Peter Olson and Dave Sawyer. After a significant amount of recriminating and name-calling among the Fairleigh Dickinson trio, Marlo had informed Peter and Dave, to their enormous relief, that Alison's father had no real interest in seeking retribution from them. Ned's head was the one he wanted served up on a platter. Alison had told Porter, when she'd spoken to him earlier that morning, that Ned had been the mastermind of this escapade. He was the one Porter wanted delivered to his doorstep.

They'd gone back to the farmhouse so Peter could pick up his Volvo. Marlo had stowed Ned's suitcase along with her own in the trunk of her car—after she'd transferred the two unloaded pistols from his bag to hers. She'd spread Alison's forgotten silk jumpsuit across the back seat and she'd stashed the neglected pearl necklace in her purse for safekeeping. And then she and her prisoner had hit the road, heading south.

"Can we listen to some music?" Ned asked.

"No."

He cursed and turned to face out the window. "I gotta take a leak."

"Hold it in," she said in her toughest street-cop voice. "We'll stop when I say so." She wasn't going to stop at a highway oasis—those places were always jammed with people, and the chances of Ned's escaping into a crowd were too great. She figured they'd use the facilities at an off-highway gas station somewhere along the way.

"Did anyone ever tell you you're a bitch?" Ned asked.

Marlo eyed him placidly. "I've been called worse."

"I mean..." He twisted his face into a petulant scowl. "It's not like I forced Alison into anything or anything, you know? She was in on it from the start. I didn't plant any ideas in her head. She's the one who should be handcuffed and stuck in this damn car."

Marlo didn't respond.

"I mean, you think you're so tough? You chicks, you want a man to do all the thinking and the planning, and then, when we're this close to getting it right, you fall apart."

"Sure. I'm all in pieces."

"She was crazy about me," he rambled.

"She said you hit her."

"So what? If she didn't like it she coulda left."

"She did," Marlo pointed out. "She's home, Ned, and you're here."

"I could hit you," he remarked, as if the idea had just occurred to him. He grinned maliciously. "I could, you know. Or I could kick you. My feet are free."

"Try it," Marlo dared him in a steely voice. "Just try it and see what happens."

He gave her a hard, measuring stare, then sank back in his seat. "If you weren't driving, I would."

"Safety first," she quipped dryly. "That's what I like about you, Ned."

"You're a bitch," he repeated, evidently running out of insults. "I bet you stink in bed. At least Alison was good in bed. At least she loved me."

"True love," Marlo muttered, trying not to think about her own recent encounter with that particular emotion. "If she loved you so much, she wouldn't have gotten on that plane with Jeremy."

"She went with him 'cause I'm broke," he insisted, slouching in the seat and effecting a pout that was curiously similar to Alison's. "She's just a gold digger. She would've stayed with me if I'd had the bucks."

Marlo didn't point out that Ned had been the one digging Alison's gold. "If you needed money," she said, "you could have pawned that earring of yours."

"This?" He fingered the diamond stud and guffawed. "What could I get, maybe a few hundred bucks? It's not even a full carat."

"Gee, I didn't realize," she said sardonically. "I'm really sorry, Ned. Less than a carat. What a shame." Still, it had to be worth more than Alison's forgotten pearls. Such cheap trinkets, Marlo thought. A few hundred here, a few hundred there—Ned's earring and Alison's necklace put together were worth more than Marlo earned in a good week.

"I'm starving," he announced.

"Look in the bag by your feet," she said, gesturing toward the shopping bag with the leftovers from Jeremy's and her supper.

Ned poked around in the bag and pulled out a brownie. "This is all you got?" he complained as he unwrapped it, a task he executed clumsily due to the handcuffs.

"Eat it and shut up," she snapped. Her mind drifted stubbornly back to Jeremy. How nice it would have been if they'd been able to spend all last night together, thinking of nothing but each other. They could have brought their general-store purchases inside and had a picnic on the bed. They could have fed each other pieces of the brownies, and then they could have licked the crumbs off each other's fingers, and tasted the flavor on each other's lips....

A heavy warmth seized her. She sucked in a breath and willed the sensation away. She mustn't think such things. She was on her way to the Connecticut Gold Coast, a place where people like Jeremy hired people like her to clean up their messes.

He'd had his thrill for the year. He'd held a revolver and aided a detective. He'd made love to a woman who made noise. He'd taken his little walk on the wild side. If, for some unfathomable reason, he wanted to see Marlo socially once they were both back in Connecticut, she wouldn't see him. She wasn't going to date a guy who thought the most exciting thing about her was her gun. She wasn't going to be his charity project or his exotic entertainment.

She wasn't going to fall in love with him, because if she did... If she did she'd be vulnerable. She'd let her defenses down. And when he got tired of her, or found himself a woman with a better genealogy or a more reputable address, Marlo would be bereft. She'd be demolished. When you gave yourself over to love like that you were left with no protection.

She wasn't going to love him. That was that. Mind over matter, head over heart. Whatever that dark, sinuous, possessive emotion filling her soul was, she refused to call it love.

IT WAS EARLY EVENING when she finally steered onto the circular driveway that curved to the oak and leaded-glass front door of Porter Havelock's house. Ned had dozed through the final two hours of the drive. He'd told her he hadn't gotten much sleep last night, and she'd invited him to go ahead and rest. His snoring was far preferable to his snarling and empty threats.

"We're here," she said, nudging him awake.

His eyes fluttered open and he sat up. He scrutinized the imposing Tudor-style mansion and swore under his breath. "This is her old man's house?"

"That's right."

"It looks like a prison."

"A pretty classy prison, if you ask me," said Marlo. She bet a lot of convicts would volunteer for incarceration in Havelock's Southport estate. "Buck up, kid. It's show time."

"What's her old man gonna do to me?"

"I have no idea."

He looked momentarily panicked. "Alison was with me on it, you know? He can't lay the whole thing on me. If he has the police here I swear I'm gonna finger her. She's going down with me."

Alison rolled her eyes at his melodramatic language. The boy had obviously spent too much time watching inferior cop shows on television.

In a meaner mood, she would probably tell him he was headed straight for jail. But after so many hours of driving, she was feeling reflective and melancholy. Delivering Ned to Porter marked the end, not just of this one case but of her silly daydreams about belonging in a rich man's house, in a rich man's arms, in a rich man's world. It was over now, and she felt too drained, both physically and spiritually, to give Ned a hard time.

"As far as I know, he's not going to have you arrested," she said, swinging open her car door. "Come on. Let's get this over with."

Porter's housekeeper responded to the doorbell, opening the heavy door wide and beckoning them into the marble-floored foyer. "What's his mood?" Marlo asked as Ned shifted nervously from one foot to the other and mopped at the sweat accumulating along his brow.

The housekeeper shrugged. "Not so bad at all," she said in her lilting calypso accent. "He hasn't touched a drop of liquor all day, and he and the others have been talking."

"What others? My father—?"

"Oh, no, he hasn't been around here today. He's gone back to his office. He said now that you've got Alison back home he can take care of other business."

"So who else is here?" Marlo asked.

"Just Alison and her boyfriend."

"Hey, wait a minute," Ned objected. "*I'm* her—"

"You know, the tall fellow, the architect," the housekeeper clarified. "The fellow she goes out with."

Marlo felt her lunch return on her. She swallowed it back down, a sour-tasting lump that lodged somewhere below her rib cage. She was too wiped out to face Jeremy right now—especially in the Havelock house, this bastion of wealth where he felt right at home, where he was referred to as "Alison's boyfriend."

She didn't belong here. She didn't feel comfortable in posh vestibules of elegant mansions. Even Ned, with his ruffian style and his hands manacled, looked more in his element than she felt here at Porter Havelock's house.

But Jeremy… He did belong here. He fit right in. This was his milieu.

What an idiot she'd been to think they could make a go of it. Up in Maine, for one insane night, she'd let herself forget about how very different they were. But now the truth was staring her in the face. Jeremy belonged here, and she didn't.

He might have managed to capture her heart—which she had no intention of letting him keep—but she did have her pride. What she had to do was marshal her defenses for a few minutes, put up a good front and hand Ned over to Porter—and then get the hell out of here. She could do it without lashing out at Jeremy for his life of privilege, for his unforgivable ability to convince her that reality didn't count. She could deliver her prisoner in a professional, dignified manner and then return to her own world with her ego more or less intact.

At least she hoped she could.

"Okay," she said, taking Ned's elbow and steering him down the hall behind the housekeeper, who led them into Porter's study—a cloyingly decorated room Marlo had been in only once before, the morning after the kidnapping, when Porter had briefed her about his daughter's abduction. He was currently sitting on top of his desk, looking remarkably chipper. Jeremy had been seated on the pink-hued leather sofa across the room, but the minute the housekeeper ushered Marlo and Ned inside he jumped to his feet. At the sight of Marlo his face brightened with a radiant smile.

Before Jeremy could say anything, Porter had her in a crushing hug, the awkwardness of which was magnified by the fact that the top of his head came only up to the bridge of her nose. "You," he boomed, "are everything your father said and then some. You got my daughter back, you brought me this . . . this vermin—" he favored Ned with a distasteful look "—and the media never heard one word about it. You're the best, Marlo. I don't know how to thank you.''

"It's my job," she said, disengaging herself from Porter and twisting her key ring until she found the key to the handcuffs. She opened them, and Ned made a big show of rubbing the chafed skin of his wrists.

Porter ignored the kid. "I'm a new man, thanks to you," he crowed. "My daughter's back, in more ways than one, and it's all thanks to you."

She offered a modest shrug.

"I'll bet I owe you a fortune," he said, moving around his desk. He wagged a threatening finger at Ned as he passed him, muttered, "You stay put, mister," and then rummaged in the top drawer of his desk for a pen.

She felt Jeremy edging toward her from behind. "How was your drive?" he asked.

The last thing she wanted to do was exchange small talk with him. "It was fine," she managed to answer, keeping her attention focused on the self-described new man groping through his desk drawer. "Porter, I'm really exhausted. I'd like to go home. Do you want me to talk to the police first?"

"No." He stopped pawing in his desk drawer long enough to shoot a venomous look at Ned. "I'll take care of him myself."

Marlo suffered a twinge of apprehension. She couldn't leave if there was any chance Porter might have some unlawful fate in mind for Ned. "What are you going to do?" she asked warily.

Porter sized up the young man, who was struggling to maintain his surly expression but not succeeding. "Oh, I think we'll start by calling his mom and having a little chat. I've learned a lot from your father about parent-child relationships," he explained, turning back to

Marlo. "So, I'm going to call his mom, and then she can come up here and get him and put him on a leash until he's properly trained. She lives about an hour and a half away—plenty of time for me to make sure the kid understands how nice I'm being by not having him arrested, and for me to describe exactly what I'll do to him if he ever comes within a hundred yards of my daughter again." Porter hesitated, his brow dipping slightly. "He isn't dangerous, is he?"

"He thinks he is," Marlo answered.

Porter gauged the young man, then shrugged. "I can handle him. Me and Jeremy. Right, tough guy?" he added, winking at Jeremy. "Alison tells me Jeremy was quite a hero up in Maine."

Marlo gnashed her teeth. "Oh, quite," she echoed caustically, refusing to let her eyes meet his. "Look, Porter, if you don't need me—"

"Hang on a second," he said, resuming his search through the desk drawer. He pulled out a flat leatherbound book and opened it.

It was a checkbook. Porter was going to write her a check. He was going to pay her. Here, with Jeremy to witness it, Porter was going to provide the ultimate proof that Marlo was nothing more than an employee, a hired hand, a peon whose services could be bought by rich folks.

Anger, resentment and indignation bubbled up inside her. "We can work it out another time," she said quickly.

He glanced up to see her sidling toward the door. "No, I insist," he declared. "How much do I owe you?"

"I have no idea," she retorted, more and more anxious to clear out. "I'll have Ida mail you an invoice—"

"You've got to take something," Porter persisted, scribbling digits onto the check. "Take it, Marlo. We'll settle the balance later. Use this toward a new car. Come on, sweetheart, take it. It's yours.''

She stared miserably at the check he extended to her. She needed the money desperately. She'd expended a fair amount of her own cash on this case, and she'd had little enough to spare when she'd started. Porter Havelock's check would go a long way to resuscitating her depleted bank account.

If Jeremy wasn't there she would take it in an instant. But to have him standing less than five feet away, watching as Porter Havelock paid her off, as he handed her a pale blue rectangle that symbolized exactly who and what Marlo was and how she related to these people... It was humiliating.

"I'll have Ida send you a bill," she muttered, then bolted for the door before he could stop her.

She was out the front door before Jeremy caught up to her. He grabbed her shoulder and spun her around to face him. In the hazy lavender light of dusk he looked gorgeous—freshly showered and shaved, dressed in a crisp white shirt and fashionably tailored slacks. Marlo felt unbearably grungy from her long, exhausting drive, and he appeared as ruggedly handsome as a model for some pricy cologne.

As soon as her eyes met his they misted over. *Don't fall apart!* she ordered herself, stiffening against his touch even as his hold on her softened, as he slid his arm fully around her and tried to pull her to himself.

Clearly aware of her resistance, he scowled. "Was it that bad a trip?" he asked.

"No," she replied coldly, refusing him the satisfaction of glimpsing her bruised emotions. "No, the trip was fine. Just tiring. I'd really like to go."

He massaged the knotted muscles between her shoulder blades and she felt a surging, fluid warmth inside her, identical to the warmth she experienced every time she'd let memories of the previous night enter her mind. Averting her face, she twisted out of his embrace and marched to the trunk of her car to get Ned's suitcase.

Jeremy watched her, obviously trying to make sense of her hostility. "I'll admit Porter was pretty tactless," he said as she tossed the suitcase onto the brick front step and slammed the trunk shut. "He shouldn't have tried to force his money on you. It's just that he's so happy—"

"And his favorite way to celebrate is to buy people off," she grunted, moving around the car to the driver's side and opening the door. "Swell. I'm happy he's happy." She reached into the back seat for Alison's jumpsuit, then dug the pearl necklace out of her purse. She carried the items to the front step and draped them on top of Ned's suitcase.

"He and Alison have both learned something from this," Jeremy went on—as if Marlo was supposed to care. "She's resting right now, but Porter told me they spent most of the day talking, trying to come to terms with why she did what she did. I think…maybe I'm being overly optimistic, but I think they're going to come through this in good shape."

"Great."

"He's already been in touch with Ned's mother and stepfather," Jeremy went on. "Your father dug up the number, and Porter called them this morning. The mother said she had no idea how to get through to Ned, and she'd all but given up on him. Just talking to her gave Porter a lot of insight on how he'd messed up his relationship with Alison."

"Let's hear it for insight," Marlo muttered.

"Personally, I think Ned could use the services of a skilled psychologist."

"Of course. An expensive shrink. What an upper-class solution."

Jeremy studied her, apparently unsure of how to interpret her seething anger. "You've just spent twelve hours in a car with him. What would you recommend?"

"I'd recommend a lower-class solution: hard time at Rahway State Prison in Jersey. We don't need him in our local prisons—they're too crowded as it is." She sighed and shook her head. "But Porter won't have him arrested, because that might implicate Alison, and he couldn't bear to have his precious little princess implicated. No, he'll probably just pay someone to beat Ned up. He loves paying people to do his dirty business for him." She peered up at Jeremy and her lips twisted into a bitter smile. "Then again, maybe you'd volunteer to beat Ned up for free." With that, she turned and headed back to the car.

He stopped her, once again grabbing her arm. His fingers were gentle this time, though, as if he knew she wouldn't run away. She wished she could; she wished she had the strength to resist the sensual power of his grip, the pulsing heat of his fingers as they traced circles against her skin.

"Okay. I give up," he murmured. "What's wrong?"

"What could possibly be wrong?" she inquired disingenuously. "Porter's happy, Alison's happy, you're a hero and I'm going to get paid. Happiness all around, eh?"

"I'm not happy," he argued. "What about us?"

"What about us? You're back home now. You can go back to your job as Alison's number-one escort. I'm sure that would please her and Porter."

He seemed annoyed. "Marlo—I thought we were clear on that. Alison and I have absolutely no relationship. I explained that to Porter as soon as Alison and I got here. There was lots of hysteria, screaming and yelling and tears, but I explained to Porter that Alison and I are nothing more than friends."

"You sure know how to pick your friends," Marlo remarked dryly.

"Marlo." Jeremy's hand tightened around her, and he sighed. "Alison and Porter are determined to get things straightened out between them. I wish I could say the same for you and me." He bowed and kissed the smooth skin of her forehead. "Maybe you think what happened up in Maine was an aberration—"

Terrific. Now he was going to resort to ten-dollar words. "I think that what happened in Maine was a mistake," she cut him off.

"A mistake?" His eyebrows dipped in a frown that was part bewilderment and part sheer anger. "Correct me if I'm wrong, Marlo, but as I recall, we were fantastic together."

"Yeah, sure," she snapped. "For a few minutes there, we were actually on the same wavelength." She refused to think about how wonderful it had felt to talk to him— and to listen to him. She didn't want to dwell on their camaraderie, on the moments of pure friendship they'd shared. If she concentrated only on the sex—incredible as it had been—she might not get ambushed by thoughts of love.

"It was more than a few minutes," he argued, "and it was more than being on the same wavelength. I'm talking about *us*, Marlo, about how I see things in a new way when I'm with you. I'm crazy about you."

She let out a shaky breath and stared at the grass beneath her feet. She was crazy about him, too. She'd been crazy to let him into her life in the first place. No matter how she looked at it, the whole situation was crazy.

Evidently he sensed her uncertainty. He folded his hand around hers and lifted it to his lips, then planted a kiss on the pale scar on her index finger.

"I don't want to love you," she whispered.

He smiled hopefully. "Meaning you do love me?"

"Meaning I can't." With a fierce shrug, she freed herself from his clasp. "It's too risky."

"Where's the risk?"

She gave him a hard stare. "The risk is that sooner or later you're going to walk away. You're going to go back to your own world. And when you do I'll be left with nothing. The odds aren't with me, Jeremy. It's a sucker's bet, and I won't take it."

He appeared incredulous. "Why can't you have a little faith in me?"

"Because it's dangerous," she replied. "Faith is the stuff of heroics. I'm too realistic for that. I've got to protect myself."

Denying him the opportunity to refute her, she climbed into her car. Jeremy remained beside the driveway, visibly perturbed, as she ignited the engine and drove away. When she reached the end of the curving driveway, she peered into her rearview mirror and saw him standing where she'd left him, still frowning, still staring after her.

Her index finger tingled where his lips had grazed it. Her back smoldered in the aftermath of his sensuous caresses.

Damn it, she had to protect herself.

CHAPTER THIRTEEN

JEREMY COASTED TO A HALT near the trailer, which stood at the north end of the site some distance from where the first foundations of the office complex were being poured. He didn't notice Porter's Mercedes among the cars and trucks parked along the perimeter of the site. Porter had lately become a hard man to track down.

The foreman spotted the green MG and jogged over. He was sweating profusely beneath the hot July sun; safety necessitated that he wear heavy steel-toed work boots, thick denim pants and a bright yellow hard hat. Although Jeremy had on a summer-weight business suit, he automatically donned his own hard hat before climbing out of his car.

"Hey, Jeremy," the foreman greeted him before announcing, "if you're looking for the boss man, he isn't here."

Jeremy checked his watch and scowled. It was nearly three o'clock. "Where is he?" he asked, trying not to let his exasperation show. "I talked to his secretary this morning and she said he'd be on-site all day."

The foreman shrugged. "His daughter came by around noon. Porter was taking her out for lunch. They still aren't back."

In spite of his frustration at not being able to see Porter, Jeremy couldn't help but be pleased by the news that Porter was spending time with Alison. He knew they'd been seeing a family therapist regularly, and it seemed to be doing wonders for them both. Alison's hair was growing back, and she looked curiously younger and sweeter than she used to. And Porter...Porter was taking long lunches. Obviously he recognized that his life didn't begin and end with work, that he had to make room in it for other things. Like lunches with his daughter. Slowly but surely, they seemed to be working out their problems, and Jeremy was happy for them.

On the other hand, he had problems of his own, foremost among them the fact that Marlo McGinnis had an unlisted phone number.

He assumed that in her line of work such a precaution was essential—indeed, he'd found no listing in Bridgeport under her father's name, either. The only relevant listing in the directory was for McGinnis & McGinnis, Inc. He'd telephoned the agency dozens of times in the week since he'd returned from Maine, but every time he'd gotten through a receptionist had run interference for Marlo. The first few days, the receptionist had simply told Jeremy that Marlo was out. That morning, however, she'd said, "Look, Mr. Kent, I think she really doesn't want to hear from you anymore. So do yourself a favor and stop calling."

He took her advice, not because he was the least bit willing to give up on Marlo but because phoning her office obviously wasn't accomplishing anything. He had to reach her at her home, where there was no receptionist to screen him out. To do that, though, he'd have to wrangle her home number from Porter.

Getting through to Marlo was only half the battle, of course. Once Jeremy had her ear, he had to convince her to set aside her misgivings and trust him. Given that she was a woman who made her living investigating untrustworthy people—and given her rabid dislike of the upper class—he knew it wasn't going to be easy. But damn it, he wasn't just a member of the upper class. He was an individual, a human being, a man with emotions and passions. He was admittedly someone who had never had to work too hard for anything in the past—but he was ready to leap through hoops of flame now, if his efforts would win Marlo's favor.

He loved her. He loved her spirit and strength, her keen intelligence and her pragmatism, her beauty and her passion and even her mule-headedness. In a strange way her stubbornness increased his love for her; it forced him to exert himself, to extend himself, to prove himself. He had never before known how far he would go for someone he loved. Now, thanks to Marlo's infuriating, utterly unreasonable intractability, he was going to find out.

"So, you don't know when Porter's coming back?" he asked the foreman.

The foreman shrugged again. "No idea."

Jeremy's mind whirled. He had to get into the trailer. Porter's desk was there, his records, his on-site telephone. Jeremy had to get inside.

In Maine he had discovered he possessed a knack for deception. If he could lie there, he could lie here, where the stakes were so much higher.

He lifted his briefcase from the passenger seat of the car. "I have some papers here I promised to drop off for Porter," he ad-libbed. "I won't be able to come back later. Do you suppose I could just leave them inside on his desk?"

The foreman considered for a minute, then started toward the wooden steps that led up to the trailer door. "Sure, go on in and leave them," he said, unlocking the door and then clomping down the steps. "Make sure you lock up when you leave. I gotta get back to where they're pouring." He nodded toward the concrete mixers and then gave Jeremy a farewell wave. "Catch you later."

Suppressing a triumphant grin, Jeremy returned the foreman's wave and then vaulted up the stairs and into the trailer. The interior was gloomy and cluttered with file cabinets, tables, desks, folding metal chairs, a water bubbler and a small refrigerator. Plot maps were pinned to the walls and the aroma of coffee permeated the dusty air.

Jeremy moved directly to Porter's desk and opened the metal Rolodex sitting on it. He spun the wheel to *M* and then scanned the cards one at a time. None for Marlo McGinnis, but he found one with her father's home address and phone number typed onto it. He tore a pink message slip from the pad near the phone and jotted down the information, then folded the paper and stuffed it into an inner pocket of his suit jacket.

He closed the Rolodex and left the trailer, locking the door behind him. Tossing his briefcase and hard hat onto the seat next to him, he settled behind the wheel, started the engine and drove away. This detective business wasn't so difficult—if you were willing to sneak and snoop and lie through your teeth.

When he returned to Pace & Hartley he was met with pandemonium. His design for the hospital extension had just been chosen by the hospital's board of directors and everyone had been hunting for him in the warren of offices, conference rooms and drafting rooms that com-

prised the firm's headquarters. As soon as he reappeared
in the reception area he was besieged with well-wishers.
Several people thumped his back; someone shoved a glass
of Cutty Sark into his hand; his secretary rattled a two-
inch stack of specs and contracts beneath his nose.

He was thrilled. He was gratified. But he was in no
mood to celebrate. More than a lucrative contract for the
firm, more than the exhilaration of creating a successful
architectural design, he wanted Marlo. He wanted those
dark eyes of hers gazing at him in desire, and those long
legs of hers wrapped around him, and that sharp mind of
hers focused on him, only him.

Typical rich guy, he thought disparagingly. He had so
much and still he wanted more. He wanted the one thing
that seemed beyond his reach.

"Thanks," he said to the three young associates currently gathered around him, singing his praises. He
handed one of them his glass of Scotch and extricated
himself from their circle. "If you'll excuse me—"

His secretary hounded him down the hall to his office,
still waving the specs and contracts at him. "Jeremy,
you've got to review these—"

"Later," he snapped, shutting himself inside his office and locking the door. He pulled the pink slip of paper from his pocket, carefully unfolded it and punched
the numbers on his phone.

Not surprisingly, no one answered.

Stan McGinnis probably wouldn't be home for at least
an hour. Jeremy couldn't remain shut up inside his office all that time, not with a party in his honor raging
outside the door and a secretary well practiced in the art
of nagging ready to ambush him. He'd have to go out
and join the festivities. He'd have to pretend nothing was

more important in his life than his work, his colleagues, his brilliant designs and all the money they garnered for the firm. He'd have to pretend he wasn't obsessed with an ex-cop from the wrong side of the tracks, a woman who thought freshwater pearls were precious jewels, who could wrestle a twenty-one-year-old man to the ground without blinking an eye, who was a connoisseur of fast food and knew the words to "Paradise," who hated being helpless and who made love with joyous vocal abandon....

Damn. How was he supposed to go outside and accept congratulations for all he had when he honestly believed that without Marlo he had nothing?

He'd fake it, that was how. Like a detective, he'd put up a false front. He'd lie his way through it.

Sighing, he tucked the pink slip of paper back into his pocket and left the office to join the party.

STAN HAD JUST UNWRAPPED a cigar when the doorbell rang. If it was Marlo, she'd give him hell for smoking—but if it was Marlo she'd use the back door. He balanced the cigar between his teeth, struck a match and lit the end, taking his time, making sure he had the thing going.

The doorbell rang again. He shook out the match, filled his mouth with flavorful smoke and left the kitchen. On his way to the front hall he glimpsed the television in the living room. The Red Sox were playing the Yankees. Whoever it was at the door, he'd better not waste too much of Stan's time. On those occasions when the notorious baseball rivalry between Boston and New York was being put to the test, Stan McGinnis didn't take kindly to interruptions.

He switched on the porch light and opened the door. Through the screen he recognized Jeremy Kent.

Stan had been puzzling over Jeremy Kent for some time now. He'd met him a couple of times at the North Stamford office complex Porter was building, and thought the architect seemed like a pleasant young man. When Porter had mentioned that Kent was taking Alison out, Stan had thought they made a good pair. But how on earth Kent had infiltrated Marlo's car and traveled up to Maine with her Stan couldn't begin to figure.

It wasn't like Marlo to do something that irregular. She was always so cautious, so straight. The only thing that kept Stan from worrying about her in the business was that she didn't take stupid chances. Even though the kidnapping had been a fraud, chasing after Alison and her schoolmates could have been dangerous. Why had Marlo compounded the risk by letting Jeremy Kent tag along?

When he'd asked her about it, she had mumbled something about how Jeremy knew how to fix cars and since her Honda was on the fritz she'd thought he would come in handy. A shabby excuse if ever Stan heard one. He'd noticed the way her eyes had avoided his, the way her cheeks had darkened and her breath had caught. It didn't take a trained detective to guess that she was infatuated with the guy. But when Stan had continued interrogating her, she'd sworn it wasn't so. "I brought him along because I thought he'd come in handy," she'd insisted. "As it turned out, he did. Get off my case, Dad."

She'd been in a terrible mood ever since. Six days now—too long for the monthly blues. This was a genuine funk, and he couldn't seem to shake her out of it. Praising her on the success of her work in Maine didn't help. Receiving a bonus from Porter actually seemed to make things worse. Stan wished to hell he knew what was eating her.

Seeing Jeremy Kent standing on his front porch gave him an idea of what it could be. "What do you want?" he said.

"May I come in?" Jeremy asked.

Stan sized him up. He was wearing a pale gray suit that reeked of good tailoring and good taste. The collar of his shirt was unbuttoned, the knot of his tie loosened. He looked as if he'd come here straight from work. "I'm watching a game," Stan alerted him, then nudged open the screen door. If Jeremy started getting on Stan's nerves, he'd blow cigar smoke at him.

Jeremy stepped inside and followed Stan through the arched doorway into the living room. "The Yanks and the Sox," he observed.

"You follow the sport?" Stan asked as he settled himself in his easy chair.

"Actually, I'm a Mets fan."

"The Mets," Stan grunted disdainfully. Still, that was better than being a Yankees fan.

Jeremy lowered himself onto the worn cushions of the sofa and watched the game for a minute. Without looking at Stan, he said, "I need to talk to Marlo."

Stan was cagey enough not to let his expression change. "She hasn't lived here in years," he said, also addressing the television.

"I know. She's got an unlisted phone number, though, and—"

"So do I. You found me, didn't you?"

"Yes. And now I'm hoping you'll help me find her."

Stan turned to study his visitor. Jeremy Kent had always struck him as a cultured fellow, not the sort to go pushing his way into other people's lives. But now, as he looked the kid over, he acknowledged that there was a helluva lot more to him than the polish of affluence. Jeremy had broad shoulders and a pugnacious chin. This was a guy who could fight if he had to. "Why should I help you find her?" he asked.

Jeremy turned as well, ignoring the television and staring earnestly at Stan. "I'm in love with her."

For some reason, Stan wasn't surprised. He should have been—while he considered Marlo an exceptionally lovable woman, she was standoffish around men in general, and she'd never had anything to do with men like Jeremy Kent.

But Stan knew as soon as Jeremy spoke that what he'd said was the truth. "In love with her, huh," he repeated, puffing on his cigar and mulling over his words. "You know, Marlo's a modern woman. It's not like you've got to come and ask me for permission to date her."

"I'm not asking for permission," Jeremy explained. "I'm asking you to help me find her. She's hiding from me, Stan, and I don't know why."

Stan scrutinized him through the gray smoke. "Sure you know why," he said.

Jeremy lowered his eyes to his hands. "Because she thinks I'm too wealthy," he guessed, then thought again. "There's got to be more than that."

"She's afraid of getting hurt," Stan told him.

Jeremy lifted his gaze to Stan again. "Who isn't?"

"You think she could hurt you?"

"She *is* hurting me." Jeremy sighed. "Tell me how to reach her, Stan, or I swear I'm going to camp out overnight in front of your office and tackle her when she arrives at work tomorrow."

Stan could believe Jeremy would do that—and the fact that he would elevated him in Stan's esteem. He smiled and tapped the coal of his cigar against the ashtray at his elbow to remove the loose ashes. "I can't tell you her home address," he said. "That would be a real breach of trust."

"Then tell me what you can."

"She isn't home tonight, anyway."

"Oh, God," Jeremy groaned. "She's on a date."

"No—on a job."

Jeremy looked greatly relieved. "Where?"

"She's doing a stakeout on some two-timer. But look, you really can't go messing with her when she's working. You'll break her concentration."

"I won't," Jeremy vowed. "I'll wait until after she's done with the stakeout—"

"And then what'll you do?" Stan asked, both curious and wary.

"I'll tell her I love her," Jeremy replied simply.

Stan gave him one final, assessing look. Jeremy Kent was all right. He didn't need Stan's approval to court Marlo, but Stan did approve. All his fine breeding notwithstanding, the guy had moxie. Stan liked that.

"Okay," he said. "She's in Stratford. I'll get a map and show you where."

MARLO STARED at the house, waiting for the second-floor bedroom light to come back on and thinking about the insanity wrought by love. Love made people act dangerously, irrationally, selfishly. That morning, love had driven Loraine Novicki, a thirty-four-year-old mother of two, to enter Marlo's office and agree to fork over a sum of money in return for information about where her husband was spending his Monday nights. Forty minutes ago, love had brought Joe Novicki to this modest split-level house a few blocks from Wooster Park in Stratford. He'd let himself in with his own key—Marlo had recorded the event with her camera—and, judging by the lights in the windows, the party had moved with undue speed from the living room up the stairs to the bedroom.

Marlo was parked a couple of houses down and across the street, under the cover of a leafy maple tree that shielded her car from the glaring light of a street lamp. She cradled her camera in her lap. One quick call on her cellular phone to Angie at Southern New England Telephone informed Marlo that at that address the telephone service was billed to Cynthia Shirer. Usually if a woman was married the phone was listed in her husband's name, so Marlo deduced that Cynthia Shirer was single—divorced or whatever.

Only one marriage was being torn apart by this adultery, Marlo concluded. Love was wreaking only fifty percent devastation. Most of the time in cases like these, there was a cuckolded husband along with a betrayed wife. Sometimes the two forsaken spouses teamed up and split Marlo's bill.

Just one embittered spouse this time—one spouse and two children. Why would any reasonable person voluntarily open herself to the risk of this sort of hurt?

Obviously, it wasn't voluntary. Sometimes, despite your best efforts, you fell in love with the wrong person. Sometimes the most cautious woman could be suckered by a pair of gentle gray eyes, a soothing voice and a pair of hands that could string a pearl necklace around her throat and make her believe the impossible. Sometimes it happened.

The best you could do was shore up your defenses before it was too late, fend off the emotions before they overtook you, keep your head on straight and play it safe. Eventually the danger would pass.

Or so she hoped.

She glimpsed a flash of white in her side mirror, the reflection of a pair of headlights as a car turned the corner onto the street. She slithered down in her seat, trying to be as unobtrusive as possible. Peeking over the sill of her open window, she watched the headlights grow progressively brighter in her side mirror as the car neared her. It was cruising slowly, much too slowly....

An MG. A green MG convertible.

She bolted upright as the car pulled to the curb behind her. Cripes. Of all the people she didn't want to see, of all the times she didn't want to see him—*how had he found her?*

She listened with increasing dread to the sounds of his car door opening and closing, then his footsteps against the asphalt as he approached her. Her stomach twisted, her heart raced and her palms grew clammy. This was not a good state to be in during a stakeout.

Jeremy leaned over her open window and gazed in at her. "Why have you refused my calls?" he asked.

As if there was nothing else going on in the world. As if Marlo wasn't trying to do her job, trying to keep a low profile on this quiet residential block, trying to earn what passed for a living. As if all that mattered was Jeremy and Marlo, the ultimate mismatch.

"Jeremy, please," she whispered, "I'm working."

He braced his hands against the roof of her car and stared in at her. His stance had the unfortunate effect of parting the flaps of his unbuttoned jacket and stretching his shirt taut across his chest. Marlo didn't want any reminders of his alluring torso. For that matter, she didn't want any reminders of the rest of his body. She didn't want to remember the tenderness in his eyes, or the sweetness of his mouth on her. She didn't want to be tantalized by him the way she'd been tantalized by Alison's freshwater pearls. She didn't want unattainable things dangled before her eyes, taunting her.

She didn't want to be vulnerable to Jeremy Kent.

"Are you going to answer my question?" he asked.

"No, I'm not," she whispered through clenched teeth. "I wish you'd get the hell out of here."

"After trying so long and so hard to talk to you, Marlo, I'm afraid I can't grant that wish."

In spite of herself she felt a rush of pleasure at the thought that he'd tried long and hard to reach her. It was awfully flattering. But flattery was merely a ploy, just another way to sucker her, and she resisted its power to sway her. "You're going to spoil my stakeout," she muttered. "Can we talk about this some other time?"

"You've lost the privilege of picking the time," Jeremy declared. His tone grew gentle. "Marlo, I—"

The porch light went on at Cynthia Shirer's house. Marlo lifted her camera to her eye. "Get out of the way," she said, her tone low but urgent. "Now. I'm not kidding, Jeremy."

The front door opened. Praying that Jeremy would make himself scarce, Marlo blocked him out of her mind as best she could and concentrated on framing the scene with her viewfinder and capturing it on film. Luck seemed to be with her—the straying husband stepped out onto the porch accompanied by an attractive young woman dressed in a terry-cloth robe. She gave him a quick good-bye kiss, which Marlo caught with a snap of the shutter. She kept the shutter depressed, nailing at least three more pictures of the amorous couple before the woman in the robe went inside and closed the door. Joe Novicki romped down the porch steps, jogged toward his car parked across the street from Marlo's, and then spotted her.

She cursed. Joe Novicki cursed. Jeremy, bless his high-class breeding, only said, "Uh-oh."

Ignoring him, Marlo shoved her camera under the passenger seat and groped for the ignition key. Joe Novicki was charging toward her, his face contorted in a rabid grimace. "Loraine sent you!" he roared, tossing aside any pretense at discretion. "How much did she pay you, huh? How much? I'll pay you more. Gimme the film!"

Not bothering to answer, Marlo turned on the engine.

"Double!" he pleaded, his face growing florid as he advanced on her car. "I'll pay you double. Gimme me the film."

Marlo wanted to drive away. But Jeremy had started forward to intercept Novicki. She couldn't just abandon Jeremy to Novicki's flying fists.

"Go, Marlo!" he shouted over his shoulder to her. "Get out of here!"

Novicki shoved him toward the front bumper, then lifted a fist-sized stone from the side of the road and hurled it at the open window of her car. She shifted into reverse and hit the gas. The rock bounced off her front fender and landed in the road. Envisioning the scratch it would leave, she cursed again.

Maybe Jeremy "Grease Monkey" Kent could handle a dinged fender, she thought. This whole foul-up was his fault. He'd been too conspicuous, he'd called attention to her, he'd let himself be pushed in front of her car so she had to drive backward to elude Novicki's rock.

Which Novicki had retrieved, she noticed with alarm. He stood in the middle of the street, winding up for his next pitch. She shifted into first gear, floored the pedal and let out a shriek as the rock soared directly toward her windshield. Sliding her foot from the clutch, she let the engine stall out and buried her face in her arms an instant before impact.

"Are you all right?" Jeremy murmured. His voice was coming from her right, and when she lifted her head she saw that he was climbing into the car beside her. Bewildered, she turned to view her windshield. The entire driver's side was splintered into a spiderweb of cracks, but the glass had held against the stone. She couldn't see through the windshield, but it had kept the stone from hitting her head.

"Three cheers for safety glass," she muttered.

"He's gone," Jeremy said, pointing to the Beretta zooming down the street.

Marlo ignited the engine and tore after him.

"Marlo, what are you doing?"

"Chasing him."

"You've got the photographs," Jeremy observed calmly. "You did your job. Why—?"

"That man could have killed me!" Novicki turned the corner and she followed him. She had dangerously little visibility through the splintered glass, but she wasn't going to let a minor obstacle like that slow her down. "He could have killed me, and he demolished my windshield. I'm going to make him pay."

Jeremy said nothing for a minute. Then: "We should have taken my car."

"Twenty-twenty hindsight," she grumbled. "Help me out here—I can't see a thing."

"Wonderful." Jeremy stopped staring at her and focused on the road. "There's a red light coming up."

"I see it." Actually, she saw what looked like fifteen fragmented red lights. "Where's Novicki?"

"Who?"

"The sleazeball. The philanderer. Never mind," she grumbled, angling her head out the open window so she could identify the Beretta.

"I think he's going to make a right turn," Jeremy observed.

"Yeah." She followed Novicki onto Huntington Road.

"Marlo—there's a lot of traffic here. You shouldn't be driving with your car in this condition."

"Do you want to get out?" she asked. She knew Jeremy was right; she ought to cool off and take her film full of incriminating evidence home. But this was a matter of principle. Novicki could have killed her. She wasn't about to let him get away.

"There's a van cutting in front of you," Jeremy said in an admirably calm voice.

Nodding, she swerved out of the van's way. "You understand this is your fault," she said.

"My fault? What did I do?"

"You got my windshield destroyed. I was doing just fine until you came along."

He didn't respond immediately. Squinting through the fractured glass, she reflected on the profound truth in her words. She *had* been doing fine until Jeremy entered her life, until he'd insinuated his way into her heart. Until she'd let herself fall for him.

"Yeah," he murmured, reading her thoughts. "I was doing just fine, too. But you came along, and I don't want to let you go. I love you, Marlo."

She almost drove up onto the curb. She could have blamed her bad driving on the sorry state of her windshield, but in her heart she knew that what made her lose track of the road were Jeremy's words playing on her mind, on her soul.

"How did you find me, anyway?" she asked, unable to comment directly on his profession of love.

"Your father told me where you were—red light!"

Seeing Novicki's Beretta scoot through the intersection, Marlo ran the light. "What did you do to make my father tell you? Torture him?"

Jeremy winced at her illegal maneuver. "I told him I was in love with you," he said.

Oh, God. He'd told her father. He must be serious. Her eyes welled with tears, making her already hampered vision even worse. "I can't handle this," she moaned. "Oh, Jeremy—did you really tell him that?"

"I really did. I guess he believed me, too, because the next thing I knew he was pulling out the map and showing me where I could find you. Look out here—the road wiggles around—"

"I know. We're heading into Main Street. You really love me, Jeremy?"

"I told you you were the most exciting woman I've ever met, and I meant it. Right now—" Marlo came within inches of clipping a double-parked truck, and even Jeremy's exemplary upbringing couldn't prevent him from swearing under his breath "—you're a little more exciting than I'd like."

The Beretta pulled to the curb in front of a bar. "He's stopping," she shouted triumphantly, slowing down as Novicki leaped out of his car and vanished inside the bar. She double-parked next to him, pinning his car in, and climbed out.

The bar was dark and dingy, the only illumination coming from neon wall signs advertising various brands of beer. Jeremy eyed the building with obvious distaste. "Are we going in there?"

"I am," she said, then wrapped her arms around him and gave him a swift, hard kiss. "I'll be right back." She yanked open the door and elbowed her way past the crowd of men loitering near the entry. Once she settled the score with Novicki, she could entertain a discussion about love with Jeremy. She could clear her mind and analyze the situation rationally. Right now, however, she was too enraged to think straight.

And anyway, it was easier to deal with revenge than love. Marlo couldn't help suspecting that she had less to fear from Novicki and a bunch of burly barflies than from Jeremy.

The bar was definitely a working-class joint. The din of voices was decidedly baritone, the proportion of tattooed biceps was well above the national average, and the television set above the bar was tuned to the Red Sox-Yankees game. The only other woman in the place turned out to be a waitress. Marlo spotted Novicki weaving his way to the rear of the narrow room and she chased after him, ignoring the suggestive remarks and propositions tossed her way by the bar's clientele.

A small alcove at the back of the bar led to the men's and women's rooms. Glancing frantically over his shoulder, Novicki cringed at the sight of Marlo advancing on him and ducked into the men's room, pulling the door shut behind himself.

He had almost killed her. He had done serious damage to her car, and despite Porter Havelock's recent largesse, Marlo couldn't very well afford to replace it with a new vehicle. If she paused and took a deep breath, she might be able to consider an alternative way of getting reimbursed by Joe Novicki.

But if she paused and took a deep breath, she might start thinking about Jeremy, thinking about what he'd said: "You came along, and I don't want to let you go." She would think about the honesty and forcefulness in his voice when he'd said, "I love you, Marlo."

She would think about his suave top-drawer life, his fancy modern house, his Westport address, his well-made clothes and his leather suitcase. She would think about his class—in every sense of the word. She would realize how deeply she loved him, and she'd be frightened.

Marching into a public men's room in a bar seemed safe in comparison.

Her invasion caused an uproar. A man at the urinal let out a resounding expletive, and one of the two brawny fellows at the sink literally grabbed her by the arms and lifted her off her feet. "Wrong door, sweet cheeks," he growled, carrying her toward the door.

"I need to talk to the creep in the second stall," she demanded.

"You need to talk to him someplace else, sugar."
Someone opened the door and he gave her a shove.

She stumbled back into a pair of familiar arms. "No
heroics," Jeremy whispered as he guided her away from
the door.

She twisted around and met his gaze. He was right.
Blind heroics rarely achieved the desired result. He had
learned that lesson up in Maine, and now he was teach-
ing Marlo, who should have known better.

"Wait here," he urged her, loosening his hold on her.
"I'll get him." He turned and disappeared into the men's
room.

She thought about Jeremy trapped in there with Joe
Novicki and those gorillas. She thought about his impeccably tailored suit and his elegant hand-stitched loafers, his sweet gray eyes and his golly-gee attitude toward
investigative work. They were going to tear him apart,
she concluded morosely. He'd gone into the bathroom in
response to some misplaced chivalrous impulse, and they
were going to make mincemeat of him.

A minute elapsed, then two, then three. Her heart
pounded frantically against her ribs. Why hadn't he come
out? What was happening to him?

The door opened, and Jeremy and Novicki emerged,
Jeremy gripping Novicki's elbow to prevent his escape.
Not that Novicki looked much like a man plotting an escape. He appeared crestfallen, although Marlo detected
no evidence that he'd been roughed up.

"All right," he grumbled, refusing to look at Marlo.
"What do you want?"

"A check for three hundred dollars ought to cover it,"
Jeremy interjected.

"Three hundred—?"

"That's a modest estimate on the cost of a new wind-shield. Consider yourself lucky."

Novicki snarled something under his breath, but he pulled out his wallet. "You don't take credit cards, do you?"

"Cash or check," said Jeremy.

More snarling. Reluctantly, Novicki pulled a blank check from his wallet. Jeremy supplied him with a snazzy gold pen and spelled Marlo's name for him, and he wrote the check. As soon as he handed it to Jeremy, Jeremy released him. Novicki shot out of the alcove, through the bar and outside.

A few onlookers chuckled, and one slapped Jeremy on the back. "Hey, stranger, those are mighty fancy threads for a bone-crusher."

Jeremy appeared confused. "Bone-crusher?" he mouthed to Marlo as he tucked the check into Marlo's shirt pocket.

"A collection agent for a loan shark," she explained as she led Jeremy through the crowd and out of the bar. She saw Novicki cowering in his Beretta, clutching the steering wheel and waiting for her to move her car so he could flee. She signalled through his closed window that he might as well cool his heels, then turned to face Jeremy. "What in God's name did you do to him?" she asked.

Jeremy grinned. "I told him he could be brought up on charges of attempted murder and assault with a deadly weapon. After that, reimbursing you for damage to the car didn't seem so bad to him."

"You really told him that?" She gave Jeremy an awe-struck look. "How did you get him to believe you?"

Jeremy shrugged. "I told him I was an agent with the FBI."

"The FBI!"

"I'm getting to be a good liar, thanks to you," he said, brushing her cheek with a kiss. "I told him you had received threats on your life, and he was currently the Bureau's prime suspect. I also told him that if he paid for your windshield like a nice boy, I'd see what I could do about getting you to hand over the film in your camera."

"But—" Marlo was about to retort that there was no way he'd ever get his hands on the film. Then she realized this had all been part of his deception. "You're pretty convincing," she said.

"I sure hope so," Jeremy murmured, gathering her into his arms. "I have the feeling I've still got a lot of convincing to do when it comes to you and me."

He did, and she didn't know how successful he'd be. But right now his embrace was convincing enough. She tilted her head back, eager to receive his kiss. Before his mouth met hers, Joe Novicki began pounding on his horn.

She sighed. "I guess we'd better let him go before he figures out you conned him." She unlocked her car and started to get in.

"Do you want me to drive?" Jeremy asked, scowling at the smashed windshield.

"No—just navigate me." She waited until he was settled in the seat beside her, then pulled away. "Can I really get this repaired for three hundred dollars?" she asked.

"Shop around. You'll probably find someone willing to do it for two hundred. You can use the balance to get your air conditioner recharged."

She tossed him a quick look, then laughed. "Let's go get your car."

They found the green MG where Jeremy had left it, on the block where Marlo had been staking out the Shirer house. Marlo stopped her car and turned to him. He was watching her, looking devastatingly handsome in his now rumpled suit and loosened silk tie. His tawny hair glinted with blond highlights beneath the street lamp, and his lips curved in a tentative smile. "What happens now?" she asked.

"You tell me you love me," he cued her. "And then I follow you home."

"To my place?"

"It's closer than mine."

She pictured her small, untidy apartment with its second-hand furnishings, her chipped dishes and all-weather carpeting, her cheap stereo and nineteen-inch portable TV with the rabbit-ear antenna because she couldn't afford twenty-five dollars a month for cable. She pictured her twin-size bed with her and Jeremy tangled up in the sheets and wondered if, after he was forced to contend with the gritty reality of her life, he would even get as far as her bedroom.

He would be better off knowing exactly who Marlo was before he made any more grand proclamations about love. "Okay," she said. "Follow me."

"Would you rather drive the MG?" he offered. "I could drive your car."

"Not when you don't know the territory. Speaking of which..." She glanced at his car. "You'd better put up the top. We'll be driving through a pretty rough neighborhood."

Jeremy nodded. He knew from experience what could happen when the convertible top was down.

The drive to Marlo's apartment seemed to take longer than usual, because she had to strain to see the road. Still, it didn't take long enough for her to sort through her tangled thoughts. She contemplated not so much Jeremy's words as his actions. In spite of her efforts to keep him from reaching her, he'd found her. He'd actually persuaded her father to reveal her whereabouts. And he'd protected her, not just from the incredible hulks in the men's room at the bar, but from her own rashness. If it weren't for his natty attire and his cute sports car, she could easily have forgotten that he was an aristocratic architect from the Gold Coast. This evening, Jeremy had been her devoted friend.

As he'd been in Maine, she reflected. As he'd been every step of the way. If he wanted to hurt her, he'd had plenty of opportunities. Sometimes, you simply had to have faith.

So he dressed well. So he drove an MG. So he lived in Westport. If he could accept her as she was, why couldn't she accept him as he was?

Then again, he might not accept her as she was, she reminded herself as she missed the driveway outside her building by inches and bumped over the curb into her parking lot. Jeremy pulled in behind her and parked in one of the visitor spaces. They entered the impersonal brick-front building together, strolled through the equally impersonal lobby and rode the glaringly lit elevator to the third floor.

"It isn't the Ritz," she pointed out unnecessarily as they headed down the hall to her door.

Jeremy seemed noncommittal as he took in the bland cinderblock walls and sidestepped the empty baby stroller the Santinis always left outside their door because, with three kids in a two-bedroom apartment, they simply didn't have room for it inside. At least the building was clean, Marlo consoled herself. No graffiti, no cigarette butts on the floor, and the silverfish were all in hiding.

She unlocked her door and ushered Jeremy inside. He looked around the living room for a minute, then ventured inside her minuscule kitchen. "Now this is bad," he muttered.

Lingering in the living room, she groaned. So much for having faith, she thought dolefully. One look at her kitchen and he was ready to reject her. "What's bad?" she asked, trying to keep her anger and disappointment under wraps as she joined him in the kitchen.

"Whoever designed this room planned it poorly. They put the refrigerator right next to the stove. When you take something out of the refrigerator, you can't put it on the stove. There should be a counter here."

"When your kitchen is six square feet, you haven't got much room to fit in the appliances," she pointed out.

"Your sink, refrigerator and stove are supposed to create a triangle for maximum efficiency," he explained, then smiled sheepishly. "I'm sorry, Marlo—it's a habit of mine. Whenever I come into a new place I start critiquing it like an architect."

"Actually," she corrected him, "what you were critiquing was the fact that this place is so small and cramped, and—"

"And you live in it, so I love it," he cut her off, circling his arms around her and pulling her to himself. The kiss they'd come close to sharing outside the bar in

Stratford was completed now, in Marlo's crowded, poorly planned kitchen. Jeremy's lips covered hers, softened them, coaxed them apart to allow his tongue access to the inner recesses of her mouth. He slid deep, stroking every surface, consuming her until she was trembling all over.

A breathless minute passed and he pulled back. "You still haven't told me you love me," he whispered.

"It isn't fair for you to ask after a kiss like that," she protested feebly.

His arms remained tight around her waist. "I'm going to be a lot less fair. Where's your bedroom?"

"Jeremy—"

"I know. It isn't the Ritz," he said, misinterpreting her hesitancy. Or maybe he wasn't misinterpreting it. Maybe she was still suffering from insecurity about how her life-style compared to his. He must have read the apprehension in her eyes, because he continued, "I don't want the Ritz, Marlo. I want a bed—with you in it. There isn't enough room in the kitchen to do what I've got in mind."

Another shiver rippled through her, hot and fluid. "Are you going to seduce me into loving you?" she questioned him.

"If that's what it takes." His smile faded as he absorbed her worried expression. "Marlo, what *would* it take? How about if we got married?"

"Married! We hardly know each other—"

"We know everything we need to know."

"We've spent all of maybe forty-eight hours together—"

"Forty-eight intense, incredible hours. It didn't take longer than that for me to realize what I want in a woman, what I need in my life. What I love about you."

He kissed her brow. "I know you're worried about the differences in our financial situations. But marriage would solve that. If you were my wife, everything I have would be yours, too."

"I don't want to be rich," she argued.

He shook his head. "What you don't want to be is cruel and self-centered," he corrected her. "You don't want to be pretentious or snobbish. You don't want to take advantage of other people or exploit them." He lifted his hands to her cheeks and cupped them gently, framing her face so she was forced to look into his eyes. "Don't you see? You couldn't do any of those things even if you wanted to. It isn't in you, Marlo. You're a good person. That goodness comes from within. Money can't change it."

"But..." She drew in an anxious breath. "When you put those pearls on me that day in Maine, Jeremy..." She was admitting to her most private failing, her greatest fear. But if anyone deserved to hear this confession, Jeremy did. "When you put that necklace on me, I wanted it," she admitted. "I wished it was mine. I wished I was rich and could afford all those nice things, and—"

"That's normal, Marlo. It's not a sin to want nice things. It's not a repudiation of your values, or an act of disrespect to your mother's memory. There are things I wish I owned, too. Some of them I might be able to get someday. Some of them I'll never have." He touched his lips lightly to hers. "This afternoon I found out my design was chosen for that hospital extension," he said.

She frowned at this abrupt change of subject. She recalled his mentioning in Maine that a design of his had made the hospital board's first cut, but she wasn't sure what that had to do with values or sins or materialism. "Congratulations," she said uncertainly.

"I found out about it this afternoon," he repeated, "and everybody in the office was celebrating, and all I could think of was how I had to get to you. Winning the contract was good, but in the grand scheme of things it doesn't matter. What matters is having a woman who challenges me, and makes me want to go to the ends of the earth for her. I would go to the ends of the earth for you, Marlo."

Marlo understood the truth in his words. She felt it. And suddenly she realized she was the richest woman in the world. To have a man love her so much—a man she loved every bit as much—was truly all that mattered. The rest was just the trimmings.

"I guess I've got to believe you," she said, this time initiating the kiss. "You went into that bar's men's room for me. That was pretty close to the end of the earth, wasn't it." She kissed him again, a longer, more poignant kiss. "I do love you, Jeremy. I love you so much it frightens me."

"A fearless woman like you?" Laughing, he lifted her into his arms. "Where's your bedroom?"

"I'm too heavy for you," she warned.

"I'm tougher than you think. Where is it?"

She pointed toward the living room. "You have to go through the living room to get to it," she told him. "There's no hall. Isn't that an architectural flaw?"

"Not if it means we get to your bed sooner," he said, struggling slightly under her weight as he moved through the living room.

Reaching her bedroom, he dropped her onto the mattress and then tumbled into her welcoming arms. Bowing to her, he kissed her thoroughly, profoundly, warming her body and soul. She accepted his love as she gave her own, freely and fully—and fearlessly.

Harlequin Superromance®

**This August, don't miss Supperromance
#462—STARLIT PROMISE**

STARLIT PROMISE is a deeply moving story of a
woman coming to terms with her grief and gradually
opening her heart to life and love.

Author Petra Holland sets the scene beautifully, never
allowing her heroine to become mired in self-pity. It
is a story that will touch your heart and leave you
celebrating the strength of the human spirit.

**Available wherever Harlequin books
are sold.**

STARLIT

Harlequin Superromance®

CHILDREN OF THE HEART
by Sally Garrett

Available this August

Romance readers the world over have wept and
rejoiced over Sally Garrett's heartwarming stories of
love, caring and commitment. In her new novel,
Children of the Heart, Sally once again weaves a story
that will touch your most tender emotions.

You'll be moved to tears of joy

Nearly two hundred children have passed through
Trenance McKay's foster home. But after her husband
leaves her, Trenance knows she'll always have to
struggle alone. No man could have enough room in his
heart both for Trenance and for so many needy
children. Max Tulley, news anchor for KSPO TV is
willing to try, but how long can his love last?

"Sally Garrett does some of the best character studies
in the genre and will not disappoint her fans."
Romantic Times

**Look for *Children of the Heart* wherever
Harlequin Romance novels are sold.** SCH-1

This August, don't miss an exclusive
two-in-one collection of earlier love stories

MAN
WITH A PAST

TRUE COLORS

by one of today's hottest
romance authors,

Jayne Ann Krentz

Now, two of Jayne Ann Krentz's most loved books are
available together in this special edition that new and
longtime fans will want to add to their bookshelves.

Let Jayne Ann Krentz capture your hearts with the love
stories, MAN WITH A PAST and TRUE COLORS.

And in October, watch for the second two-in-one
collection by Barbara Delinsky!

Available wherever Harlequin books are sold.

Take 4 bestselling love stories FREE

Plus get a FREE surprise gift!

HARLEQUIN
Romance

**This August, travel to Spain
with the Harlequin Romance
FIRST CLASS title #3143,
SUMMER'S PRIDE
by Angela Wells.**

"There was a time when I would have given you everything I
possessed for the pleasure of taking you to my bed and loving
you...."

But since then, Merle's life had been turned upside down, and
now it was clear that cynical, handsome Rico de Montilla felt
only contempt toward her. So it was unfortunate that when she
returned to Spain circumstances forced her to seek his help.
How could she hope to convince him that she was not the
mercenary, unfeeling woman he believed her to be?

If you missed June title #3128, THE JEWELS OF HELEN (Turkey) or July title #3136, FALSE
IMPRESSIONS (Italy) and would like to order them, send your name, address, zip or postal
code, along with a check or money order for $2.75 plus 75¢ postage and handling ($1.00 in
Canada) for each book ordered, payable to Harlequin Reader Service, to:

In the U.S.	In Canada
3010 Walden Ave.	P.O. Box 609
P.O. Box 1325	Fort Erie, Ontario
Buffalo, NY 14269-1325	L2A 5X3

Please specify book title(s) with your order.
Canadian residents add applicable federal and provincial taxes.

JT-B8R